A Beautiful Death

4/96

Also by S. T. Haymon
in Thorndike Large Print ®

A Very Particular Murder

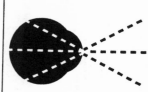

**This Large Print Book carries the
Seal of Approval of N.A.V.H.**

A Beautiful Death

S. T. Haymon

Thorndike Press • Thorndike, Maine

3 1969 00780 1367

Published in 1994 by arrangement with St. Martin's Press, Inc.

Thorndike Large Print ® General Series.

The tree indicium is a trademark of Thorndike Press.

The text of this Large Print edition is unabridged.
Other aspects of the book may vary from the original edition.

Set in 16 pt. News Plantin.

Printed in the United States on acid-free paper.

Library of Congress Cataloging in Publication Data

Haymon, S. T.
   A beautiful death / S.T. Haymon.
      p.   cm.
   ISBN 0-7862-0265-3 (alk. paper : lg. print)
   1. Jurnet, Benjamin (Fictitious character) — Fiction.
2. Police — England — Norfolk — Fiction. 3. Norfolk
(England) — Fiction. 4. Large type books. I. Title.
   [PR6058.A9855B43   1994b]
   823'.914—dc20   94-12231

A Beautiful Death

1

'Time I was moving on, then,' the young man said and stepped jauntily off the window-sill into the fourteenth-floor air. Even in sleep Jurnet, pressed into a shallow embrasure a few feet away, remembered not to look down. This time round he had no need to, anyway, his dream obligingly vaulting time and space to call up an instant picture of the young man skewered upon the ornamental railings fourteen floors below like a sucking pig ready for roasting. The dream went further, transporting him — in the same instant that he choked down nausea and faced anew the dreadful necessity of extricating himself safely from his own precarious perch — into the room behind that now-vacated ledge where a young woman and two small children lay dead on a bed soaked in their blood.

And what had he and the murderous young man talked about as they clung like flies to the outside of that desirable apartment block?

Had he tried to convince a bloke who had just bumped off his wife and kids in circumstances of the most revolting cruelty that — despite the evidence to the contrary, despite the blood already stiffening the posh shirt, the Armani jeans — it was all a regrettable mistake, that nobody could possibly be all that desperate in a flat which boasted three en-suite bathrooms and a kitchen fitted out with more peninsulas than the map of Europe? No, he had not. That would not have been psychology. Instead, following all the textbooks, the two of them had chatted about Angleby's chances for the cup, agreeing that the club's management must be out of its tiny mind letting Tony Alpert, the best attacking forward of the century, go to Real Madrid, no matter how much money was dangled. Oh, they had got along like a house on fire, weighing up the pros and cons of who could best be brought in to fill Alpert's place, everything going swimmingly until, between one moment and the next and whilst he, Ben Jurnet, had been racking his brains to recall the name of that promising youngster who had done so well last season at Cardiff City, the young man was gone, without even saying goodbye, the unmannerly bugger.

How was it possible to be so tired when you were already asleep? Tired, moreover, with a tiredness that was a kind of drowning, an ocean out of which it was a waste of time to shout for help, no one would hear you, and yet you went on doing it. Or would have done, if it hadn't been too much of a fag.

Thank heaven — asleep he congratulated himself — at least he hadn't had to drive home, which in the circumstances would have been an undertaking little less hazardous than trying to get a maniac down from the stratosphere to terra firma in one piece; hadn't used the Rover all day, as a matter of fact, Jack Ellers, his faithful sidekick — for some reason which in his dream escaped him — having picked him up in the morning and, after it was all over, brought him home again, insisting gently, as they drove through Angleby streets touched with the first magic of dawn, that the young man had been a schizo and there was nothing anybody, not even Detective Inspector Benjamin Jurnet in all his glory, could have done to stop what happened happening.

Jurnet was pretty sure that the little Welshman, a voluble type, had said more, if only he had managed to stay awake to hear it. Already overwhelmed by that fatigue which even sleep, it seemed, was unable to assuage, the most his dream could dredge up was some vague recollection of Ellers parking his car next to his own, edging into the narrow space left by the bulging black plastic bags which, as ever, awaited the coming of a phantom dustman; of being led up stairs his feet trod with unthinking familiarity, and where the pervading smells of Nappisan and joss sticks, of cabbage and slow-simmered underwear, advertised the proximity of home.

Home! Jurnet surfaced briefly, seeking Miriam beside him, only to sink back into the abyss when his questing hand could not find her. Had she been there, her wonderful bronze hair spread out as usual on the pillow when he had tumbled into the old brass bed, barely conscious? Had he woken her up? Surely the jangling bed must have awakened her.

His dream provided no enlightenment.

Up on the fourteenth floor the young man said chattily for the umpteenth time before stepping from the window-sill into eternity, 'Time I was moving on, then . . .'

'Ben!'

Going down for the third time, Jurnet heard Miriam's voice, a raft to cling to, a promise of salvation. He sensed that she was bending over him. He smelled the lovely smell of her and the images of the night, of his failure, his guilt, fell away. The ocean receded and with it the need for rescue. He let go the raft and fell instantly into the dreamless sleep of a copper who had had a heavy night doing what he was paid for.

'Ben — please wake up!'

Incredibly, with all the noise he was bound to have made, she must after all have slept through his return home, her lover thought confusedly, trying, truly trying, to take in what she was saying. Otherwise she would never have tried to drag him out of his blissful oblivion with something about her car — or his, was it? — and being late for a train she simply had to catch or something would — or would not — happen. Something too about a cab which either had or had not arrived as promised. Something about Heathrow — at least it sounded like Heathrow except that the young man was called Heath and maybe she had got the names muddled. Unless it was the wife and the children she was on about, lying next thing to headless on the posh bed which had telly and a bar built in, no expense spared.

On the other hand, could be the Super-intendent had been on the blower, demanding to know what the hell was keeping the dumb cluck who had let a poor, crazed kid slip through his clumsy fingers. Correction. The Superintendent would never in any circumstances have let words like hell and dumb cluck pass his patrician lips — good gracious, no — only imply them in syllables as impeccably styled as his tailoring. Unless it was one of those days when he chose to dress as if for a grouse moor rather than Angleby Police Headquarters, in hairy tweeds that smelled to high heaven of heather and a private income.

Jurnet smiled in unconscious recognition that not even sleep could quite deaden the sweet-sour sniping which was an integral part of his relationship with his superior officer. The essential part. Ten to one, the detective decided drowsily, turning over and rolling deeper into the dip in the middle of the bed, a manoeuvre which, on better days, better nights, brought him and Miriam, willy-nilly, even closer together than they were already, it would be a tweeds day, a veldschoen and pipe day, a day-at-the-butts day and he, Jurnet, the inevitable butt.

Had Miriam called out 'Ben!' yet again? Before Jurnet could be certain, he was beyond answering, dead to the world. Did he feel her lips warm on his forehead or only imagine it, before her crisp, light footsteps

12

hurried from the room?

Did he, hell?

Jurnet slept.

Jurnet slept.

Sleeping, he did not actually feel the block of flats rise up a little and shake itself like a wet dog before settling back on its inadequate foundations: at least, looking back later, he was unable to conjure up any such awareness. The window was what had awakened him. It cracked across its width with the sound of a pistol shot, exactly the kind of sound to reach a copper however lost in sleep.

Thus roused, Jurnet sat up and looked at the window; whereupon, as if only waiting to make sure it had attracted his attention, the upper pane fell out. He heard the glass tinkle prettily as it shattered on the paved yard two floors below.

By the time he had swung himself out of bed he became aware of other noises — of shouts and cries that seemed to be coming from the front of the building: a general impression of alarm. A stumble across the bedroom floor to the window provided no clue as to what was amiss, its view over the muddy playing fields of the neighbouring Comprehensive as dispiriting as ever. However, the brisk October air which poured through the newly opened gap completed the waking-up process and served to remind Jurnet that he was naked.

He grabbed jeans and a sweater, thrust his bare feet into sneakers and came muzzily out of the flat on to a landing masked by a curtain of yellow dust which revolved slowly in the draught emanating from a vacancy normally occupied by a stained-glass window on the half-landing allegedly depicting the defeat of the Armada. This window, unlike the one in the bedroom, had fallen in, not out, and the stairs were thick with shards of blue and green and red, Spanish galleon and English man-o'-war crunching impartially under the detective's feet as he descended to the chaos which awaited him.

There, at ground level, the dust was even thicker. Outside the O'Driscolls' flat, its hood shredded, its bodywork in pieces, the pram in which seven young O'Driscolls had progressively taken their infant ease would never welcome the imminent eighth. The door of the flat had been blown off its hinges.

'Any one there?' Jurnet shouted, wishing he had thought to wind a scarf or a towel over his mouth. His voice hoarse with dust, his heart beat faster at the thought of those seven children. The older ones, at least, must

14

surely have gone off to school by now —
or had they? He had no idea what time it
was — but the babies, God, the babies.

Here too, in the O'Driscoll flat, the windows had imploded, letting in, it seemed,
not daylight, but a dust made up of dust
mixed lethally with pulverized glass and
shreds of the fancy swagged nets which had
been Mrs O'Driscoll's pride and joy. Trying
not to breathe, Jurnet groped his way through
the ruined rooms, stumbling over disembow-
elled upholstery and overturned cots until
satisfied the place was empty and no gas
was escaping from the clapped-out stove in
the kitchen.

The noise outside seemed to have died
down a little, become more official: bells
and sirens and whoopers, lovely sounds that
betokened fire engines, ambulances, the police his brothers: everything under control.
A sudden, immense feeling of relief, almost
of happiness, surged through Jurnet.

Resolutely refusing to knot together in his
mind the fact that O'Driscoll was an Irishman
with the further fact that there had undoubtedly been an explosion, Jurnet squeezed past
the splintered remains of the mock-Tudor
front door which had once lent the whole
jerry-built construction a spurious dignity,
and went outside.

After the dust the abrupt contrast of the autumn sunshine was, for a moment, an additional affront before he had the sense to raise his head gratefully to take in its purity and light. He blinked hard and had the satisfaction of seeing that the O'Driscolls, at least, were safe — Mrs O'Driscoll, her dressing gown torn and filthy, her hair in curlers, still contriving to look like a lion-hearted mother of antiquity as she stood, magnificently pregnant, her arms round her brood. Mr O'Driscoll, never an assertive personality unless he had drink taken, hovered on the outskirts looking haunted but not, Jurnet would have said, either guilty or proud of himself. Miss Whistler, the late-blooming spinster on the first floor, had obviously run out of the building just as she was, in what she had on — or hadn't, as the case might be — which had happened to be a black silk petticoat trimmed with lace, nothing above the waist. But then, Miss Whistler boasted nothing much above the waist either, so decency was scarcely offended, if at all.

The only serious casualties, so far as one could judge at first glance, were the black plastic bags of rubbish native to the ill-kempt forecourt, those staple furnishings without which home would not be home. One and all, with what looked like joyous abandon, had seized the opportunity to burst at the seams, carpeting the fractured concrete with everything in the way of domestic waste from potato peelings to used sanitary towels. The air was spiced with vegetable decay and another odour the detective chose not to identify.

Two ambulance men, who could not be expected to know that that was the way she always looked in the mornings, were gently urging Mrs Petherton, the alcoholic widow whose flat was next door to Jurnet's, towards an ambulance drawn up hospitably at the kerb. PCs Hinchley and Bly, Jurnet noted with a pleased nod of recognition, were prudently ushering the small crowd which had already gathered on the pavement to the safety of the further side of the road. A van drew up, disgorging purposeful young men armed with wrenches and other implements designed to turn off gas and water. Jack Ellers, unaccustomedly pale but as chubbily alert as if he had passed an undisturbed night in his Rosie's arms, arrived in his car with a passenger — Sid Hale, a detective inspector forever saddened by the world's follies, but never surprised by them; his long, melancholy countenance looking marginally content that for once life had matched up to his expectations.

Everything under control.

Only then, when it was absurd to go on pretending any longer, did Jurnet move towards what was only too clearly the fount and origin of the explosion — the contorted composition of buckled steel which might have come straight from an exhibition of modern sculpture were it not for the masked fireman still engaged in smothering a small fire within its vitals with some kind of chemical foam.

Whoever had done away with the Rover car had made a good job of it. Jurnet, always an admirer of expertise whenever he came upon it — even a skilful safebreaker earning his reluctant admiration — had to give him that. It was the only thought of which he was capable, any other so monstrous as not to be entertained.

Close to, the smell — that other smell his senses until then had refused to acknowledge — was overpowering: petrol, burning oil, the acrid tang of hot metal. And something else beside.

Suddenly Jack Ellers was at his side, a hand on his mate's arm, his face shadowed with shock and grief. The fire out to his satisfaction, the fireman turned off his spray and removed his mask, revealing the homely, freckled features of Ted Gorman from the

18

Postlegate fire station. Jurnet smiled at him gratefully. Good old Ted. Trust him to get everything under control.

Kindly but firmly Jurnet put away his friend's restraining hand and stepped forward, two steps only but the longest journey he had ever made in his life. A journey that had to be taken alone.

He moved to where a shoe lay on the ground a little distance away from the destroyed car; a shoe that, with its understated black elegance, was just the job for an executive lady with a busy day ahead of her. What made the shoe something deserving of a second look was the fact that there was a foot in it, a foot with an ankle attached, out of which, challenging as Excalibur protruding from its stone, rose a jagged lance of bone — tibia? Fibula? Feeling it somehow important to get the details right, Jurnet made a mental note to check with Dr Colton: the police surgeon would be sure to know — that shone white and virginal in the sun. He took a deep breath, filled his lungs deliberately with the tainted air, at last isolating its remaining ingredient.

Incinerated flesh.

Miriam's.

2

'If it isn't the IRA,' declared the Superintendent, tight-lipped, — 'though it's hard to imagine why Angleby should be singled out for its attention — it has to be an act of personal revenge. Who do we know who's been let out within the past two or three months, say, with an outsize grudge against the Force, or more particularly against Ben?'

The inquest, the mulling over of possibilities, went on and on — around Jurnet, above, across him, never directly addressed to his face. Bereavement, he thought, in so far as he was capable of the act of thinking, was itself a kind of death, a pervading embarrassment, the unspoken suggestion that someone had committed the ultimate social gaffe: the same low voices as at a funeral, the same avoidance of eye contact, the same difficulty of finding anything to say. Except that it was worse than death in a way, with no coffin to lower into its neat hole, no pretence that the dear departed had left for a better place where all was Hosannas and Hallelujahs. No tea and titbits after the cemetery.

No wreaths, either. Jurnet wouldn't have said no to some lilies, a whopping sheaf of them tied up with purple ribbon and with a black-edged card attached, 'In Deepest Sympathy.' Their scent might have drowned the smell of burnt Miriam which still lingered in his nostrils. Always would, he supposed, so long as he lived, if living was the right word for the continuing irrelevance of drawing breath.

Still, like it or not, they had not been able to prevent his having his say before this strange, living rigor mortis set in. No, he had shouted into the Superintendent's unsparing face, he had *not* given his fiancée permission to appropriate CID property to her own use. He knew the rules, and so did she. She had never once entered the Rover except as a passenger and ordinarily, he'd take his oath on it, would no more have dreamed of taking a bloody police car than anything else that didn't belong to her. That must have been why, even with her own car unexpectedly out of action and his car keys lying there plain to be seen on the bedside table, she had done her level best to wake him up so that he could give her a lift to the station. There had been something about a train to catch and a plane to meet, and a cab that hadn't turned up as ordered; only unfortunately he hadn't taken it in at the time, still hadn't completely. For some reason the kerfuffle with that bugger Heath had tired him out and once home he had gone to bed and out like a light.

No car of her own, no cab, train due to leave at any minute — no wonder the poor girl had been desperate.

'If only I hadn't been so bloody dozy I'd have got up and driven her to the station as she asked.' He finished, low: 'It wasn't much to ask, was it, a lift to the station?'

'What station had you in mind? Not Angleby Central, that's for sure,' the Superintendent had pointed out with an astringency which was the only possible mode of address in the circumstances. 'If you *had* got up as she asked, the only difference would have been there'd have been two of you blown up instead of one.'

The beauty of this scenario, which had never occurred to him before, was Jurnet's undoing. He buried his face in his hands. There was a long silence in the room. Through the open window the sounds of the Market Place, footsteps on the cobbles,

22

stallholders crying their wares, entered as from another planet.

'Sorry . . .'

Only then, when he lifted up his head in attempted apology, did Jurnet see waveringly, like shapes seen under water, that he was not the only one in the room with a damp face. Even the eyes of Sid Hale, to whom the worst was no more than the expected norm, were bright with tears.

The Superintendent's eyes, too, were bright, but not with tears, or not with tears only: with that cosmic rage which always possessed him in the presence of murder. After years of working with the man, Jurnet knew that unforgiving anger; had never as yet been able to decide whether it was aimed primarily at the murderer or at the God responsible for a universe in which such abominations were allowed to happen. What he was certainly unprepared for was the unequivocal compassion the Superintendent turned in his direction.

'Ben — ' the Superintendent began, and stopped. That fount of eloquence, that paragon of articulacy, at a loss for words! Though it broke Jurnet's heart that Miriam had to die to produce such a unique revelation, in some obscure way he was comforted by it; or, if not comforted, at least a little better able to endure the unendurable.

He got up, moving stiffly like an old man.

'I've still got that report on Heath to do — '

'No problem. Jack will take over. Don't give it a thought. After this, you're going to need some time off. Rest. A bit of peace and quiet.'

Jurnet looked at his superior officer with something like panic. *Rest? Peace and quiet?* How, for Christ's sake, was he expected to occupy this generosity of emptiness added to emptiness? Reliving interminably Miriam's last moments? — her quick footsteps full of energy and expectation on that dismal stair; even that turgid stained-glass of the Armada, he always fancied, calling a halt to hostilities whilst the streaming pennons of the fighting ships — English and Spanish alike — saluted her. Out through those ridiculous doors into the October day, the misty sun catching her glorious hair. How beautiful she had been, the woman who amazingly, against all the odds, had said that she loved him and, what was more, given ample proof of it: beautiful as the Song of Solomon.

Behold thou art fair, my love; behold thou art fair. Correction: Behold thou wast fair. Got to get one's tenses right.

Funny to remember how he had promised himself that one day, when at last, all obstacles surmounted, Rabbi Schnellman and the Beth Din had satisfied themselves that the candidate for conversion really wanted to become a Jew and not just because Miriam wouldn't marry him if he didn't (as if that weren't reason enough!), he would celebrate his reception into the ranks of the Chosen by learning the whole Song of Solomon by heart in the original. Lying together, two Jews become one, he would surprise her with King Solomon's very own words, the genuine article as, in all probability, murmured into the shell-like ear of the Queen of Sheba. How would they sound in Hebrew? *Thy two breasts are like young roes that are twins, which feed among the lilies —*

No. No lilies, with or without the purple ribbon and the black-edged card. And now, it seemed, no work either to fill the nothingness that was the rest of his life. Only a wilderness of rest, of limitless time in which to follow Miriam endlessly out into the morning sunshine, elegant in her business suit as she carefully negotiated the black plastic bags, got into the Rover, placed her handbag and her briefcase on the seat beside her and — a little troubled, undoubtedly, by her own boldness in driving away a police vehicle with intent — turned on the ignition.

The impossibility of remembering what

came next, the impossibility of not remembering it, had Jurnet shouting into the face of a Superintendent pale with shock but alight with love: 'How the hell can I take time off, when I have to find out why?'

Jack Ellers drove Jurnet to the synagogue. As a destination it was a compromise, the little Welshman's first intention having been to deliver his bereaved pal to Rosie, who had been a good friend of Miriam's and who knew all about comfort, if anybody did.

'She'll kill me, when she hears, if I don't bring you back with me. You know we've got a spare room and it'd be no trouble. I could nip over to your place and pick up whatever you need — '

'Ta, but no. I'd rather go home.'

'Not on, boyo! They cleared everybody out, you know that, and they'll not be letting them back yet, that's for sure. The whole bloody place could fall down any minute.' Which was, as Jurnet knew very well, a pretty transparent pretext for keeping him away from that forecourt where, in all likelihood, the forensic lot were still at it, looking for bits and pieces of his golden girl. When Jack Ellers said: 'The air there won't be breathable for a week at least,' he wondered how he would feel, breathing in and finding

26

a scrap of Miriam in his nostrils. A Holy Communion scarcely appropriate for an aspiring Jew, but there! — the consecrated wafer on the tongue, the body and the blood.

The O'Driscolls' flat had taken most of the blast. Thank goodness, the detective thought, the kids at least were all right. He suddenly remembered that the O'Driscolls had recently taken in a lodger, some kind of relation from County something or other — Kerry? Donegal? somewhere like that — a fresh-faced youngster with a touch of likeable impudence to leaven his hobbledehoy shyness. Jurnet couldn't remember having noticed him among the crowd on the forecourt. An emissary of the IRA sent over to blow an English copper to smithereens? Could it be that the O'Driscolls, in all innocence, had written home to boast that they possessed a genuine detective inspector among their neighbours? Jurnet leaned back in the car seat and let the suspicion go, less out of moral principle than because he couldn't take it — or anything else — on board. The tiredness was welling up again, like a returning tide.

He said nothing of this to Ellers, who was busy finding additional reasons why Jurnet should not think of returning to his flat, even if it were given the all-clear structurally.

Out of the blue he found himself in complete agreement, not because of anything his pal had said — he had not even been listening — but because, when it came to it, he could not face going back. Not yet, anyway, not whilst those dedicated seekers could still be turning up a finger joint here, there a nipple with a plump little cushion of breast still attached . . . Jurnet covered his eyes for a moment. He took his hands away and suggested calmly, as if he had forgotten their already stated destination: 'You could run me over to the synagogue. There's things to be done — Miriam's mother to be told, I don't know what else. The Rabbi'll know what to do.'

3

'Nineteen, six.'

Ordinarily Jurnet took care not to beat the Rabbi — who once, in his svelte youth, had played to international standards — by such a wide margin. The Rabbi was a man you wanted to be kind to, in every possible way. The detective could not understand why, today of all days, he found himself possessed of a merciless skill, finding the edge of the table time and again, dropping cross-shots where Rabbi Schnellman's short, varicosed arms could never reach them.

He could not understand, either, why the Rabbi's childlike face, the eyes magnified by thick lenses, looked marginally less crumpled with grief than before they had begun their ridiculous game.

He could not understand what the hell they were doing anyway, playing table tennis in the synagogue hall whilst back on the forecourt they were busy separating Miriam from the Coke tins and the remains of Chinese takeaways. What did the fat slob think he was doing, *yarmulke* askew on his bald head, sweat darkening his armpits, batting a ping-pong ball to and fro when what he should have been doing was getting answers?

Maybe the line was busy. More likely, the old geezer up in the sky had left the receiver off the hook. Very sensible. What was there to say?

Jurnet had waited until Jack Ellers had gone — reluctantly, insisting he be summoned back for chauffeur's duties once his superior officer had finished his business there, the car disappearing slowly round the dog-leg of the quiet suburban street — before pressing the bell for the flat above the synagogue hall. The swiftness with which the door had been opened could only mean that the Rabbi must have been there, in the little hallway at the foot of the stairs, waiting for his ring. Taken aback, Jurnet found himself without words for what he had come to say; only to discover that words were not necessary. The Rabbi had enfolded him in his arms — those arms too short to reach for an artfully placed ping-pong ball but long enough to encompass a grief that filled the universe — and for the first time since Miriam's death

Jurnet had wept, truly wept, an assuaging flood.

Upstairs, in the sitting-room crowded with the Louis Seize furniture which was a memorial to his dead wife, the Rabbi had had tea ready, the fussy china, floral and gilt, set out in readiness on the lace-edged cloth placed cater-cornerwise on the table as his lost Rachel had long ago instructed him.

'Have you had anything to eat today?' Frowning at what he clearly felt was a dereliction of duty on the great man's part: 'I asked your Superintendent. He could not tell me.' A glance at his visitor's face, haggard, uncomprehending, sufficient answer: 'I felt sure you would have had nothing, so I made you a sandwich — cheese and piccalilli, your favourite. Sit down, my dear young friend,' Rabbi Schnellman instructed. 'Sit down and eat. However much we may sometimes feel we know better, it is necessary to keep on living.'

The Rabbi had already been in touch with Mrs Courland, Miriam's mother. From the way the freckles on his plump cheeks stood out at the mention of it, brown against a milky pallor, it had not been an easy telling. Fortunately, the Rabbi said, taking out an outsize handkerchief and wiping his forehead as if the very recollection of that telephone conversation was overheating, she had had somebody with her at the time, a cousin or something of the sort recently arrived from Israel — perhaps Jurnet was acquainted with the gentleman? It had been a great relief, in the circumstances, to know that she was not alone.

Jurnet bit into his sandwich and put it back on the plate. *Who said it was necessary to go on living?*

'Eat!' commanded the Rabbi however, and, like a child, Jurnet ate; picked up the sandwich again and demolished it to the last crust; drank the heavily sweetened tea that was handed across the table. Miriam had long ago weaned him off sugar, so completely that a sip of sweetened tea was ordinarily enough to make him feel sick. Now he drank and asked for another cup of the same, feeling that the nausea which, as ever, beset him was in some obscure, infantile way a settling of accounts.

'Name of Galil,' he came out with finally, forcing himself to concentrate on what the other was saying. 'Miriam did say something. Not a cousin — some kind of relative by marriage, I believe. Works for her in Israel.'

'Ah — Tel Tzevaim!' said Rabbi Schnellman, mentioning by name the settlement for the disabled which Miriam, by setting up a successful knitting enterprise there, had put in a fair way to becoming a seminal influence on the fashion world. 'What wonderful work she's done there! How they'll manage without her I can't imagine.'

'Thanks to me, they'll have to, won't they? We'll all have to.' Mouth twisted in pain: 'She was right, wasn't she, Rabbi — dead right literally? She didn't want me to go on being a copper. I didn't listen, and now I've killed her.' Anger rising in his throat like the sweet tea: 'She was right, you were right, her mother was right, your whole lousy Beth Din was right, everybody right but me. The world overflowing with doctors, lawyers, accountants, dress manufacturers, every one of them strictly kosher, each and every one of them falling over themselves to lead her up the aisle and under the *chupa* and she has to choose an uncircumcised rozzer! Next thing you'll be saying, the lot of you, she deserved what she got!'

Jurnet pushed back his chair, its fussiness of gilt and satin a sudden intolerable insolence in a universe where such tarted-up nonsense could survive whilst Miriam was a bag of bloody gobbets waiting to be scraped off the pavement. He had to rein in an insane urge to up-end the chair, wrench its foolish legs from their sockets and break them over his knee for the matchwood they were.

For the matchwood the world was.

He saw, or thought he saw, fear in the Rabbi's eyes for the safety of his dead wife's heritage: straightened the chair, patted its fleur-de-lis upholstery in apology, and announced, 'It doesn't mean I don't want to go on with the conversion.'

As if seeking reassurance from the contact, the Rabbi felt for the skull-cap perched precariously on the bald spot at the back of his head. Looking troubled, he answered: 'You don't have to decide anything in a hurry.'

'No hurry. I know what I want. I just wanted to let you know. I don't want Miriam to have died in vain. One Jew less in the world, but also one Jew more, eh? It will even things up. Maybe that's what He's had in His mind all along. There has to be a reason.'

Rabbi Schnellman shook his head, his skull-cap hanging on like a desperate limpet. His face alight with conviction, he said: 'The reason is not important. What matters is believing that there is one.'

'Oh, I believe all right!' Jurnet moved round the table, appraised the dumpy little man with eyes bright with a bleak amusement. 'Funny, isn't it? All the months, the years, that I've been knocking myself out trying to become a Jew and you've been putting me off because you've said — quite rightly, I suppose, from your point of view — that when you came down to it I only wanted to convert because Miriam wouldn't marry me without it. Not enough, you said. You said — your own words — that you had to want with every fibre of your being to be a Jew for its own sake, for the sake of Judaism, not for the sake of getting a girl — not even a girl like Miriam — into bed with you. Right?'

'That is the essence of what I said.'

'Well, then! Miriam's gone, isn't she? She's out of the equation. All the king's horses and all the king's men can't put Miriam Courland together again. So, if I still want to become a Jew it can't be sex, can it? Henceforth, my motives have to be pure. So how can you still go on doubting my sincerity?'

In a quiet voice the Rabbi said: 'I don't doubt your sincerity, Ben. Only your love of God.'

'Hang on!' Jurnet glowered. 'Who said anything about love? Not fair to keep on moving the goalposts. Belief was what you were always on about — the necessity of belief. And I *do* believe. After what happened this morning I'd be crazy not to, wouldn't I? A really powerful guy, your Master of the Universe. I'd need my head examined not to want to keep on the right side of him.' In a voice drained of all emotion Jurnet intoned: '*Shema Yisroel adonai elohaino adonai echod* — Hear O Israel, the Lord thy God, the Lord is One.'

The Rabbi rose from his chair in turn, but carefully, so that the equanimity of the Louis Seize furniture was not disturbed. He straightened his *yarmulke* with a trembling hand. By contrast, the hand he placed on Jurnet's forearm was steady as a rock.

'Do you know what I fancy, Ben? A game of ping-pong.'

They were in the middle of their third game when the phone rang outside in the little vestibule. The Rabbi took the call reluctantly, rightly fearing to interrupt the therapeutic continuity of their exercise. He returned to find, as he had feared, all his good work undone, a whey-faced Jurnet bent over in a corner bringing up his cheese and pickle sandwich.

'My poor Ben!' Pulling out a chair: 'Sit down while I get a bucket and mop.'

Jurnet, gasping: 'Sorry about that — '

'Not another word! Stay quiet while I get

the bucket. I'm going to turn a shower on for you. I'll tell Sergeant Ellers you can't talk to him.'

Jurnet roused himself.

'Him, is it?' The other nodded. 'Tell him he doesn't have to come and fetch me. Say I'll get myself home under my own steam.'

'I'll say no such thing. I'll tell him that for the present you'll be staying here with me.'

Jurnet protested harshly: 'Don't be kind to me, Rabbi, for Christ's sake. I don't think I could stand any more kindness.' Shakily, the taste of piccalilli-flavoured vomit sour in his mouth, he went out of the synagogue hall to the telephone; leaned against the side of its little hood watching the receiver which dangled from the apparatus on the wall.

'Ben! You there, Ben?' Jack Ellers' voice came through, loud and anxious. 'Rabbi Schnellman? Ben!'

After a while, as if tiring of the game, Jurnet replaced the receiver gently, pushed himself upright with an effort and went back to the synagogue hall. He noted as an interesting but unsurprising fact that not even the strong antiseptic with which the Rabbi had been busy during his absence was enough to mask the smell of carbonized Miriam.

The detective picked up a table tennis bat, twiddled it a few times and put it down again.

'You know,' he remarked to Rabbi Schnellman who was having difficulty removing some daffodil-yellow plastic gloves from his plump hands, 'one thing I've always had against that Jewish God of yours — I can tell you now, I couldn't before — He's too damn proud by half.' Putting up a hand to ward off an expected objection: 'Oh, I know what you're going to say — that a geezer who can create a whole universe in six days flat has something to be proud about. But has He, when you come down to it?' With a face screwed up in a strained concentration which brought a troubled tenderness into the other's eyes: 'Have you taken a good look at the world lately, a really good look at what goes on?'

The Rabbi had succeeded in getting the gloves off, but inside out, all bunched up, no sign of fingers. Jurnet reached over and took the gloves from his hands; blew into them one at a time, their plastic ballooning, the fingers popping out one, two, three, four, five, like udders ready for a milking. The Rabbi drew a deep breath, the worry went out of his face. He smiled with the innocent pleasure of a child.

'That's marvellous!'

'Trick I picked up from Dr Colton. Every time I've had to attend at one of his autopsies there he is, blowing up his gloves like a kid at a party.' After a moment's silent contemplation of police surgeons and post-mortems — to wit, Miriam's — Jurnet looked up sharply. 'Well? *Have* you taken a good look? You never said.'

The Rabbi quoted without guile: ' "On the sixth day the Lord God saw everything that he had made, and behold, it was very good — " '

'On the sixth day — maybe that was the whole trouble! The guy was in too much of a hurry. Easily done. You get what seems like a brilliant idea and press on regardless. He should have taken it slower, stopped for a beer, for second thoughts as to what exactly he was getting into. He got carried away. Understandable. Unforgivable.'

'I want to help you, Ben.'

'That's OK.' The detective's tone was kind. 'You know what they say. God helps those who help themselves. Speaking personally,' announced Jurnet, 'I'm sorry for that God of yours, I really am. All day long, twenty-four hours of it, pestered with prayers like a phone which never stops ringing, everyone wanting something — and Him the only one in the whole wide universe with nothing, no one, to pray to. The only one who is on His own. Enough to drive even a god round the bend. If only, before He created anything else, He'd said, "Let there be God" — *His* God, if you take my meaning, someone for *Him* to turn to when it all went terribly wrong. Even if only someone to curse, put the blame on. As from today, Rabbi, I want you to know that I understand loneliness. I understand God.'

The telephone began to ring again.

'That'll be Jack having another try,' said Jurnet, making no move to answer it. The Rabbi's lips moved. 'Sorry — all that jangle. I didn't hear what you said.'

Rabbi Schnellman said it again.

'Teach me.'

By the time Detective Sergeant Ellers came for him, as Jurnet had known all the time he was bound to do, the detective was asleep on the Louis Seize *chaise-longue,* a blanket over his legs, his shoes carefully removed out of respect for its satin-striped upholstery. Rabbi Schnellman, who had exchanged his usual baggy slacks and ancient sweater for a dark suit and darker overcoat, garments he wore with an inbuilt air of apology for giving himself such airs, received the little

40

Welshman with relief.

'You'll be able to stay with him while I'm away. He shouldn't be left alone — not for a little, anyway. Mrs Courland — I should like to be there when she arrives. The cousin who is driving her down from London said they would go straight to Miriam's flat. I mean of course,' he finished delicately, with an approving nod for the dead girl's regard for the proprieties, 'her own place down by the river. Apparently the mother has a spare key Miriam left with her in case of emergencies. The cousin did not feel she would be up to going straight to the police station to make the identification.'

'No identification.' After a silence pregnant with all that was contained in those two stark words, the Sergeant added: 'Not in that sense. We have the dental records, fortunately.'

'Fortunately.' The word hung between them in all its awful absurdity. Then the Rabbi said: 'He's been sick, but I still think it's important he should eat something. I've cut bread and butter. And tea — give him tea with plenty of sugar. I've left everything on a tray in the kitchen . . .'

Jack Ellers glanced down at his superior officer, glad that the dark Italianate features which — at Headquarters and strictly behind

41

his back — had earned him the nickname of Valentino, were turned away from him.

'I'm sorry,' he said, 'but I have to wake him up. Take him back with me.'

'Unkind!' cried the Rabbi, with unaccustomed force; a noise loud enough to cause the sleeping man to stir, turn over on the narrow couch so that the two watchers could no longer escape the full frontal view of the dreadful blankness of his face. 'I will telephone your superior. Explain — '

'Not on, I'm afraid. As it is, the Superintendent's been holding things up for him, and he's not the most patient bloke around — '

'Holding what up?'

'Things,' non-committally. 'Where d'you put his shoes? Ah!' Locating the missing objects, Jack Ellers picked them up and approached the recumbent figure purposefully. 'If you're off down to the river,' he offered over his shoulder, 'we can give you a lift best part of the way.' He smiled at the Rabbi, sharing his concern for their unconscious friend. 'You know I wouldn't wake him up if it wasn't absolutely necessary.'

'You've caught the assassin?' demanded the Rabbi, sounding uncertain whether to be glad or sorry.

Without answering, the little Welshman knelt down and began to lever Jurnet's sneakers on to feet whose toes curled up protesting the intrusion.

The other repeated: 'You've caught him?'

'You'll be the first to hear soon as we've anything to report.' The shoes were on at last. 'Ben,' Ellers chided cheerfully, not a bad performance all things considered, 'time to rise and shine, boyo . . .'

Jurnet sat up, opened his eyes and promptly shut them again.

'I told you. Tell Rosie I'm grateful, but no. I have to go home. Things to do — '

'All in good time. Won't cut much ice with the Super, will it, to tell him that. Mustn't keep His Nibs waiting. He's got someone with him he wants you to meet.'

4

Father Culvey did not look like a man who derived a lot of job satisfaction from his work. Lines of disappointment were etched deep into a face where small froths of cotton wool adhered to shaving nicks like pink-tinged thistledown. It was not immediately apparent at what or at whom the priest's dissatisfaction was directed — whether his flock, his boss, his boss's universe, or merely a blunt razor blade — only that, from the depths of the furrows ploughed into the low, broad forehead, the problem had been with him for a long time.

The moment Jack Ellers came through the door, Jurnet following as reluctantly as if he were himself a felon brought in to help with inquiries, the priest launched into a combination of explanation and complaint.

Fastening his eyes on the Superintendent with no indication of liking what they saw: 'I am a very busy man, sir, as I don't doubt you are yourself. May I take it that I can at last claim a few minutes of your undivided attention to be told why I — why we are here?'

The Superintendent replied with that blend of deference and condescension which — had Jurnet been in any state to appreciate it — his subordinate would have recognized as the tone he invariably reserved for the cloth, of whatever denomination. 'You have been very kind, Father, and very patient. I would not have kept you waiting had I not felt it was vital that Detective Inspector Jurnet should hear what this young man has to say.'

The young man at the priest's side appeared to have nothing to say. The cheerful impertinence Jurnet had remarked in the past as distinguishing Mrs O'Driscoll's lodger was no longer in evidence. Pasty-faced and frowning, he looked lumpen in his jeans, T-shirt and anorak, shoulders rounded, hands dangling between his legs; his head down and moving slightly from side to side like an animal behind bars.

Father Culvey said bad-temperedly: 'I would wish it to be noted down that he is here of his own volition.'

'Detective Sergeant Ellers is making a note accordingly. Though I am bound to point out — ' the Superintendent permitted himself a smile too small to provide cause for offence — 'that for somebody who has called in at Police Headquarters of his own free will, he has been remarkably uncommunicative so far.'

'I will amend what I said,' the priest conceded with evident reluctance. 'After what occurred this morning, Mrs O'Driscoll, with whom Terry here lodges and who is his auntie as well as one of my congregation, rightly suspecting that as an Irishman it was only a matter of time before the police arrived to interrogate him, sent him to me for my advice, and it is pursuant to that same that he is here at this moment.'

'Excellent counselling, if I may say so — ' the Superintendent's compliment was only partly disingenuous — 'even though based on a totally false premise. No doubt Mrs O'Driscoll had her reasons, or what she thought were her reasons. Obviously, in due course, we shall be questioning *all* the tenants of the block of flats where the bomb went off, irrespective of their ethnic origin.'

'In the name of the saints,' Father Culvey returned harshly, his own accent thickening noticeably as he spoke, 'let us not bandy words. A bomb in a police officer's car — a young Irish lad conveniently to hand. *Quod erat demonstrandum.* We do not need to be instructed as to how the wind blows, Superintendent.'

'I am quite sure that you do not, Father — even though it would be a remarkably maladroit terrorist who set up an explosive device to go off outside his own windows.'

'On the contrary, my good sir.' The priest made a noise only with difficulty to be construed as laughter. 'What could better conform to your accepted image of Paddy, thick as two planks?'

'*Your* image, Father, not mine.' In a completely neutral tone the Superintendent went on: 'I imagine what Mrs O'Driscoll wanted to know from you was whether, in the circumstances, she ought to sit tight until the law came knocking on her door or pack her nephew off to Holyhead without waiting.'

From the other's expression it was almost comically obvious that this was exactly what Mrs O'Driscoll had wanted to know. Before the priest could recover himself the young man raised his head, his long hair falling back from his forehead.

'I should 'a gone without asking.' For the first time he turned and looked at Jurnet directly. 'Not that I done anything to be ashamed of, Mr Jurnet. She was a real lovely lady an' I like it here in England — ' He

47

suddenly choked, ramming back the rest of what he might have said, and ended miserably, 'I like it here.'

'Then why,' the Superintendent intervened gently, 'why, if that is so and you have nothing to conceal, do you say you should have run away, just like that?'

'Not run away — gone home to where they don't lock up people for what they are, on'y for what they done. Because I'm Irish an' because of me old man. Once you got on to him what chance I got? I wouldn't have a hope in hell!'

'Terry . . .' Looking puzzled, the Superintendent fiddled among the papers on his desk. 'Terry Doran, isn't it?'

'It is and it isn't.' The boy spoke defiantly. 'It's all according. Doran's my rightful name ever since I were seven an' me stepfather adopted me legal when he married my mum after the Specials shot dead me real dad.' The boy sat up straight, squared his shoulders as if readying either to receive or to land a blow. 'What chance I bloody got once you find out I'm Danny Cardo's boy?'

The Superintendent sat back in his chair and contemplated the young, unforgiving face.

'The Ennerlough ambush,' he said at last. '*That* Danny Cardo?'

'What other kind is there?' The boy spoke without pride, with a weary resignation. 'Fifteen soldiers killed, twenty-one wounded and a kid passing got his legs blown off. A national hero, there's a lot of people would have it. There's always people happy to stand me a pint for being Danny Cardo's boy. I reckon you'd never so much as let me into the country if you'd known who my natural daddy was.'

'Reckon we wouldn't,' the Superintendent readily agreed. 'Bearing in mind what the IRA has done in Northern Ireland and here on the mainland, could you blame us?'

'I tole you!' the boy cried. 'I'm me! Not my bloody fault what my old man did when I was a nipper.' He stood up trembling, his anger, it seemed, directed more at the priest who had brought him to Police Headquarters than towards his interrogator. Turning, he commanded: 'Come on, Father. I told you we'd be wasting our time. You know what they say, don't you?' The young lips twisted with a bitterness beyond their years. 'Once a mick, always a mick.'

'Sit down,' said the Superintendent in a conversational tone which nevertheless had in it something to secure instant compliance. 'I want you to know,' he went on, his voice modulating to a blandness that invested his

49

words with a kind of absurdity, 'that Section 12 of the Prevention of Terrorism (Temporary Provisions) Act 1984 provides a power of arrest without warrant and allows for the detention of persons arrested for a period of up to forty-eight hours — a period which the Home Secretary may extend to a maximum of seven days.'

The boy looked suddenly devastated, very young.

'I'll get the push! They're very strict at Furling and Broome's. First thing they said to me, we don't want you if you're not serious. On'y reason I could come here now is I'm on day release. It'll be bad enough as it is when they get back the attendance sheets from the Tech and find out I missed a couple of classes without any excuse — '

'If you had indeed gone back to Ireland,' the Superintendent pointed out, quite jovially, 'it's more than a couple of classes you'd have missed. Furling and Broome — they're the architects in Martineau Street, aren't they? An architect — is that what you are hoping to become yourself?'

'An architect — me?' But the longing, the ambition, was there, plain and poignant to see. 'A draughtsman, with luck. Mr Furling seems to think it's a useful talent I have for drawing an' plan-making. When he came to

Larrakil last year for the fishing Mr Gibson at the hotel showed him some of my things and he said as how I should come to England to work in his office, it could be the making of me so long as I were serious. With an auntie living in Angleby already — well, my mother's cousin actually but I've always called her auntie — it seemed the hand of Providence.' Anxiety getting the better of him afresh, Terry Doran all but wailed: 'You keep me here, I don't care for how little or how long, they'll be sure I've been up to something, no matter what. They'll never be letting me stay on.'

'For the love of God,' Father Culvey intervened, instructing, not pleading, however. 'You see how it is. There's no harm in the lad. He came here of his own accord — '

'As you have already said.' The Superintendent permitted himself another small smile in the priest's direction, one that called up no answering flame in the austere cotton-wooled countenance. 'The truth is, Father, you have acted with an almost embarrassing speed, like a guest who turns up half an hour before the time stated on the invitation. To be frank, we aren't yet ready for you and your disclaimers on this young man's behalf. We are still putting our house in order, as it were, getting ready for visitors.'

The smile petering out for total lack of encouragement: 'The trouble is, if I may say so with all respect, that here we operate no confessional. People seldom arrive at Police Headquarters unsolicited to say they have sinned because, unlike your good self, we can neither promise confidentiality nor pronounce absolution; and if they nevertheless persist in arriving, we are obliged by the terms of our employment to seek independent corroboration before we can accept a word they say. As a consequence we have to proceed strictly on a basis of evidence, a commodity which — after the dreadful occurrence of this morning — is, as you will understand, taking a little time to get together.'

Transferring his attention to the boy, who met his eyes with some effort, the Superintendent went on: 'You are a lucky young man, Terry, to have your auntie and Father Culvey here to worry about you, and put themselves out to protect what they see as your interests. Hard as you may find it to believe, we here at Police Headquarters share their concern entirely. If you have done nothing wrong you, any more than everyone else innocent and presently at large in Angleby, have nothing to fear. For the moment, at any rate, I do not propose to exercise my powers under the Act, and you can hurry back to the Tech or to Messrs Furling and Broome with, I sincerely hope, a clear conscience — an architect in the making, eh? One whose proper function, I'm sure I don't need to remind you, is to erect, not destroy. All I require in return is your word, freely given, that you will leave neither Angleby nor the country whilst our inquiries are proceeding.'

Father Culvey pounced.

'How can it be freely given, tell me that now, when you make conditions? I will stand surety for the lad.'

Nodding a good-humoured acknowledgement that the priest had made his point, the Superintendent did not take his eyes off Terry Doran. 'With respect, Father, it is this young man himself from whom I need to hear.'

The young man pushed his hair back from his shoulders, glanced pleadingly at Jurnet, whose expression remained remote. Mumbled: 'I'm not figuring on going anywhere.'

After the two had gone, the priest hustling the boy ahead of him with the impatience of a nurse with no aptitude for the job, the Superintendent sat back in his chair and announced: 'We're going to be in a spot of trouble.' He spoke as if something pleasurable were about to happen.

'Sir?' Jack Ellers, putting away his notebook, looked up, puzzled.

'The Yard!' The Superintendent's eyes were bright with the anticipation of battle. His subordinates did not need to be told the man's views on what he invariably regarded as unjustified encroachments on his bailiwick from the centre. 'A bomb! Can't leave a bomb to the peasantry, can we? That would never do! I'm only surprised the Anti-Terrorist boys haven't turned up already.'

Ellers, greatly daring, ventured: 'Doubt they'd have let the young 'un go so easy.'

'Doubt they would.' Though the tone remained light the gleam in the Superintendent's eyes had been replaced by another, frosty, implacable. 'His luck there must be the usual jam on the bypass holding them up.' The man gave the dry little cough which only his underlings knew to be a sure sign of deep feeling. 'If we're down to holding a suspect on no better grounds than that he's Irish and his father's son, we might as well shut up shop and call it a day. Or better still, send some men over to the Pike and Bittern — isn't that where our local Paddies tank up after work? — pick up whoever happens to be leaning on the bar and to hell with merry England.' His mood changing with the quicksilver swiftness typical of the man: 'Might not be such a bad idea at that. Most of them are working out on the bypass, aren't they? Take them off their excavators and concrete mixers and, with luck, the traffic building up will keep the posse from London off our backs a while longer.'

'Yes, sir.' Having rendered up the obligatory smile, the little Welshman felt safe in pointing out something that was troubling him. 'The youngster told Ben he'd done nothing to be ashamed of. Not exactly the same, was it, as coming out and denying he'd had anything to do with it?'

'You noticed that too — the ambiguity? Deliberate or just clumsy with words? Certainly no sign of that Celtic lyricism we're always hearing about. You think I shouldn't have let him go?'

'Not for me to say, sir.'

'Very wise and circumspect!' The sight of Jurnet, slouched against the window frame, recalled the Superintendent to matters other than the defence of his territory. He even conceded: 'A specific anti-terrorist cadre — they have the expertise, I suppose. They can perhaps recognize correspondences which might conceivably escape us, read things we might have overlooked.' Not sounding too convinced, he got up from his seat and crossed the room to the window, next to the hollow man who stood gazing vacantly out. Inquired gently: 'What did *you* think of young Doran, Ben?'

'Sorry.' Jurnet straightened up with an effort. 'I wasn't listening.' Making the effort to face his superior officer directly: 'Reckon I *will* need that bit of time off, after all.' He looked about the room as if for the last time, impressing it on his memory whilst all the time aware that it was a fruitless effort, not worth the expenditure of energy. With a sigh of something near relief he let the scene go, took leave of his past and of his future alike. 'I've got to be going.'

Jack Ellers came quickly to his side.

'I'll take you back to the Rabbi's. Unless you're absolutely sure you wouldn't rather come back to ours. Rosie'd be only too glad — '

Jurnet interrupted with a shake of the head, affectionate but monumentally dismissive.

'You can drop me off at Miriam's place, if that's all right.'

Ellers looked troubled. He knew that his friend had always made a special point of avoiding his lover's trendy pad in the converted warehouse down by the river — a world, as he had confided more than once, which had had nothing to do with their life together and was better kept altogether separate from it.

'Is that a good idea, Ben? Miriam's mother may not be feeling like visitors.'

'I have to give her the chance to spit in my face.'

5

The short-lived sun was setting as they came to the bridge and turned right along the riverside. It tipped the stealthily moving water with gold, struck diamonds off the windows along the quay, imparting an extra sheen to the painted front doors embellished with knockers in the shape of lions' heads or curly fish with their tails entwined or serpent-haired Medusas. The sleek cars parked alongside and the sleek people who came out of them carrying expensive-looking document cases or carrier bags printed with the names of the best shops in Angleby, did not need a sun's gilding. They carried their own inner illumination, successful cars, successful people. Only a rabble of seagulls, refugees from the autumn gales on the coast, squabbling over some unidentifiable carrion stranded at the edge of the up-market water, added a leaven of reality.

Ellers parked alongside a BMW. He

switched off the Rover's engine and the two sat quietly until the gulls, having only half disposed of their unmentionable meal, departed in haste, as if they had suddenly become aware that they did not fit into the picture.

The little Welshman persisted: 'You'd do much better to wait a few days. Give the woman a chance to come to terms with what's happened.'

Jurnet did not answer. Moving with a geriatric stiffness, he got out of the car, looked about him frowning as if unsure of where he was and of his own purpose in being there. Ellers, watching, distressed, leaned over and spoke through the open window. 'Take as long as you need. If the Rabbi's still there I can give you both a lift back to the synagogue.'

The other took a deep breath, gathered his wits together.

'Not on, thanks all the same. Rosie'll be wondering what's keeping you. You shouldn't have bothered to park.' Jurnet looked vacantly to left and right. Some of the passing cars had switched on their lights, hastening the sun's departure, the glory in the sky fading. In the converted warehouses, wall fittings and table lamps — nothing to spill out into the street with a vulgar splash —

had begun to brighten the posh windows with the miserly discretion which was all the go. Any minute now the fancy street lights sporting the golden bird and winged shoe of the Angleby arms would be springing into bloom along the waterfront, their reflections in the river illusion added to illusion. 'I'll see you out.'

Jack Ellers made no move to turn the key in the ignition. His superior was still dressed, or undressed, in the sweater and jeans he had grabbed in the morning, a lifetime away.

'You can't go about the streets like that, boyo, letting the side down. Not even any socks! And the weather report said frost tonight.'

'I can always take a cab.'

'Oh ah? You got any money with you?' Thus prompted, Jurnet felt obediently in his jeans and came out only with his house keys, seized automatically in that far-off frenzy of haste.

His subordinate said: 'You see!'

'You can lend me a fiver, if it'll make you feel any better.'

Ellers got out of the Rover, came round to the passenger side and took his friend's hand. 'You're planning to go back to your place regardless, aren't you?' he stated rather than asked, trying not to look hurt when

60

Jurnet moved away a little.

'You said yourself I needed to get some socks on.'

'But they'll have disconnected all the mains! You won't even be able to spend a penny — assuming, that is, you can even get through the door. Last I heard, they were planning to board the entire place up.'

'They must have meant the front. All the damage was done there, apart from a few windows. There's a service door round the back. And the tanks on the roof — nothing could have happened to them or we'd have had Niagara down the stairs.' With more animation than he had shown hitherto, Jurnet added: 'Don't worry. Hygiene and the proprieties will be preserved. I promise you.'

Sick at heart, Sergeant Ellers made one last effort.

'I don't like the idea of you on your own.'

'Too late for that, boyo,' Jurnet responded brightly.

There was a bell as well as a knocker on Miriam's front door. The knocker was a fish complete with fins and scales — 'Well, naturally,' Jurnet said aloud — and in case this guarantee of *kashrut* was not of itself sufficient to satisfy the visiting orthodox, a *mezuzah* was affixed higher up the lintel. Unlike the

61

bell, which Jurnet pressed in preference to disturbing the fish, this latter object, the small but visible sign on his doorpost by which a Jew reminded himself with every coming and going of his duty to his God, did not incorporate any talk-back.

The voice which came through the door-phone was male and heavily accented.

'Who is it?'

'Police,' Jurnet said.

'But I have already explained that Mrs Courland is not able — '

'She'll want to see me,' Jurnet said.

There was a pause, and then a voice said: 'A moment.'

Jurnet waited. In a little while he heard through the front door the sharp click of a gate engaging, a whirr of mechanism as a lift ascended and presently returned to ground level. The man who opened the street door, swinging it back boldly on its hinges, was stocky but of striking appearance, his mop of white hair contrasting with the tan of a face which looked battered but invincibly good-humoured, the laugh lines at the corners of the eyes too deeply scored to make themselves scarce even in the presence of tragedy; the scar that, beginning at the mouth, puckered the left cheek, unthreatening and best construed as the continuation of a smile. Himself dressed formally in a dark, double-breasted suit whose English tailoring only made even more explicit the patent foreignness of its wearer, he appeared in no way put out at being confronted by a self-announced emissary of the police brandishing a torch and clad in stained jeans and a sweater scorched and holed from having been positioned too close for comfort to Miriam's funeral pyre. Across the chasm which now separated him from the human race Jurnet felt some warmth, some welcome.

'It is Benjamin,' the man said. 'Come in.'

During the brief journey from the street up to Miriam's flat on the second floor Rafi Galil introduced himself, the relation from Israel providentially over on a visit and staying with his cousin when the terrible news came.

'Providential.' He repeated the word twice over, contriving somehow to infuse horror and sorrow into features carved ineradicably into the aspect of happiness. 'At such a time there is no substitute for one's own. And now you too are here. I am very glad.'

'How did you know I was Benjamin?'

'From Israel, how else? Did Miriam never tell you I work for her in Tel Tzevaim, manage the finances and so on while she is over here, in England? In Tel Tzevaim she has your photograph in her desk drawer. "What is that photograph you take out and look at so many times?" I asked her once, and she showed me. Detective Inspector Benjamin Jurnet. A good photograph, very handsome, very like, except there you are laughing and now, understandably, you are not laughing.' On the landing, his hand on the door to the flat, Rafi Galil turned to the detective as to a friend.

'I mean it when I say I am very glad you are here. You too are family, held tight in the bonds of love. At such a time — isn't it so? — we must take strength one from the other. So I say to Eva, and Rabbi Schnellman, he tells her the same. He tells her that you have been studying to become Jewish, that you are a good man who would have made her daughter a good husband. But Eva — ' For the first time the man looked at Jurnet uncertainly. The scar on his cheek began to ripple slightly. 'The shock has been so great. Perhaps, after all, it is a little too soon.'

'Ask the Rabbi. See what he says.'

'The Rabbi has gone half an hour ago.' The other hunched his broad shoulders and then straightened them, coming to a decision. The scar calmed down. Smiling, the purveyor of good news, he opened the flat door as wide as previously he had opened the front one, and announced to the space beyond: 'What do you think? It is Benjamin who is here. Miriam's Ben.'

The room was too much for Jurnet. His sole previous view of it had been when the flat had been newly acquired, unfinished, unfurnished. Now the sight of it complete, the walls so smooth, the couches so white, the single abstract on the wall so modishly dissociated from flesh and blood, struck terror in his soul. Where in all this chic zilch was the laughing girl who had daily run up the stairs past the stained-glass Armada to make love with him on a bed that jangled like the tambourine in a Salvation Army band? The place was so filled with the absence of Miriam there was no room left for air. Jurnet felt he might die and was disappointed to find himself still living.

'Bring him over here.'

Stumbling, Jurnet followed the Israeli across the acres of parquet to a leather armchair in whose depths a woman lay curled up as if in the womb. Her face was too swollen with crying for Jurnet to be troubled by possible resemblances to his dead love, her hair too limp to invite comparisons with Miriam's burnished bronze. When the two men approached she raised herself to a sitting position, pulled her crumpled skirt down over her knees; peered up at the detective through puffy lids, a prolonged scrutiny to which he submitted as to a well-merited punishment.

At the end she sank back, exhausted.

'All right, Rafi. You can take him away now.'

Jurnet turned to go.

'But Eva — !' the Israeli began in protest, until Jurnet stopped him.

'That's OK.'

'I needed to see him,' Mrs Courland explained, rolling the handkerchief in her hand into a soggy ball. 'I needed to put a face to Miriam's murderer. It was too aggravating, having only a blank space where his face was supposed to be. Now I know.'

'Eva darling!' Rafi Galil insisted. 'Don't be like that! He loved Miriam too. How can you say such things?'

'Let it be, Mr Galil. Mrs Courland's entitled to say whatever she wants, especially when it's the truth.' Jurnet looked down at the bedraggled figure in the armchair feeling a surge of tenderness for the woman who had once carried Miriam inside her body. What was his loss, compared to hers? Addressing her directly, he said: 'I hope it has

66

helped a little, knowing the face.'

In a voice stripped of all feeling Eva Courland replied: 'Burn in Hell.'

Jurnet stood by the river watching himself. That part of him which, honed by his years in the CID, was compulsively — one might say automatically — obsessed by the springs of human behaviour noted with scientific detachment that he no longer felt as if he were grieving, did not even feel particularly sad. Simply that life, like a holed bucket, had drained itself of all meaning.

Night had fallen. Exactly as Jack Ellers had prophesied, he had begun to feel cold in his ruined sweater, proving at least that he was not entirely lost to all feeling, only to those that mattered. Looking out over the river, where the dancing reflections of the street lamps invited him to come on in, the water's lovely, he debated with himself whether it was worth while going home to the half-life — the half-death, rather — which was all that remained on offer, or if it wouldn't be altogether more sensible to vault the low brick wall which was all that stood between him and the sweet healing of oblivion: get it over and done with. He would feel cold for a little, that was certain — if the autumn air was cold, the autumn river would be colder — but what was that opposed to the endless procession of empty days, the endless absence of love?

The absence of Miriam.

Jurnet had put a hand on the wall in readiness when his sweater was grabbed from behind, the fabric tightening under his armpits.

'You forgot something,' said Rafi Galil, not letting go but smiling as, with his free hand, he held out the torch, 'I thought, when I saw it, "Tomorrow I will take it to the police station," only then Eva asked me to draw the curtains and when I went to the window there you were, standing, looking at the river.' With complete artlessness the man finished: 'I'm glad I caught you.'

He let go the sweater and looked away, out over the water, perhaps giving the detective time to gather his wits together. 'Beautiful!' he pronounced. 'But as I told Miriam, when I was over here three years ago and she showed me over the flat before taking it, I could never live here. The damp, the rheumatism! And then, I should be afraid. Rivers are like wild beasts. You think you have them caged safely between banks and then one day they break out in floods and drown you in your bed.'

In command of himself again, Jurnet

pointed out: 'Miriam's flat is on the second floor.'

The Israeli shook his head nevertheless. 'Not high enough,' he pronounced. 'There is more than one way of getting yourself drowned.' Under the light of the street lamps the man's white hair, his unwavering expression of good humour, were calming. His eyes on the dancing reflections on the other side of the wall, he said: 'I do not know what Miriam told you about me.'

'Some kind of cousin, so far as she said anything. We never discussed anything to do with her business, it was an understood thing, and you came under that heading.'

'Because I too work at Tel Tzevaim I am separate business!' The other raised a hand in rueful protest. 'I am family! Only a third or a fourth cousin, but to Miriam always Uncle Rafi. Did she never talk to you about Uncle Rafi?'

'No,' faltered Jurnet, destroyed afresh by the thought of all the things he and Miriam had never talked about and, now, never would.

'She did not want to upset you,' the other asserted, only his words contradicting his unwavering cheerfulness. 'It is not a funny story. About my family, that is to say — my mother, my father, two brothers, three sisters, aunts, uncles and cousins too numerous to mention — all dead in the camps, in Auschwitz, in Buchenwald. Each and every one of them lovely people, hearts of gold — yet only I, the *lobbus,* the wild one, the least deserving, survived. Who can hope to know the mind of the Master of the Universe?' The Israeli sighed, his air of happy expectation not noticeably abating. 'The day, or rather, the night the Germans came to the ghetto — they came at night because they knew it would be easier for them when we were all asleep, we went to bed early in those days, sleep was the only escape — I and my friend Berl were the only two not there dreaming of freedom. Some weeks before we had found a secret way out, through some old drains which had been begun and then left unfinished, and many times at night we crept out through them into the city to steal food or kill a German. In those days — ' with a little laugh — 'it was, I tell you, easier to find a German to kill than a fowl to take home, or a few eggs. So! They rounded up everybody in the ghetto, they would not even let them stop to put on their clothes. In their vests and their nightshirts they took them, many of them naked in the night air. Took them away to the camps and the gas ovens, and next day, so soon as it was light, they brought in bulldozers to demolish the ghetto, every brick, every stone, until at last it was as if the Jews of that city had never existed.'

'You and your friend got away.' For want of something else to say, Jurnet spoke into the silence that followed.

'We got away, we the wild ones. We got away to the forest, we became animals, hunted and hunting. And at last — it is a long story with which I shall not bore you — we got to Israel — Berl, alas, only just. A soldier of the British Army shot him dead as we ran from the boat up the beach, heading for cover.' Rafi Galil turned from his contemplation of the river and smiled up at Jurnet. 'After the ghetto, and the forest, and the unimaginable horrors that had become the things of every day, he reaches Erez Yisroel only to die on the beach, before he has taken two steps on the soil of the Promised Land! I tell you, after I had killed that British soldier with my bare hands I cried for my friend Berl as I had never cried for all my slaughtered family. I cry for him still, except that now I cry for that British soldier also; only, as they say, obeying orders. But most of all I cry for the God who has to carry all these things on His conscience.'

The man nevertheless gave a little laugh, almost a giggle.

71

'Why do I tell these things to a policeman, one who knows more than other people how terrible the world is? I see you looking at the river, thinking of death, and I speak as I do to remind you that — no matter what happens — life is the important thing. Who will remember Miriam, her beauty, her brightness, if you jump into the water and drown yourself? Her mother, you may say, her family, her friends: all true. But who will remember her as only you, her lover, can?' The Israeli reached up and touched Jurnet's cheek, tenderly. 'You have a duty to live, my friend. A duty to Miriam.'

6

Protesting that their destination ought by rights to be the synagogue, Rafi Galil drove Jurnet home.

'You will have to defend me to Rabbi Schnellman. He said that you would be staying with him.'

Ignoring the man's pronouncement out of an exhaustion which made it unthinkable to get into an argument, Jurnet pointed out: 'Mrs Courland will be wondering what happened to you.'

'Is quite all right. I told her I might be a little while. I think she is glad to be left alone, for a little. There are times — isn't it so? — when sympathy is itself an insult. Now — ' turning in the driving seat with a smile — 'direct me the way to the Rabbi.'

'I have to get some socks,' Jurnet offered inadequately.

'Fine! Tell me the way to the socks first

and I will wait outside while you go in and fetch them.'

'No!' The tone of this disclaimer precluded any further discussion. 'Take the second left at the end of the street and follow the one-way system round.'

The Israeli protested no further; turned obediently, following the serpentine way which, with indifferent success, did its best to put Angleby's medieval town plan on terms with the twentieth century. 'When I was here before, three years ago,' he remarked chattily, 'I came by train. Miriam met me at the station, drove me around — to the workshop, to see the sights, all over — and I said then that wild horses would never get me to drive in this city of hers, the streets made me too dizzy. Ah well!' A sigh, followed by the smile that seemed more congenial to him. 'As it turns out, I am only too thankful to have already hired this car, so soon as I came to London. The state she is in, Eva could never have travelled in a railway carriage, so public, so many people.'

Jurnet, making an effort, the moment of seeing again the forecourt, that hole in the ground, growing nearer and nearer, managed: 'Ford Fiesta, is it?'

'Something like that, I think. A Ford, yes. A very nice little car. A sad, a terrible, journey down, Eva beside herself, but at the same time very smooth and the petrol very economical. The bypass was at last open and we arrived without any of the usual delays or hold-ups. Even coming into the city centre, into this maze, I found the way without difficulty. Only once, when I am going the wrong way up a one-way street, one of your policemen stops me, very stern with his notebook ready, but then I speak with my strongest foreign accent and he puts it away and is most kind. Stops the traffic and makes everybody wait so that I can turn, and then explains exactly how I must go to get to the river. He is so sorry for me, not an Englishman! Now — ' Rafi Galil finished — 'we are coming to a junction. You must tell me which way I must go.'

'Stop here,' Jurnet instructed, when they came to his street. He had issued the order some yards down from the block of flats, childishly postponing the moment of confrontation. 'You can let me out here.' He undid his seat belt, put his hand on the door catch.

The Israeli drew into the kerb. 'Please — ' he begged, worry, a poor fit, overlaying his cheerful countenance. 'Collect your socks, my dear young man. Your socks and anything else you may require for your comfort, and

75

then let me take you to the Rabbi.'

Jurnet got out of the car as if he had not heard.

'Thanks for the lift.'

Even then, the car did not move off immediately. Jurnet, walking reluctantly up the street, the night air cold on his bare ankles, was overcome by an unwarranted anger at the Israeli's continued presence, the little squirt's compassion an intolerable intrusion. This was *his* private business — or rather, his and Miriam's.

He turned and gesticulated at the car, stepping into the roadway to signal his meaning the more visibly.

'Bugger off!' he shouted. 'What you hanging about for? Go away!'

The detective stood there, waving his arms about, until a cheery toot on the Ford's horn acknowledged 'Message received.' He watched in dour satisfaction as Rafi Galil made a badly executed three-point turn and the car was on its way again. Only when he saw its rear lights dwindling in the distance did he whimper 'Come back!'

They had strung a red tape between the brick pillars on either side of the entrance to the forecourt, and filled the space between with a number of traffic cones. Beyond, Jurnet could see winking yellow lights, placed presumably to warn any short-sighted cats who might be passing of the gaping hole in the tarmac. The flats looked boarded up, derelict.

He had just begun to move away some of the cones when a police car drove up, and braked suddenly. Doors flew open, an officer sprang out from either side; came running, shouting. The fuss of it all made Jurnet's head ache. He felt colder than ever.

'What the hell do you think you're — ' PC Blake's voice modulated to an astonished, a concerned 'Mr Jurnet! Sir!'

Blake, thought Jurnet, desisting from his labours: very young, very keen, a dedicated bird watcher. Images of black-headed gulls, of long-legged herons, of the plaster geese which skeined across the wall above Mrs O'Driscoll's mantelpiece, swam like fish incongruously into his mind. He made a mental note to check if the geese had got safely away.

He said: 'Only here to pick up a few things and have a general look around.'

Bly, the second constable, objected: 'It's all boarded up. You won't be able to get in.'

'I'll manage.' Jurnet raised his head to look at his violated Shangri-La. 'Most of the damage is here at the front. The back's OK,

I think, bar a few windows.' Lips twisted in some kind of smile, he watched as the two policemen looked at each other uncertainly. He could see that it was his torn sweater, his unwashed scruffiness, as much as anything, which added to their unease. 'Take it from me, no suspicious circumstances. I live here, remember.'

'Of course, sir.' PC Blake hesitated, then ventured: 'Didn't see any car, sir. We could wait till you've finished and then give you a lift — '

'That won't be necessary.' Turning away purposefully: 'Goodnight.'

'We've been coming back once an hour, sir . . .' Except for Jack Ellers and the Superintendent no one at Police Headquarters had known about Miriam: she had been strictly private business. Now, from the way the youngster floundered, it was clear to Jurnet that his relationship to the female unlucky enough to have been on the receiving end of that day's bomb incident had permeated down to the ranks. 'We could pick you up next time round, if that's more convenient — '

'That won't be necessary either.'

'Right, sir!' they said then, and 'Goodnight, sir!' as they went off unhappily with none of the flamboyance which had garnished their arrival. Jurnet stayed where he was, waiting for the quiet to flow back — the solicitude of his own tribe had unmanned him a little — before turning again to the traffic cones.

This time the interruption was of a different kind. A shadow detached itself from the tangle of shadows at that side of the block where a mess of elderberry, holly and briar had long ago taken over what had once been hopefully designated a garden. A shadow with a suitcase and a voice that said in a foreign accent, 'Mr Ben? I am Pnina.'

Moving awkwardly, the girl selected a patch of light where she stopped, as if awaiting clearance before proceeding further. She stood as one used to waiting, expecting no special favours. The sodium street light tinged her olive skin with a purple which became denser round her large, dark eyes and in the hollows under her cheekbones. The straight hair that hung well below her shoulders was purple also, though Jurnet knew it must be black really, a Mediterranean blackness like his own, one the normal Angleby spectrum was not equipped to take on board. The white track suit she wore looked grey and sad.

'Did Miriam not tell you?'

The girl, he could hear, was close to tears.

79

Her childish vulnerability rekindled all Jurnet's guilt, all his anger. Death he could deal with, being cursed he could deal with, but not pathos. He answered harshly: 'Miriam's dead.'

'I know. I heard them talking.'

'Who? Who did you hear?'

'The policemen. When they were here before.' The girl gave a great sob, instantly throttled back into some sort of inarticulate apology. 'While I was waiting for you to come.'

'Why me?'

'Please!' Her thin shoulders bent with weariness, but still carrying the suitcase as if she must not be separated from it in any circumstances, the girl left the patch of light and came towards Jurnet moving as before, awkwardly. Worse than that: she was a cripple, he now saw, one leg shorter than the other. Must be one of Miriam's lame ducks from Tel Tzevaim, too late, too bloody bad. As she approached him, Jurnet retreated. He wanted to say that he was sorry, he simply could not take her on, not on top of everything else; but he said nothing.

'Please!' she cried again. A certain wildness had come into her purple-shadowed face. 'I waited at Heathrow. I wait and wait and Miriam does not come. Then I phone the two numbers she gave me. One is the work-shop. The other one, she says, is where she lives with her Ben.'

'Not any more,' Jurnet said.

'Now I know. There, at the airport I did not know. I only know that Miriam is not there to meet me as we arranged. It is not like her. I can rely on Miriam as my life. Something terrible must have happened or she would have sent a message. I phone the workshop, but there is no reply. By then, I realize, I have waited so long it is closed for the day. Everyone has gone home. So I phone the other number, over and over, even though the operator tells me the line is out of order. I have very little money. What am I to do?'

'There must have been people at Heathrow who could have helped you. El Al or the airport police. Welfare workers, the Israeli consul. Somebody.'

'I do not need people.' Jurnet had un-wittingly touched a chord. The girl changed the suitcase from one hand to the other, the tired shoulders straightened themselves. Her voice became proud and firm, a voice he could cope with. 'It is not the first time in my life things do not go right for me. I make inquiries, I find that, if I go to Victoria, there is a bus which goes from

81

there to Angleby cheaper than the train, and I have just enough money to pay my fare. So that is what I do. When I arrive in Angleby I know it is no use to go to the workshop, so I come here. A woman at the bus station tells me it is a long way, I should take a taxi, but I have not enough money, so she tells me the streets to take and I walk.'

All that way, crippled and lugging that heavy suitcase! Against his will, Jurnet felt the first stirrings of compassion. All the same he said: 'You should have gone to the police. Or the Rabbi.'

'I tell you — I do not need people to tell me what to do. I walk, and when I get here I see what has happened to these apartments. I know what bombs do and I know something has happened to Miriam. Is she in the hospital perhaps? I decide, in case she is there, I will find the hospital when I have had a little rest. The woman at the bus station was right — it is a long way. Only then the policemen come and I hide in the bushes and listen to what they say, and so I know it is no use to go to the hospital. To go anywhere.' Another sob, as rigorously suppressed as the first, prefaced: 'So I wait for Mr Ben.'

'How did you know I would come?'

82

'Miriam spoke to me many times about you. I knew.'

Jurnet had guessed correctly. The back of the block was not boarded up at all, not even the few windows on that side which had been broken. Jurnet added to their number by finding a plank with which to smash the pebbled-glass panel which filled in the upper half of the service door.

Leaving some further strands of his ruined sweater impaled on the jagged residue, he reached inside and turned the old-fashioned key, in place in the lock. The door opened with difficulty — there seemed to have been some settlement of the entire structure and the bottom of the door scraped protestingly along the worn quarry tiles — but at least it opened, Jurnet using the torch to illuminate the passage within and the narrow stairs, their concrete treads flaked with plaster from the walls which rose steeply to the floors above.

He went ahead, lighting the way for the girl behind him but making no offer to carry her suitcase for her. In other circumstances her lameness, her laboured breathing, would surely have evoked his sympathy, or at least shamed him into some pose of civilized behaviour; but that night sympathy and shame were alike beyond him. Only when, coming up to the second floor, he became aware that her ugly clippity-clop no longer sounded behind him and, directing his torch down towards the half-landing, saw her stranded there in utter exhaustion, did some remembrance stir of what it was to be part of humankind.

He retraced his steps and picked up the case without speaking, relieved, if anything, by the flash of anger in her eyes — anger, he knew without being told, directed not at him but at her own weakness. He did not insult her further by offering to carry her, as well as her luggage, the rest of the way.

The flat door was ajar, just as he had left it that morning, centuries away. Yellow dust coated everything and still hung slowly re-volving in the air that came through into the hall from the space where the bedroom window had once been. It comforted him, a little, that for the first time in all the years of his tenancy he could smell neither Nappisan nor joss sticks, neither cabbage nor the slow-simmered underwear which to-gether, rising up the stairs from some never-failing source, had combined to make up the unique and wonderful air of home: proof — if proof were needed — that it was home no longer.

Dumping the suitcase inside the door, he guided the girl to the sole armchair, then went into the kitchen and took candles and matches from the drawer where Miriam had kept them. The sight of the candles — the plain white candles with which, every Friday evening, the two of them had welcomed in the sabbath, almost destroyed him. It had been the one small ceremony which, of all his experience of Judaism, had made him feel a part, not so much of the fellowship of Israel particularly, but of a universe presided over by a loving God. Always, after she had kindled the two lights, Miriam would spread out her hands in a kind of loving greeting towards the brisk little flames so that her long, elegant fingers showed translucent round the edges, themselves part of the sabbath light. Reciting the blessing, she would raise those same hands to cover her face as if — or so it had seemed to her lover — by that small sacramental gesture she was fusing her own beauty and the beauty of the sabbath into one incomparable whole.

Loving God my eye! Jurnet felt laughter choking him like vomit; forced it back, glad for the first time of the presence of the crippled girl collapsed in his armchair in the dark to remind him to keep the stiff upper lip flying. He put a match to one candle, found a pile of saucers and came back into the living-room ready to inaugurate a festival. The girl sat up and looked pleased as he lit the candles one after the other and set each in melted wax on a saucer, ignoring altogether the small silver candlesticks on the sideboard, the ones he and Miriam had bought for their first sabbath together.

The candle flames swayed in the breeze that came in from the broken window, ten little flames in all.

Himself unaccountably better for the sight of them, Jurnet said: 'Let there be light.' The girl, he now saw, looking at her properly for the first time, had, by candle-light at any rate, a strange bony kind of beauty that teetered on the edge of ugliness. Unless it was the other way round, ugliness on the edge of beauty, he could not summon up enough energy to decide which. 'Let there be light,' he said again, for a wonder without irony.

Encouraged by his tone, or by the dancing arrowheads of flame, the girl asked timidly: 'Do you perhaps have a piece of bread? On the plane I was too excited to eat. Now I am very — hungry.' The final word came out in an abandonment of control, a childish wail. 'After I bought the bus ticket I only had money left for a very small biscuit . . .'

Resentful afresh of her demands on his attention, Jurnet took one of the candles and went back to the kitchen. Who the hell was this waif Miriam, from beyond the grave, had lumbered him with, this cripple with the nerve to thrust her private needs between his grief and his own uninterrupted enjoyment of it? Yes, enjoyment. Appalled by this hitherto unknown lout who was himself, Jurnet clenched his fist and banged it against his forehead, once, twice. Shaken by the waves of perturbation set in motion by this act of despair, the candle in his other hand flickered and almost went out.

Grief as masturbation, a solitary vice — ye gods! A double violation here, between walls where he and Miriam had loved with a total joy, each finding fulfilment in the other. Grief, it was apparent, did more than make you feel sorry. It made you despicable.

Atoning, he opened the fridge, to find inside a mess of broken eggs and rancid milk upon which he shut the door quickly, unequal to any attempt at salvage. In the cupboard over the sink where he and Miriam had kept their meagre stores — even in his present state, he recognized, no amount of posthumous canonization could ever resurrect Miriam as a good housewife — he found a packet of Ryvita barely started; also a tin of sardines which he took out, held in his hands for some little time before setting it down on the draining board. He was sorry but he simply did not feel up to getting the damn thing open.

The girl, when he returned to the living-room, greeted the crackers with such gratitude, downed them with such appetite, that, despite himself, Jurnet again felt some vague stirrings of pity; returned to the kitchen and, with what seemed to him positively heroic effort, succeeded in getting the tin of sardines open. So far as he could tell by candle-light, not a single dish or container into which to tip the oily morsels remained whole, so he brought in the opened tin as it was, without explanation or apology.

'Oh good!' Radiant, the girl — what had she said her name was? — scoffed the lot. 'It's horrible, isn't it?' she commented afterwards, with an honesty which, even as it aroused Jurnet's reluctant admiration, shocked him to the core — 'You feel yourself full of mourning, yet at the same time all you can think about is how hungry you are.' She sucked her fingers to get rid of the oil. 'It was the same with my father and my mother. We came from Morocco and we had been in Israel less than a week. We were going to go out to a restaurant — a restaurant! — in celebration that at last, after all the years of disappointments, we were there, in Jerusalem the Golden, the city of our dreams. I was a child, I had never been to a restaurant before, and all day long I ate nothing in preparation for the wonderful feast. Only then — ' the high-cheekboned face between beauty and ugliness went a little askew — 'we took a bus to go to the restaurant that some terrorists had put a bomb on. We had two more stops to go when it blew up. My mother and my father were both killed, people were lying about without arms and legs, and all I could think about was how hungry I was!'

'Shut up!' Jurnet wanted to shout. *What the hell had got into everybody?* First that fellow Galil and his family slaughtered in the concentration camps, now this girl and her bloody bombed bus. What were they trying to tell him? That he wasn't the only one in the world to suffer? That others had suffered worse than he? If that was what it was, OK, point taken. He got the message. So what?

Suddenly, shamingly, he too felt ravenous: went back to the kitchen, back to the cupboard over the sink. All he managed to turn up were a few Twiglets which he bolted down on the spot, hating the girl for showing

89

him up for what he was: wanting to think only of Miriam instead of the hamburger that hovered in front of his eyes recumbent on its bun like a houri brazenly tempting him. He could even smell the onions.

He sent his tongue round his mouth seeking out the last salt crumbs of the Twiglets before returning to the living-room to demand peevishly: 'What did you say your name was?'

'Pnina. Pnina Benvista.'

'Pnina.'

She could tell from the way Jurnet said it, elongating the first syllable so as to make its three syllables of equal length, that in some way she had offended him.

'Pnina,' she repeated timidly. 'It means a pearl.'

'Oh ah? Well, Pnina Pearl, pick up your suitcase. I shouldn't have let you drag it all the way up here in the first place. It's time I found you somewhere to sleep tonight.'

'Oh please!' Tears showed in the girl's eyes. With some effort she sat up in the armchair, her legs, of unequal length, hanging down awkwardly. 'It is late. I am so tired. Why cannot I stay here?'

'Out of the question.' Jurnet could not bring himself actually to put into words that he could not stand a moment longer the way she came between him and his grief. If only he'd been a Jew, he thought wryly — a *real* Jew, circumcised and guaranteed kosher by the Beth Din instead of a Jew in waiting — things would have been different. Then, for a week he could sit *shivah,* mourning his loss as he sat on a low chair in carpet slippers, not shaving, not alone but glad of it, so far as, in that situation, he could be glad of anything. His friends would come to share his grieving, thus lightening his own burden; to say prayers at the prescribed intervals, to chat over tea and sweet cakes, thus letting him know, in the most delicate way possible, that outside that room of mourning there was still waiting a world worth living for . . .

The realization that his animus against his uninvited visitor was not personal, that the presence of anyone else would have been equally unwelcome, softened his tone a little, not all that much. He pointed out: 'No water, no food, no bed. You can't possibly stay here — '

'Oh please!' she begged again, retreating into the depths of the old chair, burrowing into its lumpy cushions. 'I can sleep here, where I am, very well . . . It is very comfortable. And only for tonight,' she added appeasingly. 'Miriam said she had made arrangements for me to stay with the lady who is in charge of her machinists here in Angleby — a Jewish lady, she said, keeps a kosher house and is very kind: I would be sure to like her. Tomorrow, when it is time for the workshop to be open again, I will go there and speak to her — '

'No reason you can't speak to her to-night,' Jurnet interrupted. 'If she's Jewish, the Rabbi's bound to know who it is and where to get hold of her.'

He went into the bedroom where the tele-phone was, and found it askew on its cradle, as he should have known it would be. As he trod the uneven floorboards the bed jan-gled its customary welcome, one that Miriam had always asserted to be the opening notes of an otherwise unknown Enigma Variation, but which Jurnet knew incontrovertibly for the introduction to the song of songs which is Solomon's: *Behold thou art fair, my love, behold thou art fair.*

With a ceremonial, almost an hieratic ges-ture, he extinguished the candle he was carrying by toppling it off its precarious perch on the saucer and then setting his foot upon it as it lay guttering on the floor. He not merely stood on it, he trampled it with dedication, flattening the white wax un-til it lay a ghostly patch in such light as came through the broken window. When he had made, as he thought, a good job of it, he completed the ritual by smashing the saucer itself hard on one of the little brass pinnacles which decorated each corner of the bedstead. The pieces flew in all directions, one needle-sharp sliver grazing his cheek in passing. He felt the wetness of blood on his cheek and bawled like a child in a tantrum, furious it had not found his jugular.

He fell on to the bed, tearing at the flowered duvet, the bed jangling crescendo. He screamed in a passion of anguish at not being dead.

Timpani were added to the score: the clip-clop of the crippled Israeli girl as she hurried into the room as fast as she was able. In the candle-light she carried with her, her face showed pale and shocked, her dark eyes despairing.

She stood at the side of the bed imploring, 'What is it, Mr Ben? What is it?' But Jurnet was past answering, drowning in sorrow as earlier that night he had so nearly drowned in the river. Grief closed over his head with the finality of those dark waters.

'Mr Ben — oh, Mr Ben!'

Crying herself now, Pnina Benvista reached out with her free hand and touched the shuddering body, only to withdraw instantly as if guilty of an inexcusable intrusion. It was perhaps the same delicacy which made her, with trembling breath, blow out the candle; set it down next to the silent phone. She stood by the bed and did her own grieving.

Miriam.

Losing her always precarious balance in the dark, she stumbled and fell on the bed herself, rolling down its declivity towards Jurnet who clutched at her as a drowning man might clutch at a lifeline. Bewildered as children punished for something they did not do, they clung together sobbing, until presently the sobs died away and they slept in each other's arms.

7

The Courland Collection said the elegant black italics, an enlargement of Miriam's own handwriting, scrawled with a chic nonchalance across the low, white-painted building which was — had been, Jurnet reminded himself without mercy — Miriam's workshop. It was an additional shock to see his lover's red Renault, spick and span and doubtless ready to go, parked alongside the dwarf cypresses which lined the short drive-in.

A life for a spare part — not much of an exchange. Jurnet's eyes were stinging. He shut them, squeezing the lids tight, and reopening to find the world unchanged and Miriam still dead, dead, dead.

He paid off the cabbie and picked up the suitcase without hearing any demur from its owner. After their night together and without a word spoken, his relationship with the Israeli girl had moved on to the different, if precarious, footing of those who have rendered each other a service and received one in return.

Not gratitude, since both had benefited equally from that catharsis of tears, but not especially friendship either. More a subliminal recognition that, one way or another, both were in the same boat and sinking fast.

No: Jurnet made a mental correction. Whatever else she might have in mind, it was plain from her air of adamant resolution, from the stoic forcing of her recalcitrant body into the postures of normal movement, that Pnina Benvista had no intention of going down for the third or any other time. In her crisp white blouse and a tailored suit whose skirt length made positively no concession to the deformity below, she looked considerably altered from the waif of his first encounter.

The girl looked at the immaculate building, the shipshape greenery, and permitted herself a smile, small but, as the first relaxation of her severe aspect that he had seen, as disconcerting to Jurnet as any Cheshire cat's grin. 'I'm so glad to be clean again,' she said. 'It is necessary to make a good first impression. What would they think of me, turning up dirty and unbusinesslike?' She smoothed down clothes that were immediately thrown out of true again by the ugly protuberance of her left hip, and finished: 'Your friend Mario is a kind man.'

'Yes. A good guy.'

'He was, of course, paying a debt,' she stated matter-of-factly. 'While you were in the bathroom shaving he told me how you had saved his son's life.'

'Young Johnny's? He was having you on.'

'He said so,' she insisted, looking a little affronted, as if it were her own word which was being doubted. 'He said that without you his son would have gone to prison for drug-trafficking, that he was being framed, as they say. It was something before the boy was even born, he said, to do with old quarrels and hates in Sicily — and only you believed he was telling the truth; found out who the real criminals were, and set him free.'

'Hardly saving the boy's life.'

'Mario said that now his son is in America on a scholarship. One day he will become a great scientist and it will all be your doing. Without you he would be in prison, his life ruined. Though it is possible — ' she conceded with a certain grudging reluctance — 'that even without his son he would be kind. It is, I think, in his nature.' The surprising smile came back again, enlarged itself into a curving of lips that turned her, for an astonishing moment, into a mischievous child. 'I think only a kind man could make such good poached eggs.'

They had dressed, the two of them, in the dank chill of morning, autumn pouring over the sill of the missing window as if itself seeking refuge from the weather. Purged of emotion, they were conscious only of their physical state, unfresh, unfed. The taps, when Jurnet, hoping against hope, turned them on in kitchen and bathroom, ran brown sludge. The yellow dust which, the night before, had revolved in the draught with a certain ponderous grace, had settled thickly on every surface, living and dead.

They dressed with an exaggerated regard for each other's privacy, donning fresh clothes which seemed to them to shrink from contact with the unwashed bodies beneath. Pnina muttered shamefacedly: 'I'm hungry.'

'We'll go across the road to Mario's — he ought to be open by now. It's only a caff, no cloakroom that I know of, but he'll let us use his wash-basin, I shouldn't wonder, so long as there's no crockery waiting to be washed up.' Jurnet picked up the girl's suitcase. 'We'll take this with us, so we can go straight on to the workshop and I can drop you off there.'

'Will you stay on here?'

'Probably. I haven't thought about it.'

The girl looked about her, memorizing the place. She sat down on the bed as if, now that the moment of departure had come, suddenly unwilling to go. The bed jangled non-committally, dissociating itself from the argument. 'I don't like to think of you here on your own.'

Jurnet returned harshly: 'I shall be on my own wherever I am. Come on!'

Out in the air it was a little better, not much. Early as it was, a few spectators already stood on the pavement, beyond the cones which filled in the entrance to the forecourt, commenting in the self-important way of people privileged to be in on some disaster occasioning loss of life. The appearance of Jurnet and the crippled girl from round the side of the block was evidently an unlooked-for bonus.

'Who you reckon, then?' One of the *aficionados* accosted Jurnet eagerly, taking in Pnina's deformity with approval, more grist to the mill. 'IRA? Sinn Fein?'

'Women's Institute,' Jurnet returned firmly, setting the cones back in place. Instantly, the realization that he had actually made a joke, feeble as it was, depressed him beyond measure. Miriam only twenty-four hours

99

gone and already the quick-talking dick was settling back into his stride, cracking-wise. Pnina Benvista's inquiry, her face turned puzzled towards him as she clip-clopped across the road at his side, as to who, what, was the Women's Institute, did not make him feel any better.

In the café Mario was already at work on the day's sandwiches. It was plain from the way he buttered the slices of bread laid out on the wooden board, enriched them with cheese and salami, frills of lettuce and slivers of tomato, olives — one green, one black, to each completed work of art — that the man loved his work. When Jurnet and Pnina Benvista came through the door, he put down his long, thin knife reluctantly, as one parting from a dear friend; wiped his hands on his apron and came out from behind the counter. His broad peasant face alight with emotion — Miriam had been a favourite of his, one for whom it had been his pleasure to fashion sandwiches with extra cheese, extra salami, at no extra charge — he wrapped his arms round the detective and kissed him on both cheeks. With tears in his eyes he admonished: 'Just the same, my dear Mr Jurnet, remember it is of God.'

Unable to think of anything by way of reply, Jurnet said nothing and waited for the garlic-flavoured embrace to expend itself. Strange, it occurred to him with the eerie detachment which seemed to have taken over all his thought processes, how he still hadn't a clue how to mourn, seeing that in the course of his work he must have come up against enough mourning, one would have thought, to have made him an expert on the subject. *'Blessed are they that mourn, for they shall be comforted,'* he reminded himself. 'Oh yeah?' he mouthed, silently derisive.

The white plastic chairs in the café's eating area were still on their night-time perches on top of the plastic tables, Mario lifted two of them down and placed them in position at a table over which hung a painting of two lovers passionately conjoined in a gondola, whilst behind them the gondolier, beaming approval, sent his boat gliding through the turgid waters of the Grand Canal. 'Sit down, Mr Jurnet. The coffee is just this minute ready, good and hot and fresh, the best of the day. And the young lady, please . . .'

For the first time the café owner took a good look at Jurnet's companion, his heavy features once more softening into an expression which evidently gave no satisfaction to its beneficiary. The young lady sat down and announced composedly: 'My legs are also

101

of God, Mr Mario. Don't let them worry you. Mr Ben said you would let us wash in your wash-basin if we asked, but I am so hungry. I would like some breakfast first, if you please.'

How the two of them had tucked in! Two poached eggs each and a mountain of toast, and then two eggs each again and *cappuccinos* beyond counting. After a final topping up of coffee cups Mario, a little bemused, had returned to his sandwiches as to the eternal verities. *Snick!* went his knife in a sharp diagonal across the completed rounds, deeply reassuring.

When they were ready to think once more about washing, the café owner announced with pride that upstairs was a bathroom they were welcome to use with all his heart, a bathroom with all modern conveniences; even — this with a troubled glance at Jurnet, lest it be taken for a judgement on the dark stubble which gave the guardian of law and order, for all his dark business suit, striped shirt and quiet tie, the appearance of a Neapolitan brigand — an electric shaver left behind by Johnny when he went to America in case the American electricity was different from the English kind.

Pnina Benvista went up first, taking her

time and descending in an aura of well-being which, even as he noted that the girl was less plain than he had earlier thought, made Jurnet greet her return with a scowl, made him screw up his eyes as if the light in the café was suddenly too strong for them. He discovered without surprise that he could not bear the proximity of happiness, not even of the small happiness which came from being clean.

Yet when it came to his own turn and he stood, washed and shaved, in front of the mirror over the bathroom basin, he too was unable to repress an involuntary, if guilt-ridden, spasm of satisfaction. Out of the glass a colourable imitation of Detective Inspector Benjamin Jurnet, Angleby CID, stared back at him, not a sight that would ordinarily have afforded him much pleasure — his dark, un-English appearance something he would have preferred to do without — but one that at least testified that everything was once more under control, the cork back firmly in the bottle. Henceforth his grief was strictly something between himself and Miriam. For better or worse, the scourge of the Angleby criminal classes was back on the job.

Even as his mind proffered that consolation prize he drew back, alarmed, from its implications. Was he or was he not in any condition to go out into his altered world and seek out the killer who, planning merely to blow away a hated copper, had stumbled upon a vengeance beyond his most blood-thirsty imagining?

The eyes in the mirror image narrowed, the fists clenched, as for an intoxicating moment Jurnet savoured the ecstasy of squeezing the last breath out of the bugger who had killed Miriam.

He went back downstairs, used the phone under the stairs to call for a cab, went to the counter and paid his bill. When he came back to the table where the Israeli girl sat eating a croissant, she looked up at him and remarked, in that matter-of-fact voice which he found at once off-putting and refreshing, that now he was as handsome as he had been in his photograph. She chased the last crumbs of the croissant round her plate and transferred them to her mouth with a little sigh that the party was over. 'I'm not hungry now,' she announced, as if there might still be some doubt on the subject.

'Fine.' Resuming his seat, Jurnet said: 'I've phoned for a cab. Shouldn't be long. I'll drop you off at the workshop.'

'Thank you. And then you can get on with finding the murderer.'

'Maybe, I'm not sure.'

Pnina Benvista sat up straighter in her chair. Back to her customary severity she commanded: 'But of course you will find him. You are a policeman. It is what policemen are for.'

'I'm not the only police officer in Angleby.'

'For the rest it is not personal. None of the others will try as hard as you.'

Jurnet protested harshly against having his mind made up for him. 'Mario said it was of God. Who am I to foul up His little game?'

'What game?' Pnina Benvista demanded. 'You are talking nonsense. Alfred Einstein said God does not play at dice — or at any other game, I am quite sure.'

'Einstein, eh?' Glad of any excuse to turn the conversation in a different direction: 'Too highbrow for me.'

'You have heard of Einstein, I hope?' Pressing her lips together: 'I am Bachelor of Science of Tel Aviv University and I tell you he was a great man, perhaps the greatest.' Something in Jurnet's lack of reaction either to this dictum or to the recital of her own credentials must have riled her, for she added testily: 'Just because you are a cripple doesn't mean you have to make a profession of sitting on the ground with a hat in front of you, waiting for people to throw money into it. At Tel Tzevaim, when they found out that I was clever, they made sure that I had every educational opportunity.'

'The least they could do, after you being blown up on that bus.'

'Oh no!' The girl actually laughed, the first time the detective had heard her do so: a short-lived sound, however, an experimental dipping of the toe into mirth followed by a hasty withdrawal. 'I myself was hardly scratched. The way you see me is the way I was born. In the hospital in Morocco, when I was a baby, they tried to put it right and only made it worse, and by the time we came to Erez Yisroel the doctors said it was too late to do anything.' She finished, on a note of pride that Jurnet, for all his overriding preoccupation, could not but find touching: 'That is why my mother and my father called me Pnina, Pearl — to show that I was precious just the same.'

'It's a beautiful name.'

'Yes,' she assented gravely, 'and a pearl is a beautiful thing. But never forget, my father used to say, when he was annoyed with me, it is also an irritation. Grit gets into the oyster shell and so the oyster makes a pearl to coat it and cover it up — not out of love, you understand, but because it is uncomfortable. At the heart of every pearl there is something sharp and hurtful.' Pnina Benvista ended, the bony contours of her face intent: 'I shall be sharp and hurtful to you, Mr Ben, if you do not find out who killed Miriam.'

8

Summoned by a receptionist, Rafi Galil came out of the main workroom into the vestibule; gave a shout of joy and wrapped Pnina Benvista in a beaming embrace.

'Thank God!' he exclaimed. 'Our little pearl is safe!' Turning his head to smile at Jurnet without letting his captive go: 'Our detective has found her for us — I should have known! But three o'clock this morning when I woke up from sleep with the sudden thought, what was Miriam going to Heathrow for, who was she intending to meet, what was I to think? In a minute, of course, once I was properly awake, I remembered what until then, with so much sadness and shock, had gone completely out of my mind — that she was going to meet Pnina. She had told me so on the phone. Middle of the night as it was, I telephoned the airport, I phoned El Al, I phoned the police. I would have phoned Buckingham Palace if I had known the number. Where could she be, our little genius, lost in a strange land?'

The Israeli girl freed herself, straightened her suit composedly, and said in a tone of resigned affection, as one used to the other's excesses: 'I am not a little genius, Uncle Rafi. I was not lost, and I am not in a strange land. There was no need to make such a fuss.'

'Prickly!' Rafi Galil crowed delightedly, his scarred face creasing afresh in the broad smile which seemed its most natural configuration. 'All as usual! You have no idea, Mr Jurnet, how she tells me off, always for my own good, it goes without saying! But oh my child — ' the man sobered, sorrowed — 'how are we going to manage without our darling?'

Pnina Benvista's eyes filled with tears to match his own, but her voice remained steady as she asked: 'Will the business have to close then? Is that what you mean?'

'Unthinkable! Already — perhaps it was too early to speak, but I could not stay silent — I have spoken to Mrs Courland and she says, under no circumstances. The business must go on. Not because it is her money which paid to set it up, or that from it she draws an income for her living, but because of Tel Tzevaim. A good woman.'

To Jurnet: 'Did Miriam never tell you about Tel Tzevaim?'

'She told me about the disabled people who work there.'

The other shook his head impatiently, the mop of white hair flying.

'Disabled! It is only a word, good for government reports. I tell you, there were men and women at Tel Tzevaim you would think it a mercy if they fell asleep and never woke up again. But that was before Miriam came. A miracle — the only word for it! Not that, before her, people were not kind, but Pnina will tell you — won't you, little one? — that kindness is not enough . . .'

'Kindness is not enough,' agreed Pnina, poker-faced.

'And our Pnina is one of the lucky ones. She has brains, she has legs she can walk on. No one has to convince *her* of her place in the scheme of things. But those others — in the old days, before Miriam came, it would break your heart to look at them. Miriam gave them self-respect, a sense of their own worth — that only the vessel was damaged, the spirit within unharmed. She brought in experts to make machines they could use and other experts who could teach them to use them. A real business, you understand, not therapeutic play.' The Israeli rubbed a hand over his eyes. He flung an arm round Pnina's bony shoulders and squeezed them affectionately. 'A real business, eh? One that, with the help of the Almighty, we shall keep going as before, a memorial to our wonderful girl. A day or two for rest, my child, and then you must go back to Tel Tzevaim while I hold the fort here until it is decided what is best to be done.'

'No, Uncle Rafi.' Pnina Benvista disengaged herself without making a production of it. 'That won't do and you must tell Mrs Courland so. You know it won't do. In Israel there are already others who can carry on, who are carrying on at this moment. That is the way Miriam set things up in the first place, so that she could be mostly in England with her Mr Ben and still things at Tel Tzevaim could go along smoothly. She said — ' trembling a little with the telling of it — 'that I was to come here to learn the English end of the business so that if she married Mr Ben and had a child, which was what she wanted most in the world, she would know she had somebody at headquarters she could absolutely rely on.' In a voice devoid equally of arrogance and false humility she finished: 'She hoped, too, when I had studied how things were run here in England,

111

that I might have some ideas of my own to make them run even better.'

'And on me she could not rely?' Rafi Galil made a face rueful and comic. 'Is that what she said?' With a sigh: 'More computers, I suppose. Too many complications for an old-fashioned bookkeeper with only ten fingers and ten toes to count on, but there! If that's what Miriam wanted . . .'

The Israeli smiled without reservation, first at the girl and then at Jurnet who had turned, first pale, then fiery red, at the reference to marriage and a child. 'In that case,' Rafi Galil continued, barely audible to the detective above the pitiless din of his own pounding heart, 'it remains to thank our friend here kindly for delivering you safely to the correct address, and release him to get on with his own work while we get on with ours.' To Jurnet he said directly: 'I saw the cab drive up. If there is red tape — and when is there not red tape this side of the grave? — and they have not yet issued you with another car, why not take Miriam's and use it in the mean time? The garage delivered it first thing this morning, all in working order.'

'Mrs Courland — ' Jurnet began, his voice hoarse.

'Mrs Courland does not drive and I could

never use it, even if I wanted to. It possesses gears, unlike the one I have on hire which is made with the automatic transmission designed for mechanical idiots like myself, born in the age of the horse and cart. Left in the car-park here it can only be a matter of time before it is stolen or vandalized. Don't be afraid of it,' he admonished gently, seeing the look, almost of horror, on the other's face. 'It is what Miriam would have wanted.'

Holding on to the handle, Jurnet stood at the driver's door of Miriam's red car. He raised his right foot up to the high sill, glad of the effort, and kicked with all his strength, pleased to see that some gravel which had adhered to the underside of his shoes had scratched the gleaming paintwork. If there had been an axe to hand he could have done some real damage — if there had been an axe and if Pnina Benvista had not, just that minute, come round the side of the low building holding out some car keys and clip-clopping harder than ever in her ugly haste.

Some of his anger against the car — against the garage men who had repaired it too late — spilled over on to this outsider who had dared to insert herself into his grief. Making no attempt to go to meet her, to shorten the distance covered with so much effort, he awaited the girl's coming with naked hostility.

'You forgot these.'

Timidly, as if aware she was somehow at fault, she held out the keys which he took with bad grace, resenting her thin fingers — one more, as he saw it, silent call upon his unwilling compassion. The remembrance of the enormous meal he had watched this pathetic-looking waif putting away in Mario's enabled him to harden his heart without difficulty.

Once he was in the car where, steeling himself as against a blow, he had settled himself in the driver's seat, his hands on the steering wheel, she stood by the window and inquired, with a diffidence he found altogether hateful: 'Shall I see you again, Mr Ben?'

Conscious of Miriam's fingerprints underneath his own, an invisible burning that bit like acid into his fingertips, Jurnet made no answer. After a moment, his lips twisted with the pain of it, he let the wheel go. Who was he kidding? What was the use of continuing to look for traces of his lost love when he knew perfectly well that the only ones which mattered were lying bagged and labelled in a drawer in Angleby morgue?

The Israeli girl was bending forward to speak. Her long straight hair touched the window glass.

'I hope I shall see you again,' she persisted. 'I promise next time not to eat so much and cost you so much money.' When this second approach equally elicited no response she added, for information purposes only, no plea for special consideration: 'I don't know any other people in Angleby.'

'I shouldn't worry about that. You soon will. All the people in the workshop, that woman you're going to board with. The Rabbi will introduce you to the congregation. You'll soon have more friends than you can do with.'

'Not friends.' With a shake of the head: 'People who will be sorry for me. Real friends do not pity.' After a moment Pnina Benvista added: 'You, Mr Ben — you do not pity.'

Jurnet nodded, recognizing the compliment at its proper worth. Twenty-four hours had been more than enough to teach him that pity was of all blessings the deadliest.

'Besides,' he said, kind for the first time in their exchange, 'you told Mr Galil that England was not a strange country to you. Does that mean you've been here before — know people here already?'

The girl shook her head again, sending

her black hair moving, the light on its shining surface moving with it. 'I meant that my mother was English, from Surbiton, which is near London, on the river Thames, and so I am half-English. It is my ancestry.' Her earnestness making her Middle Eastern accent even more pronounced, she explained with a childlike pride: 'That is why I speak English like an Englishman.'

'I wondered about that.' Against his will, Jurnet was touched, until the long black hair caught his eye and rekindled his memory of hair that was auburn, bright with its own inborn illumination. Rekindled his anger, his desolation.

Dismayed by the sudden change of expression, Pnina Benvista asked: 'Mr Ben, are you sure you are well enough to drive?'

Without replying, Jurnet put the Renault into motion, making no offer to drop the girl off at the workshop door on his way out. In the car mirror, until the curve of the drive hid her from him, he could see her standing still and lop-sided, looking after him.

9

Jurnet drove out of the industrial estate into the traffic of the ring road, feeling, in Miriam's car, unreal, an alien from another planet, yet with some part of him responding with an involuntary pleasure to the velvet functioning of the vehicle and to his own expert handling of it. Even its bright red, so different from the sobriety of the police fleet, in some unbidden way lightened his spirits.

He wondered if he were going mad, and decided against it. He was calm, dead calm.

Dead.

Leaving the ring road at the first exit, he drove towards the city centre, into the Angleby he had loved and shared with his lost lover. Now the ancient streets mocked him, the Market Place, the castle on its mound, Marks and Spencer's and Tesco's, all the dear familiar places — how was it possible? — utterly unchanged. Feeling betrayed, he fled from their heartless indifference towards a northern fringe of the city which had never possessed a heart to lose, an area of low, yellow-brick terraces huddled behind front gardens planted with privet, dustbins and cars long defunct that nevertheless still managed a further valedictory rattle whenever the wind was in the right direction.

Number 5 Vinery Street — some clever dick who knew the street and had actually stayed on at school to take his A levels had altered the I to an E on the name plate affixed to the house on the corner — was distinguished from its neighbours in that, instead of the statutory wrecked jalopy, it boasted a battered safe of antique design under its front window. Boast was the right word, thought Jurnet, pushing open the rusted gate which swung precariously from a single hinge. In the old days shoemakers hung a golden boot outside their premises, didn't they, to advertise their goods and services, and locksmiths giant keys. Monty Bellman, whether or not he realized it, was only following in a fine old tradition.

There was neither bell nor knocker on the front door: little enough paint either. When Jurnet thumped it with his fist, some flecks of khaki drifted down on to his knuckles in a desultory way. After an interval, a small woman who had to be younger than she looked — nobody outside a mummy case could be that old — came to the door and said: 'If you're from the probation, Monty's not in.' She took a second look and bellowed, 'Hallelujah!' Turning away without further salutation, she shouted into the interior: 'Come on out, Monty, and stump up! Tha's ten nicker you owe me!'

The man who came out of the shadows, down the narrow hallway, was a neat little person in body and dress — that is, if you discounted what looked like the best part of a bowl of porridge displayed down the front of his natty weskit. His thinning hair was plastered across his bald spot with anxious care, his complexion the healthy tan to be expected of one who had just completed a term in the latest of Her Majesty's open prisons, all the comforts of the Costa Brava save only the strippers and the lager louts. His hands were the hands of an artist, which is what he was: the best peterman in the business.

'You got to hand it to the old bag,' Monty Bellman remarked affectionately to Jurnet as he fished in his trouser pocket for the £10 note which discharged his indebtedness. 'I said as how you'd never have the nerve to show your lovely mug within a mile of here

arter what you did to our Billy, but Ma —
the minute she saw that bit in the paper
an' the pictures, she bet me you'd be round
before you could say fuck — an' she were
right.'

Jurnet said: 'I never did anything to your
Billy. How is the boy?'

'Come in and see for yourself, why doncha?
You already got a preview of his dinner.'

With a neat movement the man stepped
out of the door, into the garden; took off
his weskit and got rid of as much of the
goo as was vulnerable to a good shake.
Whether by accident or design a fair amount
of the stuff spattered the bottoms of Jurnet's
trouser legs and the tops of his shoes. 'Here,
Ma — ' handing over the unlovely object
— 'boil that up wi' a bit of bacon, it'll do
fine fer tea, especially if Mr Jurnet's staying.'

'I know you swore to get me,' Jurnet said
with a smile — *how easily one slipped back
into professional posturings, as if nothing had
happened, nothing at all!* — 'but there must
be simpler ways.'

'Swore to get you?' Monty Bellman looked
pained. 'Don't be daft! Can't you reckernize
a figger of speech when you see one? Not
that it wouldn't make my day to see your
guts spread out on the cat's meat stall, but

not by me, guv. Not by me. I gotta look arter Billy — Ma's done her bit while I bin away, an' now it's my turn. I can't take any chances, you know that, not even to dish out to a bloody bugger no more than in common justice he deserves.'

'I didn't do anything to Billy.'

Taking no notice, the man led the way to the back of the house, to a kitchen whose peeling surfaces were so cluttered with the accessories of the good life there was scarcely room left to move.

'Got my eye on a nice little property on the Newmarket road,' he vouchsafed. 'Somewhere to fit in all this blasted ironmongery Ma's so gone on, and Billy could have a paddling pool. He'd like that. You'd like that, wouldn't you, Billy? Only Ma here's so set in her ways she don't want to move, the stupid ol' fart. Says she's used to it here.'

'Billy's used to it too,' piped up Ma. 'Aren't you, Billy love?'

At a table in the centre of the room a curly-headed young man strapped into an outsize approximation of a child's high chair lifted his head for a moment before letting it loll back on to his chest, the curls tumbling about a scarred forehead.

'Aargh,' said Billy Bellman.

'Tell you what, Ma,' Monty Bellman suggested, acting jolly, 'while I put the kettle on, whyn't you go fish out Billy's last school reports? I know Mr Jurnet'll be interested.'

'Don't bother,' Jurnet said to no avail, Mrs Bellman obediently vanishing into the adjoining room regardless. 'I'll take your word for them. And don't bother with tea either, not on my account. All I want to know, Monty, if it's not too much trouble, is, what were your movements yesterday.'

The safe-breaker put down the kettle, which was a fancy one made of white plastic inset with gauges that showed both temperature and quantities. He looked at the detective, his bright little boot button eyes crinkled in a smile.

'Not my movements, Inspector — Billy's. You wouldn't believe how many times a day the feller has to go to the bog. I don't know how Ma ever coped. Whenever I fancy taking him a good long walk — it gets boring round and round the houses — I have to pad him up in disposables like I was stuffin' a bloody sofa. They love me down in Boots the Chemist, I can tell you.' Deflected by the sound of drawers next door being pulled out, he called: 'The sideboard, Ma!' Then: 'They'll do your heart good, Mr Jurnet — you havin' a personal interest, as you might say. A's in everything. Football captain, born leader, shows great promise. Wanted him to think of going on to college an' get a degree. A degree! What you think of that, then?'

'I think all the more fool you for taking the lad with you on that job.'

Monty Bellman's smile was unwavering.

'Billy always knew how to twist me roun' his little finger. Nagged me something awful till I'd say yes. Me little brother.'

'What kind of degree did you expect him to get in college, for Christ's sake? BA in Breaking and Entering? Having taken him along, the least you could have done was keep him off that area of glass roof. You took care to keep off it yourself.'

'Panicked, didn' he, poor little sod? What you expect, first time out, couple of rozzers chargin' over the horizon like Injuns on the warpath? Couldn't wait ter put the cuffs on till we was safely back on the ground — oh no! That was too much to ask.'

'And have you melt away like moonshine up one of those alleyways back of the plant? Be your age, Monty. We had reports of two men seen on that warehouse roof. We had to go in and investigate.'

'*You* didn't,' the other pointed out. 'What it is to be managerial! All *you* did was give the orders. *You* stayed safe on your flat feet at ground level.'

'Yes,' Jurnet agreed readily. 'Lucky for Billy I did, wasn't it, after him falling down four — or was it five — floors on to that concrete? If there hadn't been somebody down there to apply a tourniquet and give mouth-to-mouth resuscitation till the ambulance got there, he wouldn't be here today.' Realization dawning: 'Is that what's eating you, Monty? Is that what this is all about? You wish I'd let him die?'

'Aargh,' commented Billy Bellman.

'Get out of here!' Monty Bellman ordered, his voice, however, neat as ever: but Jurnet had seen the momentary gleam of recognition in the boot button eyes, knew he had hit on the truth.

'I'll go when you've told me where you took Billy for his walk yesterday.'

The man calmed down, smoothed his hair, refurbished his smile.

'Jes' revisiting the old places, Inspector, tha's all. Renewing fond memories an' so on. Pushed the boy all the way across town an' back, uphill an' down. Nothing like a stretch in one of them new coolers to get you in tip-top physical condition. Government privatize 'em, all them overweight city gents'd be queuing up to get in — that's to say, them as weren't in there for free

124

already. I wanted Billy to see where the famous Inspector Jurnet lived when he weren't busy turning youngsters full of promise into bleeding vegetables.' When Jurnet made no comment, the man added smiling: 'Bet you didn't know as I knew yer private address.'

'Unfortunately for you, Monty, that's one thing you're going to have to find out all over again. After what happened the block's uninhabitable.'

'Bloody amateurs!' snorted Monty Bellman. 'First thing I said to Ma when I saw them pictures in the *Argus*. One run-of-the-mill car's all they're fingerin' an' they pack in enough Semtex to bring down a ruddy skyscraper!' Lips pursed in Puritan disapproval: 'Wasteful.'

'Oh? So you know it was Semtex! So far as I'm aware, no information relating to the explosive has been released to the public.'

'Do me a favour, mister. I'm in the business, in't I, not one of your fucking civilians. One look at that car, or what was left of it, and it says Semtex loud an' clear as you're standing here talking to me this minute. Bloody amateurs!' Monty Bellman repeated.

'On the other hand,' Jurnet pointed out, 'it could have been made to look like that on purpose.'

The other gave him a sharp glance before smilingly shaking his head.

'Wish I was that clever. That car, though — Rover, were it? Hard to tell. Write-off an' a half, weren't it? By the way — who was that piece they said caught it instead of you? Some slag on a one-night stand making an early getaway?'

— 10 —

Rain was slanting down thinly as Jurnet drove
along the road that divided the marsh, the
red car traversing its immensity like a toy
across a billiard table that stretched to a
horizon beneath a sky which appeared to
hang, now that the detective gave it his attention, no more than a couple of feet above
the tattered willows which edged the dykes
on either side. He could not remember how
or why he came to be driving to Havenlea,
nor how he had negotiated Angleby's incredible one-way system without apparent
injury to himself, the car, or any other vehicle
unwise enough to cross his path.

He could not remember anything except
what he had done to Monty Bellman.

'No harm done!' the man, with astonishing
magnanimity, had gasped when he was once
more capable of speech, the boot button eyes
no longer popping, the tongue back in his
mouth, and the dreadful purple fading out

of his cheeks. Ma, understandably, had been less amenable. Returning to the kitchen with Billy's school reports to find an officer of the law engaged in throttling the life out of her elder son, she had reason on her side, as well as Jurnet's undying gratitude. Only her screams had brought him back to his senses, prevented him from finishing off for good and all the bastard who had dared insult Miriam.

'What you think you up to?' she had demanded, once she had made sure her son would live. 'You a policeman an' all! You're a disgrace to the force! I've a good mind to — '

'Give over, Ma,' enjoined a Monty Bellman sufficiently recovered to be resettling the lie of his shirt collar, straightening his tie. 'Worth it to find out the bugger's got blood in his veins like everyone else, he's not something they have to wind up every morning before they send him out on the job.' To Jurnet, with sunny unconcern: 'Girlfriend was she, then? Serious?' When Jurnet, who had stood looking down with loathing at the hands which had almost committed murder, made no reply, the man had finished complacently: 'Guy what did it, didn't do so badly then, after all. Hurt you where you'd feel it most, way you hurt Billy.'

His voice only a little less hoarse than the other's, Jurnet said at last: 'I'm sorry.'

Monty Bellman drank the rest of the water his mother had brought him and burst out laughing. 'Hear that, Ma! Worth it to hear a cop apologize!'

Jurnet said: 'I'm specially sorry to have upset Billy.'

The safe-breaker regarded his brother with love. Billy Bellman, his head up and rolling from side to side, was still tremendously excited. He waved his arms about, bounced up and down in his chair. Out of his mouth, along with saliva, poured a cascade of gabble, slur and splutter.

'Upset! Look at him! More life in that kiddo than I've seen since I got back home. He wants you to do it again!'

It came to Jurnet, the red car propelling him towards the coast as if it knew where it was going, that the sky, so low over the landscape, was not quite low enough. A few feet more and that would be it — the car and himself squashed flat on the road like a rabbit that hadn't made it to the further side. Too bad about the Renault, which was innocent of all offence, but for himself no more than justice. Half-mesmerized by the purr of the engine, he watched the innocent raindrops being swished off the windscreen by the merciless wipers. Everything getting its come-uppance except the one person who deserved it.

One good thing, he told himself — if good was the word for it — had come out of his attack on the safe-breaker. It had proved beyond argument that Detective Inspector Ben Jurnet, Angleby CID, was unfit to be involved in any official investigation into the death of Miriam Courland. Even the Super-intendent would have to see that. Whether by the same token he was unfit to continue as a member of the Police Force in any capacity whatever was a question he felt un-able to cope with at the moment and put aside for further consideration.

Except . . . what if there was anything behind that remark of Monty Bellman's — *hurt you where you'd feel it most, way you hurt Billy?* Why the bugger's amazing good humour in the face of a murderous attack, as if enjoying some private joke? And what about Billy, that ex-potential candidate for a university education — could it be that among the shards of that shattered intelligence lurked the desire for revenge on the brother who had led him into that fateful scrape?

Christ! Jurnet took his right hand off the steering wheel and smote his forehead with his open palm. There he went, still playing the ruddy cop! Would he never learn?

He pressed his foot down on the accelerator and hurtled into Havenlea.

The place had all the charm of an English seaside resort out of season in the rain. Jurnet parked the car, leaving its warm red to battle his way along the promenade past the drained boating lake and the denuded strips of municipal summer bedding, passing shelters where pensioners taking their breaks on the cheap huddled out of the wind, their dismayed countenances gazing out over the grey sands, the heaving sea.

On the pier the tea kiosk, modelled very loosely on the Taj Mahal, was already battened down for the winter. In the mock-Tudor castle which housed the slot machines, the woman who dispensed change and kept an eye on things kept Jurnet waiting for service until she had checked and rechecked the number of stitches on what could well have been a knitted shroud.

After wasting £5 in 10p pieces on various contrivances which seemed to him as mysterious and threatening as the woman's knitting, Jurnet went outside again, down to the end of the pier where the rain tasted of salt and sewage and where an elderly man who sat with a line dangling into the water greeted him affably. 'Nice day for ducks.'

'Not so bad for fish either, by the look of it.'

'Oh that,' the old man returned. 'I don't mind that. Tell you the truth, I'm quite relieved. Turns my stomach putting them maggots on the hook. God's creatures too, I always say.' Above a plaid scarf folded neatly about his chest and neck his face showed like an apple long in store. He squinted up at the detective, standing tall against the sky; patted his rod, nodded towards the open creel lying empty on the boards by his side. 'Props, as you might say. You come upon me, as you come just now, an' all I'm doing is sitting here — no line, no nothing — you'd think me barmy, wouldn't you, out in this weather. So I have to dress it up a bit, don't I — do something to make it look I'm not quite ready yet for the loony bin.'

'Never entered my mind.'

'Not that I'm not doing *something*,' the old man stressed with some earnestness. 'Something that takes a lot more skill than hooking a passing plaice. I'm passing the time.'

At this unexpected mention of his new-found enemy, Jurnet felt his throat contract with remembered terror.

'You'd think,' said the old man comfortably, settling his back against a flag-pole from whose top a flag bearing the Havenlea arms flapped drearily, 'that when you get to my age and there's not a lot of it left, time'd pass a whole lot quicker than you'd want it to; only, take my word, it isn't like that at all, quite the contrary. It seizes up like your bloody circulation, it won't move, no matter what. More like constipation than anything else, if you'll excuse the expression, 'cept that, in the case of time, you can't take Syrup of Figs to make it pass quicker. It's only when you're a young chap, like you, mister, that time an' going to the WC both come easy — easy come, easy go.

'Not both,' said Jurnet.

At the end of the front, past the shuttered beach huts and an area of coarse grass out of which a phalanx of gulls rose up at his coming, screeching like witches who had mislaid their broomsticks, Jurnet came to the Amusement Park, abandoned save for the Bingo Hall whose façade, outlined in electric bulbs of which only a few were not working, sent out the message that, despite appearances, hope was not extinct, you too could be a winner.

Inside, in what, except for the front embellishments, turned out to be a marquee whose canvas walls billowed in the wind, the air of expectation was almost palpable, the stage at the far end a veritable Aladdin's cave hung about with electric kettles, hairdryers, soft toys, non-stick frying pans, everything the heart could reasonably desire. Jurnet, having paid his open sesame, settled down with an almost contented mindlessness into a rhythm orchestrated equally by the twanging of steel guys in the gale and the voice of the caller, a meagre man who struggled bravely to be jolly, despite having a nasty cold.

'Twenty-one, are we having fun! Ten, one-o, how far will she go? Fifty-six, none of your tricks! Seventy-seven, Havenlea's heaven — ' The large woman who sat next to Jurnet nudged him in the side, not out of kindness. 'You're bingo,' she pointed out sourly. 'Bingo!' she called out in exasperation when Jurnet stared at her blankly. 'Chap here's bingo!'

The prize was a teddy bear, a toy manufactured without grace and not much skill either. As large as a two-year-old child, white-pelted with black linings to the ears, it bore little resemblance to Winnie the Pooh. Its oriental cast of feature was imprinted with a stoical acceptance of whatever might befall.

Jurnet could not help feeling for it, as he always felt for loners and losers. Outside the rain had thickened, grown aggressive. It attacked the bear's cellophane wrapping as if it meant business, it poured itself over Jurnet's hair and down the back of his neck. Welcoming the discomfort as only fit and proper, the detective did not so much as turn up his coat collar in defence.

He tucked the teddy bear under his arm and walked without haste back to the car, where he stowed the toy on the back seat, its expression unaltered. After he had locked the car up again he stood for a few moments looking down at his prize through the rear window. Ping-pong with the Rabbi, Bingo on the sea front, what was the next game the caller up in the sky had in store for him? Tiddlywinks?

Parted from his furry companion Jurnet felt doubly chilled and alone. With vague thoughts of a cup of tea as something that had to make you feel better he continued towards Havenlea's main street, an undistinguished enough thoroughfare at the best of times and in the continuing downpour all but extinguished. Most of the shops were closed for the day or the winter or the millennium, the few that remained open offering seaside tat and postcards of a mythical Havenlea throbbing with tropical sun.

Half-way along the street he found a tea room, unwelcoming but well filled and with a certain liveliness among its rain-bedraggled clientele, an air of self-congratulation — not long to go now, it would soon be dark, and then the telly and bed — at the prospect of being able soon to cross another day off the calendar.

'Cup of tea, please,' he said to the waitress, a heavy-breasted woman of middle age who, after a predictable lapse of time, came to take his order.

'We on'y do set teas.' The waitress sounded as if she had been made an improper proposal. Her breasts wobbled with insult; but then, having taken in the handsome ravaged face, her manner softened. 'If it's on'y a cuppa you're wanting, there's a café six or seven doors along.'

Jurnet did not feel capable of walking six or seven doors along. He said faintly: 'I'll take the set tea, please.'

'Plaice fillet, kipper or bloater.' The waitress recited a clearly familiar litany. 'All served wi' chips an' peas, bread an' butter,

pot of tea, slice of fruit cake or jam tart.'
When Jurnet looked at her, seemingly unable
to choose between such temptations, she became positively maternal. 'Take the plaice
if I was you. No bones.'

When the food came, even under her en-
couraging supervision he could not eat it,
but he drank thirstily of the tea, the waitress
fetching additional hot water without being
asked.

'Ta very much,' she said, pocketing his
generous tip on departure. 'An' remember
termorrer's another day.'

Jurnet was glad to get back through the
rain to the safety of Miriam's car, which
seemed a little less empty with the teddy
bear in the back. On an impulse he reached
over and lifted the toy forward to occupy
the front passenger's seat, which was a mistake. It flopped against the door like a dead
thing.

Dead.

Deciding without conscious decision that
his private rites for his lost love were as
completed as they were ever likely to be,
Jurnet set the car back on to the road across
the marsh — a marsh that was no longer
green, however. Here behind the coast the
wind had died down, yielding house room
to a slatternly mist which drifted about aim-

lessly, disclosing occasional glimpses of reed beds, drainage mills, exploded Rovers and elegantly shod feet with white shafts of bone sticking up out of them.

Out of that ambiguous air the name Miriam, each separate letter of it, every curve and straight line, resonated through his being like a twanged harp; a name he dared not speak aloud for fear the sound of it would shatter once and for all the precarious balance of the universe. Yet for all that he did say it — shouted it to the elements, *Miriam!* — only to discover, the ultimate outrage, that the world went on as before, the marsh receding on either side and the sky staying unmoved as the red car sped back towards Angleby and loss.

11

Back to what his foolish mind persisted in referring to laughably as home, Jurnet parked his car opposite the violated block of flats, outside Mario's. He got out, and whilst he hesitated on the pavement, undecided whether to take the teddy bear with him or leave it in the car, a man came out of the BMW parked a few yards further along the street and hurried towards him. 'Mr Jurnet!' the man exclaimed. 'This *is* a pleasure!'

Jurnet had no difficulty whatsoever in recognizing Jolly Jim Hepton. Three years in the clink had done nothing, apparently, to reduce the ex-councillor's comfortable girth, fade the roses in his cheeks, dim the blue of eyes which, as ever, positively blazed with sincerity. Judging by the BMW and the natty camel-hair coat above tattersall-checked slacks, he hadn't had to make for the nearest Job Centre either, to sign on once the prison gates had clanked to behind him.

'Waiting for me, were you?' Jurnet asked, too tired to play any more games, not even Tiddlywinks. It stood to reason Jolly Jim Hepton would be waiting for him. Ignoring the man's outstretched hand, he went to the edge of the kerb, signifying pointedly his intention of crossing the road. 'Detective Sergeant Ellers is the one you want to see, if you want to see anybody. I'm on leave.'

'So Sergeant Ellers told me.' The other, with no visible sense of rejection, drew back on the expensive-looking glove which he had removed in anticipation of a more cordial reception. He said laughingly: 'Only wish the guys I employ were as quick on the trigger. The *Argus* had hardly dropped down on the mat, I'd barely had time to take in the pictures, let alone what it said, when your lot was banging on the door.' With the rich chuckle that went with his embonpoint: 'Me and the Sarge had a good old chinwag about old times. But, as I told him, I'd still need to have a word with you.'

Jurnet did not ask what about. He stepped out into the road.

'Hold on!' Hepton protested. 'If it's getting back into your place you're thinking of, it's all boarded up . . .' And when the detective, without comment, continued on his way, the man called out cheerfully across the widening gap: 'The back door as well as the front.'

'It's called serendipity,' explained Hepton, taking a key out of his coat pocket and, to Jurnet's surprise, inserting it into the lock of a back door which had been boarded up in the course of the day. 'I went to the reference library and looked it up to make sure. "Give me the Oxford English Dictionary," I said, "the best you've got." And what it said was: "The facility of making happy and unexpected discoveries by accident." '

'Oh ah?' murmured Jurnet, who had instantly made up his mind that nothing would induce him to go up to his flat if it meant that Hepton was to accompany him.

'Serendipity for me, serendipity for you,' the man expatiated, pushing the door open but making no attempt to enter. The two stood about in the little stone yard, cold and the night descending. 'The serendipity for you, Mr Jurnet, is that I happen to be the owner of this block of flats. I bet you never knew that.'

Jurnet stared. He had not known. 'Loverdale Properties. You aren't on the billheads as a director.'

'Nominees.' Jolly Jim Hepton waved the

formality aside. 'My Mary chose the company name.' The man's large face expanded in a smile of tender reminiscence. 'Romantic, eh? Just like a woman.'

Tight-lipped, Jurnet observed: 'If I'd known who my landlord was I might have had more to say about the maintenance of the place — or rather the lack of it.'

'Police! What do they know?' The other shook his head pityingly. 'You could have gone on asking, chum. Jerry-built old pigeon loft, money down the drain it would have been — even you must see that, Mr Jurnet. Only reason I bought it in the first place was to pull down and redevelop. The area's ripe for gentrification, convenient for the city centre and so on. Could easily attract a better class of person, no offence meant of course and present company excepted. Only then, unfortunately, as you know only too well, my trouble came along, so there was no way I could get planning permission. Politics pure and simple, but there you are!' The smile grew even wider. 'But now, look at the way things turn out! Johnny who blows up your Rover's so enthusiastic, so anxious to make a proper job of it, he uses enough stuff to bring down half the neighbourhood into the bargain. Through no act of mine, the whole block's irredeemably unfit for human habitation. Now they'll *have* to let me demolish and rebuild. Any time I run into the bugger who did it in a bar he can take his choice of poison, no expense spared. That's serendipity for you!'

' "Through no act of yours" . . .' Jurnet let an interval of silence elapse before asking, his voice carefully neutral: 'And the murder of Miss Courland — is that serendipity too?'

'Absolutely! Serendipity for the two of us! For you because, sad as it is to lose your girlfriend, it wasn't you starting up that car engine. You're still breathing, which, look at it any way you like, is a whole lot better than being six feet under. And serendipity for me — ' the humorous, bantering tone did not alter — 'because now, Mr Jurnet sir, you can suffer like I suffered when you killed my Mary.'

'When I what! You're crazy!'

'Another year,' said Jolly Jim Hepton, 'and I'd have been Mayor. Me and Mary, Mayor and Mayoress. It was the dream of her life. If she saw a dress she thought really special she'd say, "That would be nice for the reception," meaning the reception they have in City Hall when the new Mayor's installed for the year. Or if she saw a painting somewhere, an oil painting, the genuine thing, none of your wishy-washy water-colours, she'd wonder aloud if the artist would be the right one to commission to paint my official portrait for hanging on the City Hall stairs along with all the other Mayors hanging there.

'Once all those plans and dreams went up the spout she couldn't take it, it was too much. She just faded away. The doctor said it was cancer, but I knew better. She died of disappointment.' Jolly Jim Hepton laughed his jolly laugh. 'Soon as your Sergeant had taken himself off and I'd had time to read the *Argus* account thoroughly, I nipped out for the biggest bunch of carnations you ever saw, and took them over to Mary's grave. Carnations were always her favourite flower. She was going to have them on all the tables at the reception, and I wanted her to enjoy some of the serendipity too.'

His heart untouched, Jurnet said: 'If disappointment's what your wife died of, it could have been disappointment at finding out about how you'd been dipping your hands in the civic till. All that setting up of shell companies, all those illegal kickbacks — '

'What do you know?' Hepton interrupted, more in commiseration than contradiction. 'What do you coppers know in your cosy little cloister over at Police Headquarters?

144

What do you know of real life and how the game is played? Let me tell you, while I was Chairman of the Housing Committee this city built more houses, for letting at rents the working man could afford, than any other local authority in the country. Schools, hospitals, rubbish collection — you name it, we did it brilliantly. The ordinary citizens of this borough, never mind what happened after, they still call down blessings on my name. Angleby never had it so good until you had to poke your big conk in.'

'For Christ's sake, man! You tried to bribe me!'

'And aren't you kicking yourself you didn't take it?' Jolly Jim Hepton looked his jolliest. 'You'd taken what was on offer, with more to come where that came from, and you and your girl could this moment be having it off on a sun-kissed beach in the Caribbean instead of her getting herself sprinkled like confetti over the neighbourhood on account of your high principles. Think about it, why don't you, when you're next having a job getting to sleep at night.'

The man turned up his coat collar, settled his cashmere scarf in place, went through the ritual of readying for departure.

'Here's the key then,' he finished, handing it over. 'Not that you need even bother to lock up after you. There's nothing in there worth tuppence and, as I say, the whole building'll be coming down before you can say knife.' Half-turned to go, he spoke over his shoulder. 'Know what your Detective Sergeant wanted? Only to ask please sir, was it you blew up Mr Jurnet's car and his fiancée and the ruddy block of flats they were fools enough to doss down in? And you know what I said?'

Into the expectant pause Jurnet inserted wearily: 'What did you say?'

'I said, "That would be telling!" '

12

A man was sitting at one of the little tables wedged between the delicatessen counter and the wall hung with the lovers in the gondola. An open *Telegraph* concealed the upper part of his body. Not that it mattered. Only one person in the world could achieve that perfection of knife-edged trouser, that lustre of handmade footwear, bright but not gaudy.

As Jurnet came into the shop the Superintendent folded his newspaper without haste and put it away. He smiled up into his subordinate's face and greeted him: 'Ah — Ben! I was worried about you. I had Jack try the Rabbi, anywhere else he could think of where you might be. And then, when Blake happened to mention that he'd seen you come in here for breakfast, I took the chance you'd be back for your evening meal . . .'

At the other's calm assumption of ownership Jurnet felt a pleasurable surge of the old familiar anger (*'You don't own me body and soul! Who do you think I am?'*) only, at one and the same time, to be moved beyond words by the man's evident concern. He felt an absurd desire to reach out across the table and take the other's hands in reassurance, in love. As it was, he sat down without being invited to — itself something momentous in that awesome presence — and announced: 'I went to the seaside. I won a teddy bear.' When this evoked no comment, he added by way of enlightenment: 'Bingo.'

'Ah.' A pause. 'So long as you're all right.'

'I'm fine.'

After that, conversation languished afresh, the silence mercifully interrupted by the arrival of Mario with two steaming plates of soup.

'Mr Ben, I took the liberty. Fresh minestrone, home made, not out of a can or a packet. You look chilled, it will do you good. A raw day, the night will be colder.' Retrieving a basket of rolls from the counter, he set it in the middle of the table which, Jurnet noted with a twinge of ironic amusement, had been set with starched white napkins instead of the usual paper flimsies. 'Your friend said he would wait for you and have whatever you had.' Addressing the Superintendent directly, with respect but with an air of intimacy which set Jurnet wondering what confidences the two of them could have been exchanging about him in his absence: 'It will do you good too, sir, against the cold.'

'Against the cold and anything else that needs getting the better of.' The Superintendent had already taken a spoonful. 'It's glorious.'

His face aflame at the praise, Mario promised: 'For main course I make you a *scaloppine al marsala* you will not get better at the Savoy.'

'It sounds wonderful.'

It was wonderful, if either of them could have done it justice for the burden of things unsaid lying between them and their appetites. The Superintendent at least made a beginning. Ate a morsel of veal, a cap of mushroom, and said: 'They tell me that the block over the road will have to come down.'

Busy arranging the food on his plate to make it, for fear of hurting Mario's feelings, look less than was actually there, Jurnet barely nodded.

'If it helps,' the other persisted, 'there's a police house falling vacant at the end of the week. Young Warrington from Eastgate's off to join his wife's family in Australia. It might be an idea for you pro tem until you find something you really want.'

What I really want! Jurnet drew a deep breath and jumped in, if only at the shallow end.

'Matter of fact, I was having a word with the owner of the block just before I came in here.'

'Oh?'

'Not one of nature's truth-tellers. It was the first time I even knew he *was* my landlord. Loverdale Properties is what they call it. In fact, it turns out to be Councillor Hepton. Jolly Jim.'

'Good Lord!' After a moment of surprise, the Superintendent frowned. 'You don't think . . .'

'I don't think anything. All I know is he's over the moon now he can expect planning permission to go through on the nod — something otherwise, after his conviction, he hadn't a hope in hell of getting. Also, that he accuses me of sending his wife into a fatal decline by refusing to take his bribe and putting the law on to him and so preventing her from ever becoming Mayoress. Also, incidentally, by not allowing my palm to be greased, I killed Miriam.' Jurnet regarded his superior officer unsmilingly. 'He points out, quite plausibly, that if I *had* taken the money and run, she and I could by now be living it up in some tropical paradise instead of — ' He stopped, rammed a piece of *scaloppine* into his mouth as if it had become necessary to have something to bite on, even if it were only dead calf. Resuming when he was once more able to speak: 'He wraps it all up in a word he seems really chuffed at discovering for himself, and which he took pains to explain to me — serendipity.' Wiping an involuntary smile of approval off the Superintendent's face, he ended: 'Looks like we're getting a better class of criminal these days. That has to be progress.'

Jurnet had made no response to the offer of a police house. Had it been available that very night, it might have been different. Even with the key to the back door of the building opposite in his pocket he did not, when it came to the point, feel able to mount those grotty stairs, go back to the flat again.

Last night had been different. Then, shock had deadened his reactions; and besides, yesterday he had had the crippled Israeli girl to share his grief with — to add her grief to his own so that, mourning in company, they were each that iota less bereaved. He almost smiled at the remembrance of the enormous breakfast the girl had put away

151

that morning, sitting at the very table where he now sat with the Superintendent and the starched napkins.

'I was wrong, Ben,' the Superintendent now admitted astonishingly. 'Wrong as regards you, wrong as regards myself. I should never have advised you to take time off.' Looking momentarily fatigued, he said: 'The Anti-Terrorist Branch, God save us, has arrived and, unless He is merciful, will stay, it is to be presumed, for the duration.' After a moment's hesitation: 'In case you haven't already heard, I have to tell you that the IRA has claimed responsibility. They got in touch with the *Mail* using the established code, so that the making of the claim appears genuine even if its truth remains to be proved or disproved, as the case may be. My information is that it is by no means unknown for that organization to claim as all its own work any outrage which, by its own peculiar standard of reckoning, it feels could enhance its image and give it publicity.'

'What do you think, sir — you yourself?'

The Superintendent twisted the starched napkin in his elegant hands.

'After letting that boy go,' he said at last, 'I'm almost afraid to say. It's a wonder our Anti-Terrorists haven't put me to stand in a corner, to teach me better. I do believe,

152

if they had their way, they would round up every Irishman and Irish woman in Angleby, to say nothing of everyone with any Irish blood in his or her veins even unto the fourth generation. Forgive me — ' the man ended, an apology which seemed addressed as much to the crumpled table linen as to his companion — 'I exaggerate. But not all that outrageously.' His face set and unforgiving: 'Whilst I understand without being told that ruthlessness may well be necessary against such a ruthless foe, I tell you, Ben, between ourselves, that I can't bear to see our city poisoned with a hateful and indiscriminate suspicion which is itself a victory for the powers of darkness. The work gang from the bypass, every last one of them Irish, were in the Bittern last night, as anyone would have expected them to be, celebrating the opening of the road and the completion of their contract. Not surprisingly, considering their fat wage packets and the quantity of drink taken, there were a few — misunderstandings, shall we say? — which ended with four members of the gang and seven locals — all Irishmen though, originally from the Republic — ending up in the cells. Par for the course, I'd say. The Chief was well pleased. But when our Anti-Terrorists arrived and found them already in residence, it seemed to me, God help us, that they all but rubbed their hands together in glee. By then, fortunately, the rest of the gang had already left for their next job, a link road in Devonshire, and thankfully some of our new house guests — alas not all — immediately took off for the South-West in hot pursuit.'

The Superintendent sighed, straightened his well-tailored shoulders; smiled at Jurnet with an affection that for once — or so it seemed to its recipient — contained not the slightest element of equivocation. 'Highly improper, Inspector Jurnet. You will forget every word I have just said.'

'Yes, sir.'

'Put it down to pique, offended vanity — aversion to admitting one has made a mistake — '

'Sir?'

'Didn't I tell you?' The Superintendent looked up from his plate. Self-abasement seemed to have reactivated his appetite. 'As you will recall, I let young Terry Doran go. In my book, there were no grounds for doing anything else. Well — fool that I was, I chose to make it a matter of trust between us, and he has broken his word. He has decamped, scarpered, absconded . . . That Father Culvey, who brought the boy to us

154

in the first place, turned up again at Headquarters to bring me the good news. He seemed disappointed when I didn't clap him into irons on the spot for doing something he of all people, as a priest, should have known better than to do — to wit, putting his faith in sinful humankind . . . By now, no doubt, the young spalpeen is in the Emerald Isle, south of the border naturally. And you, my dear Ben, are the obvious person to go after him and persuade him to come back.'

'Persuade him to come back!' Jurnet stared. 'Fat chance of that.'

'Only one we have. You underestimate your powers of persuasion,' the Superintendent said blandly.

'No,' said Jurnet. Hating the saying of it, he began:

'I went to see Monty Bellman . . .'

When he had come to the end of his story — *'I'd have finished the bastard off, no doubt about it, if his mother hadn't come in'* — Jurnet sat looking down at his plate, steeled for the anger which must follow, the double disillusion. Not only had a subordinate, one of the tribe, demonstrated himself unworthy of the trust reposed in him. What was the Superintendent, the all-seeing, all-knowing, to think of his own judgement in not having perceived that fatal weakness ahead of time and anticipated its inevitable consequences? As always, in their relationship, it seemed Jurnet could do nothing, good or bad, which did not, one way or another, involve his superior officer in the tripartite, the trinitarian, role of protector, judge, God.

Jurnet forced himself to raise his head, look the Superintendent in the eye.

To his amazement the man was smiling broadly.

'Reprehensible,' the Superintendent agreed, the good humour abating not one jot, 'but, as it happens, something that, in all the circumstances, fits in remarkably well. Not, as you rightly say, conduct befitting a police officer — heaven forfend! — for which reason your trip to Ireland can best be taken as that of a private citizen unconnected with the constabulary on either side of the Irish Sea.'

He leaned back in his chair, eyes sparkling, his earlier air of depression quite dissipated. 'Let me make it clear Ben, that, no matter how great the temptation, I am not taking advantage of a heaven-sent opportunity to give you the sack — merely proposing, so to speak, to put you on the back burner for as long as it takes. You won't have to worry about the financial side. I'll have a word with the Chief. I'm sure something can be arranged.' The smile discarded its edge of irony, the eyes became strangely shy. The Superintendent leaned forward across the table, suppliant. 'We know each other too well, Ben, either for formal declarations of concern or facile attempts at comfort — '

'Yes, sir.'

'Except to say this — that for myself, in your place, even after what has happened, I would still go down on my knees and give thanks for the privilege of having loved a woman as you loved your Miss Courland.'

As if he were being accused of something, Jurnet countered: 'She loved me too.'

'Then you were doubly blessed.'

'Yes.'

'And you'll go to Ireland, then?'

'Yes.'

'Good! Then let's have some coffee, shall we?'

After the Superintendent had gone, Mario came over to the table.

'Another cup, Mr Ben?'

'I don't think so, thanks.'

'Good, then I clear. Too much coffee will keep you awake at night.' The Italian made a token gathering up of cutlery. 'Forgive me for asking. You are going back over the road to sleep?'

Jurnet shook his head, unable actually to say the no, the negative that would erase for good and all the jangling bed, the smells on the stairs, the lost ecstasy.

'Forgive me,' Mario said again. He looked troubled, 'but I heard the gentleman your friend say something — I could not help hearing — about a house for you. You are taking this house?'

'I don't think so.'

'Then where will you sleep tonight? You have hardly eaten.' Holding up a hand to ward off apologies: 'I am not insulted. You ate a good breakfast, you cannot always have appetite. But now, more than food, you need rest in a good bed, and I — ' the strong peasant face wreathed itself in smiles — 'I have a very good bed waiting for you!'

'Very kind of you. But I couldn't bother your wife — '

'Not at my home! Here — upstairs! You saw for yourself the bathroom this morning. All modern and there is a bedroom equally so, and a living-room nicely furnished. Even a kitchen, though heaven knows why, with the café underneath to supply all necessities. We fixed it up for Johnny, he was feeling too much of a baby, still living at home at his age. His mama — you know how women are — she never could stop doing things for him. Now that he is in America he said we should rent out the place, get money for it, but we did not do so. We wanted the flat kept nice for him. One day he may want to come home and there will be people in the flat who will not go when I ask them to — I know of such cases — and so we keep it empty, but everything ready, even the bedclothes. Twice a week my Maria comes in to dust, to put on fresh sheets in case her *bambino* should desire to come on the spur of the moment. Even though, in her heart — in both our hearts although we never speak of it — we know he is lost to us, an American. It would be a pleasure to know the place put to good use. What do you say, Mr Ben?'

'If you're sure — if you think it would be OK with Johnny — '

'Of course I am sure, or I would not say. When I let him know Mr Ben is upstairs he will be overjoyed to do for you a favour in some small return for all you did for him.'

'I did nothing for him. And not a favour, Mario. Only if you charge me a proper rent. Only on that basis.'

'We will talk about it later,' declared the delicatessen proprietor in a tone which signalled he intended doing nothing of the kind. 'Now you must get rest. No need for pyjamas, anything. Look in the drawers, you will find all your needs. Johnny is not, maybe, so tall as you, but he has the breadth, a boy brought up on good pasta, eh? Only first — if you are not too tired — put your car in the yard. It will be safer there than left out in the street.' Laughing: 'Out in the street — who knows? — you may get a summons from the police!'

13

Jurnet parked Miriam's car in the yard, next to Mario's van. As he locked the doors, he glanced through the rear window and saw the Bingo bear, still in its cellophane wrapping, sprawled on its back across the rear seat looking up at him. In the white floodlight which illuminated the parking space Jurnet noticed for the first time that its eyes did not even match. One was black and matt, the other green and shining, a cat's eye, not a teddy bear's at all. Jurnet studied his prize through the window. What an ugly bit of rubbish it was, with its flat, impassive face and now, on top of that, odd eyes!

Overcome by a pity that was as much for himself as for the failed toy, Jurnet unlocked the car again, reached into the back and lifted the bear out. He had forgotten how large it was, how ungainly. Its size, its weight, took him by surprise. He could not imagine it bringing joy to any child, or to anyone else.

Jurnet stripped off the wrapping with gentle hands, only to find that the creature's so-called fur, spiky and unyielding, was no more endearing than the rest of it. Mario, upon the detective's return, eyed this unexpected companion with astonishment and distrust.

'A prize,' Jurnet said, and, feeling some further explanation to be necessary, 'I thought it would be safer in here than leaving it in the car.'

'The yard is quite safe, I think. And, if you will excuse me — ' the delicatessen owner came closer to get a better look at the teddy bear — 'I do not think a thief would want to steal such a toy, not even if it was Christmas Eve and he had nothing else to put in his *bambino*'s stocking.'

'Not exactly a beauty.' Jurnet managed a laugh to mask the resentment which, to his surprise, he felt welling up within him. The privilege of criticizing his bear was his alone. 'But I don't know. He grows on you after a while.'

'If you say. In a moment, if you please, I take you both upstairs.' The Italian, frowning, made himself busy stripping the cloth off the table, bundling it up with the used napkins. When the task was done and the chairs perched safely on the table top, he drew a deep breath as one coming to a decision. 'Do not be angry with me, Mr Ben, if I ask you.'

'Ask me what?'

'My wife, Mr Ben, my wife Maria, she has a friend who has a daughter who is called Carmela, a warm girl, very loving. Young as she is, she has already had tragedies in her life. A person to understand what another is suffering.' The man's gaze moving in embarrassment from the detective's blank face to the even blanker face of the Bingo bear, he ended clumsily: 'The bed upstairs is ample for two.'

Jurnet said: 'You're offering me a woman?'

'There is no shame in it, Mr Ben,' the other protested. 'Only, perhaps, comfort. When this morning I saw you come in with the cripple I could not help thinking, there must be better than that to be found.'

'The crippled girl is from Israel, on business. Miriam was supposed to meet her at Heathrow. When she didn't show, she naturally came to Angleby looking for her.'

'My apologies. I did not understand. I thought — never mind what I thought. All the way from Israel on those legs!' Persisting nevertheless, his broad face alight with the conviction that what he was advocating was, in the circumstances, the one rational counteraction to the infamy of fate: 'Carmela, the saints be praised, has legs the whole street turns to look at when she walks past — '

'Bully for Carmela!' Jurnet put his free hand in friendship on the delicatessen owner's shoulder, the ungainly bulk of the Bingo bear held firmly in the other. 'You're a good fellow, Mario. You mean well — but no, thanks.' Inwardly wracked with a piercing mirth at the sublime absurdity of the very suggestion, he finished, in the grateful mode the occasion clearly called for: 'Another time, maybe.'

Jurnet lay in Johnny Ferdanzi's bed, a fine modern construction made, whatever else his father pretended, for solitary sleeping: one that did not sag in the middle, conspiring in the act of love, did not jangle a joyous song in celebration. In the orange glow reflected from the street lamps on to the bedroom ceiling Jurnet lay chill between Maria's scented sheets and under her piled Continental quilts, looking up at the patterns traced by the lights of passing cars, cars of people hurrying home to loved ones, going home to bed. To bed.

It troubled him that his grief should take the form of a lustful envy of others' good

164

luck. Surely there had been more to his relationship than a good fuck? He knew there had been more, but what it had consisted of escaped his recollection. No love, no tender memories, only a lubricious spite at being deprived of everything except the air he continued unwillingly to rake into his lungs and expel again: breathe in, breathe out, until the end of time. It came to him that, thanks to Mario's cooking, his breath must smell of garlic, something Miriam had always abhorred, and he half-raised himself, preparatory to going to brush his teeth; only to sink back, garlic-scented breath and all. What the hell did it matter any longer?

A small crucifix hung over Johnny's bed. By tilting his head back Jurnet could just see it, oddly out of perspective, the nailed feet the most prominent feature. Subsiding back on to the pillow, Jurnet gave himself up briefly to a hatred of all gods, Christian, Jewish, Moslem, the lot.

The orange street light caught the green eye of the Bingo bear where it sat, legs stuck out at an angle, in a wicker armchair, propped against a red satin cushion shaped like a heart. Jurnet, rolled over on to his side, watched the green eye for some time, trying without success to decipher its message, wondering even more what the other eye, black and unreflecting, might be trying to convey to him. At last, though nothing had been settled to his satisfaction, he pushed aside the bed covers, got up and padded across the floor to the bathroom where, for what it was worth, he brushed his teeth. Miriam always said that tooth-brushing only partially solved the garlic problem. The stuff, she asserted, seeped out of your pores for days afterwards.

Well, he thought: nothing he could do about that. At least he had shown willing. He came back into the bedroom where the green eye of the Bingo bear signalled unremittingly; picked the ugly thing up by a leg and took it back to bed with him. Cried himself to sleep hugging his teddy bear.

— 14 —

Ireland was a dream — good! Its unreality suited Jurnet's mood. In a dream anything could happen.

Ireland was a dream that, against expectations, was grey, not emerald — a dream of rain that drummed incessantly on the roof of the car he had rented at the airport, of the mesmeric drone of windscreen wipers, of the swish of passing cars and the backwash of the huge refrigerated lorries which from time to time loomed out of the murk like demented dinosaurs hurrying to their extinction and disappeared leaving the sodden landscape even emptier than before.

Ploughing along steadily, going west and north, Jurnet told himself that it must be his own jaundiced state of mind which had conjured up so many derelict homesteads to his view, so many outbuildings and stone walls in terminal collapse: when you were feeling down you tended to see only what was down there in the abyss along with you. Yet, even so, he could not shake off the feeling that he was heading deep into a land whose inhabitants had long ago fled from some calamity whose harrowing details were mercifully unknown to him.

It came to him that practically all the traffic, such as it was, was coming away from his projected destination. When, the main highways left behind, he overtook a solitary cyclist pedalling away, head down against the wind and the rain, and the man looked up at his passing and waved a cheery hand, Jurnet felt a grateful warmth steal over him. Against all the outward signs, he was still on the planet.

Larrakil Lodge turned out to be a large grey house with a cheerful ugliness which was disarming. For what had seemed at the time sufficient reason, Jurnet had made no advance booking. Particularly on the chance that his name might ring bells he had been concerned to avoid alerting Mrs Doran, Terry's mother and the hotel receptionist, to his imminent arrival.

He could not imagine that the place would be full up in early November; but neither, on the other hand, as he encircled the dispirited area of scrub which comprised the front garden, and drew up at steps leading to a

168

front door whose grandiosity of pillars and richly ornamented corbels had more in common with a wedding cake than architecture, had he expected such complete indifference to his coming, such an utter absence of light and animation.

For the first time it occurred to him to wonder if perhaps the entire establishment did not close itself down in November, as well it might, if that day's weather was a fair sample of what the prospective holiday-maker might expect at that season of the year. He was suddenly overcome by a longing for a steaming hot cup of tea, fortified further against the prevailing damp by a generous dollop of that local panacea, whiskey spelled with an 'e'.

Whilst he sat in the car, undecided whether the hotel too was a dream and no more real than the rest of Ireland — whether it was worth his while to unbuckle his seat belt, get out and hammer on the ridiculous door in the hope of arousing the natives within from their tranced slumbers, a man came round the corner of the house, a small, compact person who wore no raincoat yet moved unhurriedly as if he had come to a personal accommodation with the weather, whereby the rain fell to left and right of him, leaving his black trousers, white shirt, natty striped weskit and red bow tie almost entirely un-spotted.

'Can I be of assistance, sir?'

It was quite a relief to Jurnet to see, close to, that the man was as rain-soaked as one would expect any human being to be in the circumstances. It was his attitude, his cool ignoring of the elements, which signalled him out. The detective wound down the car window with some of that respect he habitually reserved for people who were good at what they did. This was a fellow who had plainly mastered the art of living in County Donegal.

Jurnet said: 'I was hoping to put up here for a couple of days. Could you tell me, is the hotel open?'

'Well now,' said the man, after a moment in which he appeared to give the matter some thought, 'it is and it isn't, if you take my meaning.' His voice was strangely precise, concentrating on each syllable as if it might be part of a foreign language, something it needed care to get right. 'Officially, I have to say that we are closed for refurbishment and rehabilitation, but I am sure the missus will be only too pleased to see you and make you as comfortable as anyone could hope to be anywhere.' Making no attempt to hide his curiosity: 'Not many tourists around here, you see, this time of year, specially, as I take you to be, sir, from England. Certainly no time at all, when one does turn up out of the blue, to turn him away when all we're up to inside is slamming on a few rolls of damp-proof and a lick of paint where it shows most.' The man looked over Jurnet's shoulder into the back of the car. 'Shall I take your bag, sir? Once you've checked in you can give me your car keys and I'll put her under cover round at the back.'

'Take 'em now if you're sure it's OK — '
'I wouldn't say if it was otherwise.'

Mrs Anthea Gibson, her hair pushed up into a paint-spattered shower cap, an immaculate white jacket shrugged on over frayed jeans and sweater, was in the kitchen stirring Madeira into a pot of Irish stew, tasting liberally between each copious addition. Responding to the warmth of the place as well as to the fragrance which rose from the stove, Jurnet felt his taste-buds expand with the passionate urgency of nestlings waiting, beaks open, for their parents' return with the goodies.

As he came into the old-fashioned room, its cluttered spaciousness, the young chatelaine of Larrakil Lodge turned from the vast cooking range with a smile that jiggled the freckles spread out in a band across her nose and upper cheeks. 'Are you here to eat or to stay, or is it,' she demanded good-humoured, 'as it generally is this time of year, just to sell me something I haven't a need in the world for, except that your ten barefoot kids will go hungry to bed if I don't buy?'

'He wants to stay,' said the small man who had followed Jurnet in. 'He's from England and he wants to stay for several days if we're open, as I said we were not, expecting you would say different.'

'What do you mean, Willie? Of course we're open!' As if to lend additional credence to the assertion, Mrs. Gibson whipped off her shower cap and, red curls tumbling about her shoulders, became instantly transformed into a hostess of bewitching prettiness. She held out a hand sticky with Madeira, shook Jurnet's hand warmly, not to say adhesively, and giggled, 'Not that we wouldn't be open to the Devil himself in November and this weather.'

'Shall I put his luggage in Number 7, then?' the man named Willie wanted to know. 'Mr G. will have finished the papering and it's the only room where the heat's been on all day.'

'It isn't that cold,' Jurnet offered helpfully. 'You don't have to worry about that.'

'Not the cold — ' the young woman cor-

172

rected him — 'the damp.' Frowning: 'But that willow pattern! I knew it was over-ambitious.' To Jurnet, in explanation: 'I'm afraid Mr Gibson put several of the rolls on upside down and they'll have to come off. Still — ' well aware of her own taking ways, she turned a dazzling smile on the newly-arrived guest — 'I'm sure you won't mind sleeping in a room with a lot of Chinamen standing on their heads, will you?'

Jurnet smiled back. 'I prefer them that way.'

'*Do* you? Don't let on to Greg then, whatever you do. He was ready to cut his throat when he found out what he'd done. He despairs so easily, the poor lamb. There isn't all that much at Larrakil Lodge to despair of, and he does so enjoy it.' Without waiting for Jurnet's assurance that he would stay mum to the death, Mrs Gibson continued. 'And about meals — I'm afraid the dining-room's out. It's the next job on the list. So you won't mind taking pot luck with us here in the kitchen, will you?'

'If it always smells half as good as it does at this moment, I'll be delighted.'

'Oh the poor man!' Mrs Gibson exclaimed, looking at Jurnet directly for the first time and taking in the detective's gaunt good looks

173

with a mixture of compassion and undisguised approval. 'You're cold and you're hungry and sad, and here I go rattling on like the rattle I am. A plate of my famous stew will put you back in circulation in no time. Willie, take up Mr . . . Mr . . . ?' The light, enchanting voice hovered questioningly.

'Jurnet. Ben Jurnet.'

'Mr Jurnet's luggage to Number 7. See that he signs in.' Correcting herself, the conscious charm very much in evidence: 'I shouldn't have said that, should I? You don't even know yet how much it's going to cost you, and I'm sure I don't know either. We've never had anyone before wanting to stay when we're, in a manner of speaking, closed for business. It's a question of how much we can decently soak you for.'

Jurnet responded: 'I'm willing to take a chance, if you are.'

'You're a lovely man!' declared Mrs Gibson. 'You may call me Anthea. You can get out the register after all, Willie. Then find Mr G. and tell him I'm serving right away, it's an emergency. You too, Willie, once you've washed your hands.'

'I told you,' said Willie. 'I have a game of cards lined up with the boys.'

'Did you tell me? I don't remember, but never mind. I'm quite relieved. I was wondering if there'd be enough for the four of us.'

Willie held out Jurnet's car keys.

'I've already put it in the garage out back, the one with a number 2 on it.'

'Thanks very much.' Jurnet pocketed the keys. 'Have a good game.'

'I will that. And you, sir — a good sleep after your journey. See you in the morning, Mr Jurnet.'

'Yes. See you.'

Replete with stew, lulled with a remarkable claret Greg Gibson brought up from the cellar, dulled with the Jamieson's which had punctuated the rest of the evening, Jurnet lay on his bed in a daze of contentment thin as a skim of ice stretched over a crevasse. One false step, he knew, one misplaced thought, and he would be through, plunging down to the depths that lay, as ever, awaiting him.

He shouldn't have said no to that last Jamieson's.

Even at the table, amid the aromatic delights of food and wine, there had been moments of danger. Greg Gibson, of kindly if melancholic aspect, a man who seemed content to let his young wife do the talking, had suddenly looked up with a sharp look in his eyes to ask where their unexpected guest had heard of Larrakil Lodge. Guidebook? Advertisement?

'Neither. Mr Furling, who was here earlier in the year, told me how much he'd enjoyed his stay with you. We're both of us from Angleby, you know.'

'Chap that took on young Terry, Frances' boy?'

Jurnet nodded. 'I believe there was a young man from the village — '

'Furling — of course! Capital man — a great one for the golf and the fishing. But November!' Mr Gibson shook his head in humorous disbelief. 'What was he thinking of, giving you a recommendation for a month when we natives all but sprout fins and the moss begins to grow over us if we stay sitting in the same place for ten minutes running? A little more wine, Mr Jurnet? It would be a blasphemy not to finish the bottle.'

Eyes on the level of the lovely liquid as it rose in his glass, Jurnet had taken a deep breath before answering the unspoken question.

'I needed to get away. I've been bereaved. An accident. My — my wife died.'

Jurnet rolled over on to his side and repeated the word aloud, rolling it round his tongue as he rolled about the bed. Wife.

176

Never, while Miriam lived, had he called her that. He might as well have spoken the secret name of God.

'Wife,' he said now, like a child daring how much it could get away with. 'Wife, wife, wife.' He said it over and over again, sensing that in speaking the word aloud to strangers he had passed some kind of milestone.

Yet the moment he had said 'wife' he had regretted it. Not because it was both a lie and the hope which had fuelled his existence, but out of guilt at having unworthily called up the instant compassion he saw take over the Gibsons' faces. So that it was a positive relief to have to field, almost immediately after, a further sharp-eyed inquiry from the husband: one with whose answer he had primed himself before ever setting out on his journey.

'If it isn't an impertinence to ask,' Greg Gibson had nevertheless asked with kindly interest, 'what do you do for a living, Mr Jurnet, out in the big world?'

'I was in the police,' Jurnet replied, pleased to note that the man's friendly regard did not waver. 'No longer, though. After what happened I'm a bit betwixt and between. Taking time out to have a good long think.'

'Very wise! And where better to take time

out than in Ireland, where taking time out is a national industry! About the thinking part I'm not so sure.' Her laughter rippling, Anthea Gibson had brought to the table a dessert smelling of almonds and apricots. 'Did you never see Terry Doran then, yourself, Frances' son?' She continued, spooning the delicious mess into glasses etched with harps and shamrocks. 'You could put his mother out of her misery with a first hand report of him, if you can give it to her. She's such a strong-minded woman I don't think she expected to miss him as much as she does. She's our receptionist — I don't know whether Mr Furling mentioned it — only we always lay her off while we're closed for redecoration. Generally speaking, it's an arrangement which suits us both because this is the time of year her husband, Andy, is usually home. He's some kind of engineer, away wherever the work is, only this year he's been called to a Norwegian oil rig out in the North Sea, so poor Frances has got both her men away together. And Balorborrean in November is not exactly a hive of activity.'

'Balorborrean? That's down on the coast, isn't it? I'd been planning to go and take a look at the Atlantic.'

'At Balorborrean you can turn up your

trouser bottoms and take a paddle in it, if you've a mind to, in this weather. The only place round here you can do that, thanks to our local hero. Balor of the Baleful Eye,' she had gone on to explain when Jurnet looked puzzled. 'He was a giant with one eye in the middle of his forehead, like the Cyclops. It was so enormous his serving men had to use a wooden beam to keep it propped open. Not a lovable character, I have to admit, and he had a filthy temper. I won't go into all the dreadful things he did, it would make your toes curl up in horror. But one good thing — the cliffs along this stretch of coast are so high that, even if you're a giant, you need ropes and crampons to get yourself down to the sea. Those cliffs made Balor so mad that one day, when he wanted to take his annual bath in the briny, he doubled up his fist and punched a passage clear through the rocks — punched and didn't stop punching until he'd made the prettiest cove you ever saw. That's how it got its name: *Balor* plus *borrean* means Balor's stony place. Except that it isn't stony any more; a lovely little beach of pure silver sand . . .' Mrs Gibson broke off for a moment, then finished: 'The picture in your room, over the fireplace — that's one young Terry did of Balorborrean beach. I'm surprised you haven't noticed it.'

Greg Gibson intervened.

'Mr Jurnet hasn't noticed it because it isn't there to be noticed. I haven't put it back up yet.' To Jurnet: 'It's nothing much, whatever Anthea says. The picture, not the place. A couple of tumble down sheds, very amateur. The boy's no Leonardo da Vinci, that's for sure.'

'It's lovely!' his wife protested. 'The old boathouses, spread out on the sands like cats soaking up the sun. It makes me feel happy just to look at it.'

Deciding that it did not take a great deal to make Mrs Gibson feel happy, Jurnet smiled at the young woman with genuine liking. He said: 'Mr Furling has a couple of the young man's pictures himself, hung up in his office. Very nice. In fact, I was thinking maybe Mrs Doran — that was the name, wasn't it? — has got some at home she'd be prepared to sell. I thought I might call by some time . . .'

Rewarding him for the suggestion with a brilliant smile, the young woman exclaimed, 'Whether she has or she hasn't, you'll be laying up treasure in heaven, bringing her news of Terry.'

Jurnet said carefully: 'I've hardly news — '

'Use your imagination, man!' his hostess

urged, dimpled and irresistible. 'Make it up. Tell her how well he's doing, how satisfied Mr Furling is with the way he's shaping up.' She jumped up from the table. 'I'll just be giving her a ring to let her know you'll be calling.'

'Don't do that,' said Jurnet, trying not to speak too hastily. 'I mean, I wouldn't want to disappoint her. It will depend on the weather and, frankly, how I'm feeling after a night's rest. The way I'm feeling this moment, I could sleep for a week. Better if I simply drop in and take my chance when I'm over that way.'

'Oh. All right.' Mrs Gibson resumed her seat, looking disappointed. 'So long as you don't forget to go.'

'I won't forget to go. I promise.'

15

Lying on the bed, Jurnet looked at the space over the fireplace, peopled by upside-down Chinamen slant-eyed and sinister in the light from the bedside lamp. Mr Gibson must have papered over the hole where the picture hook had hung. You could not have told that a picture had ever hung there.

Jurnet lay back and thought about the beach of silver sand and about Balor the Baleful. About the eye that needed to be shored up with a wooden beam — enough, in all conscience, to make anyone bad-tempered. He also reflected that if Terry Doran had returned home he was evidently not advertising the fact. Mrs Gibson would have been sure to have known of it.

That the Gibsons might know of it and were not letting on was something he simply hadn't the energy to take on board.

Terry Doran, born Terry Cardo, son and heir of the redoubtable, the execrable, Danny.

If the boy were indeed following in his natural father's footsteps he would surely never have made the elementary error of making for the one place to which he was known to have ties. At this very moment, if he were anywhere in Ireland, it would be Dublin, losing himself in a big city, safe among thugs who remembered his father and were tickled pink to welcome his son to their diabolical conspiracy. *So what if the youngster had blown up the wrong person, a pretty girl instead of a hated copper?* Jurnet could imagine their indulgent smiles. *Anyone could make a mistake — you might almost call it an Irish prerogative. Give the boy a Guinness and better luck next time!*

Jurnet turned out the lamp and still did not sleep. The dark was absolute, silent save for an incessant sussuration that was too un-accented for rain, too insubstantial for a river: an Irish water torture. By the time you had identified it, it would be too late, you would be a goner, rushes sprouting out of your ears as you sank deliquescent into the bog. Night-long Jurnet lay without sleeping a wink, an error persisted in until a knock at the bedroom door preceded the entry of a comfortable, grey-haired woman in a white starched apron, who brought him a cup of tea.

'Two cups I've brought and taken away, and you dead to the world,' she greeted him cheerfully. 'Third time lucky! I finally thought to myself, too much sleeping's as bad as too little. If the gentleman doesn't throw the cup back in my face he'll thank me for it once he's back in the land of the living.' The woman set the cup and saucer down on the bedside table, went over to the french window and opened the doors a little, briefly setting foot on the balcony outside before withdrawing indoors again. 'It's a lovely soft day,' she announced, looking out upon a greyness which seemed to Jurnet unchanged from the day before. 'By the time you've eaten your breakfast we'll even be providing a spot of sunshine at no extra cost. My name is Eleanor,' she finished. 'I'm the chambermaid and the kitchenmaid, the waitress and the general treasure without who Larrakil Lodge out of season would sink without trace. And will you be having sausage or a kipper, coffee or tea?'

When she had gone, with an order for a kipper and coffee, Jurnet sat up and drank the tea. Showered and dressed in cords and a thick sweater he in turn, before leaving the room, went out on to the balcony to assess the promise of the morn, if any. As if only awaiting his appearance, the grey mat of cloud fractured, blue sky revealed itself in the gap, coyly, its nakedness made decent with puffs of cirro-cumulus.

The November landscape exposed to view clamoured for his attention. For the first time since making landfall Jurnet looked out on a vista of Ireland: on small rushy fields hedged raggedly with blackthorn stripped to the buff for winter; on crumbling walls; on small conical hayricks that wore old-fashioned snoods like old women who had given up taking trouble with their hair; on the flash of water in hollows and ditches: the whole laid out on a receding chequerboard where black-faced sheep moved about without a clue to the rules of the game, against a backdrop of mountains tinted an improbable purple. Upon these last Jurnet turned the cold eye of one brought up to the understatement of East Anglia, to horizontal planes and gentle slopes fashioned to the same scale as the natives. Here, from what he could see, except for the sheep there were no natives — or if there were, they were not in evidence. The smoke that rose from the chimneys of the few low, white-painted farmhouses scattered like dominoes across the terrain merely added to the overwhelming inwardness of the place, apparently so open to the soft air, in reality so full of secrets. The narrow roads that crossed the area, winding round hillocks, skirting water, all seemed to Jurnet to be leading the eye, and with it the heart, away: away over the mountains, away to the hidden sea, anywhere away. No wonder the land looked so empty. Who would ever choose to stay when there were ways of escape for the taking?

Willie, the small man who had greeted him the night before, came into the stable yard as Jurnet backed the hired car out of Number 2 stable.

'Off on a day's sightseeing, is it?' The man, natty in his striped apron, came over and leaned an arm companionably on the ledge of the driver's window, close enough for Jurnet to smell the brilliantine he wore on his shining black hair, as well as the tobacco on his breath. 'A grand day. I see you've been clever enough to bring your own weather. I hope you didn't miss the pile of literature on the reception desk, telling you all the places you have to see or you haven't seen Ireland. Sure, we Irish ourselves never even knew what sights we were till the Tourist Board put it in print, but now that we know, you'd be hard put to it to find somewhere or someone in the Republic who wasn't picturesque, one way or the other.

Luckily though — ' the blue eyes bright with an innocent mischief — 'they're most of them shut for the winter, so you won't be put to the bother of working your way through them.'

Jurnet laughed. He shifted as far away from the open window as was possible without risking offence.

'Sightseeing's putting it too high. I thought I'd just potter around the neighbourhood, wherever the spirit moves me.' To get away from a subject in which he saw dangers, he asked: 'Had a good game last night, did you?'

'Very convivial, thank you, sir. Lost a packet, but there! That's life, isn't it? You win some and you lose some.'

'What do you play?'

'Only pontoon. Nothing intellectual.' The man leaned even closer, inspecting the car's interior. 'Don't tell me Eleanor let you go without a flask and some sandwiches! Mrs Gibson told her, before she and Mr Gibson left for the shopping, to make sure you didn't go off unfortified.'

'She did offer, but after the breakfast she made me I'm fortified till this evening, if not next week. In the unlikely event I do get peckish I'm sure I'll find somewhere . . .'

Willie shook his head doubtfully.

'Don't be so sure, sir. Deepest Donegal, this time of year, you won't find a lot open this side of Letterkenny, if there.'

'Surely there's bound to be a pub where I can get some bread and cheese?'

'Very rough and ready, sir. And this the Gaelthait, some of them not even speaking English. I hardly think you'll find them to your liking.'

Jurnet swivelled his body so as to face the man directly, hair oil, tobacco and all. 'You aren't by any chance trying, in your delicate way, to tell me that as an Englishman I won't be welcome in an Irish pub?'

Willie opened his blue eyes wide.

'Would I ever say such a thing, now, and the Tourist Board putting out all those beautiful brochures? Friendly faces, lovely people, Ireland of all the welcomes, you can read all about it, you don't have to take my word. I simply thought, what with the sawdust on the floor, gobs of spit flying, and language not what an English gent's used to — '

'Sounds exactly the kind of local colour we English gents drive miles to see. It wouldn't surprise me if your Tourist Board lays it on specially, spit and all, just for our benefit.' Jurnet revved up the engine purposefully. 'I'll be on my way, then . . .'

'There was one other thing,' the man said,

moving back from the car, but only a little. 'The missus said I was to tell you Mrs Doran's house is the very first you come to as you go into Balorborrean. There's five modern bungalows and hers is the first. You can't miss it. The roadway there is so narrow people visiting usually leave their cars by the shrine, which you'll come to a little before, under the hill. It's been made wider there, as you'll see, for people who stop to pay their respects, and from there it's only a matter of yards to Mrs Doran's.'

Wryly reflecting that he ought to have known the impossibility of keeping a secret in the country, Jurnet drove in his hired Escort through the scenery of which he had had a preview from his bedroom balcony. Without Miriam he had thought it impossible he could ever feel lonelier, but driving to Balorborrean he did feel lonelier, his being possessed by an autumnal despair that carried with it no promise of spring. He stared out at a landscape more brown than green, its unregarding beauty a visual mockery.

There was little traffic to speak of, which was just as well considering the way such oncoming vehicles as there were tended to hog the middle of the road — less, it would seem, out of brutish disregard for other road

189

users on the part of their drivers than because, judging from the startled expression on the faces glimpsed in passing, they knew from long experience that nobody ever came that way and consequently anybody who did so was a freak of nature whose vagaries could not be foreseen nor made provision for.

Some six miles from the Lodge, a short distance past the junction with an unmetalled lane signposted 'The Cove', Jurnet came to the shrine where, sure enough, the road widened, just as Willie had promised. Even so, had he not been going slowly, taking in, as he went, the high land on one side, the marshy swamp on the other, he might easily have missed it. True, the man had specified 'under the hill', but the words had conveyed no picture of the cave which now presented itself to the detective's somewhat abashed gaze. Jurnet's Nonconformist childhood as well as his tentative advances towards Judaism had left him uncomfortable in the presence of religious faith rendered visible to the naked eye, and once abreast of her, the Virgin who stood at the entrance, hands joined in prayer, a rosary dangling from one arm, the whole painted from head to foot in a white that was almost fluorescent, was as visible as it was possible to be, a shining presence against the dark of a hollow which appeared to have been rough-hewn out of the base of the bank rising steeply from the roadway. The statue stood on a pedestal scarcely large enough to accommodate its spreading draperies, around its base several plastic pots containing chrysanthemums long past their prime, the once-yellow blooms brown and shrunken. In rocky crevices ferns and other anonymous greenery, which in summer must have softened the unforgiving stone, hung dank and dying. Altogether, in November a sad place for all its affirmation, its implied promise to the faithful of better things to come in the hereafter.

A blue-and-white telephone box had been placed next to the shrine, and the Virgin, her head slightly tilted, seemed to be listening for a call, her eyes — albeit sightless and painted white like the rest of her — fixed on heaven. Thankful that they were not fixed on him, Jurnet parked the car with as little fuss as possible, mentally apologizing — to whom he would have found it hard to say — for any inconvenience.

16

Mrs Doran's bungalow was one of five arranged round a semicircle of coarse grass. In summer, their window boxes brimming with geraniums, scarlet against the white stucco, one could imagine them looking cheery and courageous, a welcome human statement shouted at the implacable mountains which seemed to advance and retreat as the fancy took them. November had reduced them to packages delivered by mistake to the wrong address and dumped rather than incur the expense of re-routing them to where they belonged, the respectable suburb with ornamental cherries planted along the street at intervals; where husbands always put their jackets on before answering the door and wives never went shopping without first taking the rollers out of their hair, no matter if they had a Liberty scarf to put over them.

All five bungalows had carports, Mrs

Doran's with a car in place, a Volkswagen past its youth but well cared for. All five had bright green doors, the first true emerald Jurnet had seen since arriving in the Emerald Isle. His knock at Mrs Doran's was answered almost immediately by a woman who looked more Scandinavian than Irish, a tall, handsome woman with a natural elegance which even the greying blonde hair scraped back carelessly into a bun low down on her neck could not belie. Her face had the calm assurance of one who not only knew her place in the world but had moulded the entire planet to her own specification. Only the grey eyes were watchful above the pleasant smile with which she greeted her caller before he had had time either to introduce himself or state his business.

'Mr Jurnet! This *is* a surprise!'

Whilst Jurnet, privately wondering which of them had warned her of his coming — the Gibsons, Willie or Eleanor — publicly exhibited astonishment at her recognition, she left him on the step for a moment and came quickly back holding a framed enlargement which she handed over in smiling explanation. Jurnet's heart contracted, his vision blurred. Miriam had taken the picture, one of himself surrounded by the O'Driscoll children, a moment of riotous laughter captured one August weekend as, under her direction, they had moved to and fro across the forecourt of the block of flats, vainly seeking a spot where her viewfinder would not pick up any of the ubiquitous plastic bags of rubbish waiting, as ever, for the dustman. The spot they had eventually fixed on — Jurnet reckoned, studying the print with an attention he had never accorded it before — was, just about, where his Rover had been parked the morning Miriam had died and the world ended.

He handed the photograph back unable to comment. Looking a little disappointed, Mrs Doran said: 'My cousin Lucy — Mrs O'Driscoll — sent it to us. You have a distinctive face, Mr Jurnet, and I knew you at once. My husband said you looked a devil of a fellow. You're never staying at the Lodge, not with all the redecoration going on there?'

'I am. Mr Furling recommended it so highly that when I decided to take a break — ' a pause during which Mrs Doran's air of cordial interest did not waver — 'I came on the spur of the moment, never thinking to telephone first. But the Gibsons have been very kind and made me very comfortable.'

Was it possible the woman knew nothing of what had happened back in Angleby, that neither her son nor the O'Driscolls had been

194

in touch to put her in the picture? But in that case wouldn't you have expected her first words to be: 'Have you seen Terry? How is he?' And why didn't she ask him in, proffer some of that famous Irish hospitality? Could it be that her living-room was cluttered with Terry's paraphernalia, his sketching pad open on the couch, his socks and trainers warming in front of the fire? Might not the boy, ear to the keyhole, be holed up behind one of the shut doors giving on to the little hall at this very moment, unable to make a break for it without exposing himself to view?

With no appearance of reading his thoughts Mrs Doran exclaimed: 'Whatever must you think of me, keeping you out here on the doorstep? Only, when you knocked, I had that very moment come to get my coat. There's an old lady in the village I promised to sit with while her daughter's off to the dentist and she'll be getting fretful if I'm not there promptly.'

Suiting the action to the word she shrugged on a red plastic raincoat which she produced from behind the door, cinching the belt in tightly as if consciously relishing her possession of a slender waist.

'Will you come and have a cup of coffee with me tomorrow morning instead? Or tea, if that would suit you better.' Calm, she finally came out with what was expected of her. 'Apart from the pleasure of your company it would be lovely to have news of Terry, if you have any. He is not one of the world's letter-writers and Lucy is no better.' Making for the outdoors in a way that left Jurnet with no alternative but to retreat himself: 'If you know Mr Furling, you'll likely be able to tell me if Terry is exaggerating when he says he is giving full satisfaction.'

Side by side, the two crossed the semicircle of grass to the road. Jurnet said: 'Mr Furling had some of Terry's water-colours up in his office. I didn't have the opportunity to ask Terry himself, but I was wondering if he had any more here you'd be willing to sell?'

'I'm sure he'd be thrilled.' Mrs Doran looked as delighted as might be expected. 'They're all packed away at the moment but come tomorrow and I'll have a selection fished out ready for you to see. I really must run now. You're parked back down the road, I suppose? You never walked all the way from Larrakil?'

'No. I parked by the shrine.'

'Ah. It's a great convenience. A shrine, a phone box. My husband always says all we need there is a public WC and all our needs, sacred and profane, will be catered for. He's a terrible pagan. Morning coffee, then?'

'Morning coffee,' agreed Jurnet, shaking her proffered hand. 'I look forward to it.'

He watched as the woman walked away towards the village whose slate and thatch he could see in the distance, walking with the long-limbed confidence of one who hadn't a care in the world.

Jurnet knitted his brows. Danny Cardo, that legendary first husband, had died in a welter of blood, most of it not his own. Trailing such a history, could anybody really walk like that, or was it, like everything else about their brief meeting, a show put on for his benefit? Surely she should have asked about her son the moment she realized who it was standing at her front door?

Pondering, Jurnet walked slowly back to the shrine; walked past it until he came to the turning that led down to the cove. Passing between banks which rose steeply on either side, his shoes sibilant on sand and gravel, the detective reflected that Balor the Baleful had given himself quite a job, punching his way to the sea — not one punch needed but a whole series of them, the road snaking between the rocks until it merged at last with a horseshoe-shaped beach against which waves broke in noisy satisfaction at having made it all the way from the U.S. of A. Wind and spray on his face, even Jurnet who at the best of times could take the sea or leave it alone, preferably the latter, felt his heart beat faster, his whole being in some obscure way magnified at the thought of that incredible journey.

With the exception of the wooden constructions sheltering under the cliff a short distance back from the water, the place looked much the same as it must have looked the day Balor, sucking knuckles that were bound to have got at least a little grazed in the exercise, had gone home to a well-earned dinner. A few yards offshore, on a rocky islet, an outsize pebble the giant had probably tossed there in his hurry to be done, a couple of gulls squabbled over some slimy delicacy, then took off and circled mewing before settling again amicably. One of the buildings — presumably the boathouse to which Greg Gibson had referred — was lofty and commodious and in a fair state of repair; the others a litter of sheds, some of them roofless, others patched with sheets of corrugated that looked as if they only awaited the next gale to be up and away, like most of the other denizens of this benighted land.

Jurnet strolled over to the window inserted in one side of the large boathouse and peered in. The window was small and smeared, but with a large skylight fitted into the sloping roof of the building the interior was sharply visible. After a few minutes of unhurried inspection Jurnet moved round to the front where a small door was cut into the vast double doors which formed, in effect, the fourth wall. A metal latch from which an open padlock dangled hung down from this small door.

Calmly, making no attempt at silence, Jurnet pulled the small door open, stepped inside; crossed the floor to the trestle table where a boy sat on a high stool painting, absorbed. In the light from the skylight the back of his thin neck, as he bent over his work, looked very young, very vulnerable.

'You're early,' the boy commented, not bothering to look round. So far as Jurnet could make out he was concentrating on getting the right shade of purple out of the blue and red pigments he was mixing in a small white pan. 'I want to get this finished before I eat.'

'That's OK by me,' said Jurnet.

'You!'

The boy swung round, splashing some of the newly mixed colour on to his picture. With a rag he mopped up as much of the mess as he could, succeeding only in spreading it further. 'Look what you've made me do!'

Jurnet waited, not apologizing, until Terry Doran threw down the rag and turned on him anew.

'Who do you think you are? This is Ireland the republic of, in case you didn't know, not England. You can't come policing here. I ought to tell the Garda. They'll know what to do.'

'Tell them by all means,' Jurnet said. 'It would be a pleasure to meet them — though, for the record, I haven't come policing, as you put it. I'm not policing anywhere any longer. I came to see you. What you might term a personal call, between friends.'

Taken aback, the boy picked up the rag again and began to rub it uselessly over his stained fingers. Looking down at them, he remarked bitterly: 'She tells me to keep myself out of sight yet she's the first one to let on where I was.'

'Your mother, you mean?' The other nodded. 'Quite the contrary. According to her you're hard at it in Angleby. A rotten correspondent but then, that's how young people are, isn't it? She hasn't heard from you in weeks but, as she said, no news is good news.'

'Oh.' The boy's voice remained sullen.

'Obviously you didn't believe her, or you wouldn't have come looking.'

'Oh, but I did believe! Or rather, I would have if I hadn't, until recently, been a policeman, as you know. You may think I was taking an unfair advantage. Policemen, you see, know there's such a thing as being too perfect, and your mother was altogether too convincing. Someone ought to tip her off about that, ready for the next time she tries to fob off a caller with a pack of lies. Not that we didn't part the best of friends. In fact, she invited me round for coffee tomorrow morning when she promises to have some of your paintings out for me to see. And as for my coming here looking, that was your own doing entirely.'

'What d'you mean, my doing?'

'Only that Mr Gibson back at the hotel told me you'd painted a picture of some old boatsheds that would have been hanging in my bedroom except it had been taken down while the room was repapered and hasn't been put back yet. So when, on my way down here quite innocently to take a look at the sea, I saw these old boatsheds I thought, "I wonder if they're the ones young Terry painted," and I came over to have a closer look.'

'They're the ones.' Between gritted teeth

Terry Doran asked: 'What you want with me?'

Jurnet moved away without replying, taking in the boatshed's interior: the timber stacked at the far end, the outsize sheet of hardwood which covered the best part of the floor. On the wall, transformed by the light from above into works of a calligraphic delicacy, were hung a series of drawings which — one of the odds and ends of information picked up in a career spent in a county which boasted two hundred miles of navigable waterways — the detective recognized as lines, the plans of a boat presented three ways — in profile, the hull and the body. Some portions of the same plans, enlarged to full size, had, he noticed, already been drawn in chalk on the hardboard, their details obscured by the curls of wood shavings which littered the floor everywhere.

Crunching some of these last underfoot, Jurnet remarked: 'You could do with a good sweep up here.'

'Keep off those loftings!' the boy commanded sharply.

'What?'

'The hardboard. Can't you see? My Dad's making the patterns. Or will, soon as he gets back from the rig. Till then, nothing's to be touched — nothing. He made us promise. When he gets back he wants to find everything exactly the way he left it. Now I'm back — ' with love and desolation — 'we can go on with it together.'

'Go on with what?'

'The boat, o' course! What you think?' His voice high and uncertain, the boy demanded afresh: 'What you want with me, Mr Jurnet?' Tears starting from his eyes, a child out of control, he cried out: 'I wish I *was* back in Angleby! I never blew up your bloody car!'

'If I thought you had,' said Jurnet, 'I wouldn't be here.'

17

For lack of other seating, the two of them sat together on the floor, Jurnet with an arm round the boy's shoulders; the boy pressed close against the detective's chest, a child seeking comfort. The stale smell of the shavings, their juicy essence quite evaporated, rose in their nostrils. Overhead, the sun had gone in, having stayed out, Jurnet reckoned, just long enough to provide a photo-opportunity for the people who prepared the Come to Ireland brochures. In place of a brash blue the skylight had refilled itself with the accustomed grey, a softness Jurnet was beginning to find more supportable than sunshine, the way it conformed to his mood of stoic, or rather, not so stoic, despair.

Almost too low to be heard, the boy said: 'Uncle Denis — Mr O'Driscoll — was waiting for me when I got back from the police station to that drill hall where they moved us first thing while they were trying to find somewhere for us to go to. He said the police had been asking him questions too, and how had I got on. He's a great one for going on and on and I said OK. All I wanted was to get back to the office and explain I hadn't stayed away on purpose. I asked was there a washroom in the place, I needed to clean myself up, but he took hold of my sleeve and hung on to me and whispered like he was telling a secret. Daytime he works as a kitchen porter at the Shire Hotel, but three nights a week he helps out behind the Bittern bar. What he whispered was that he had orders to see I'd be in the Bittern that night.

'Orders!' The boy shook his head in remembered distaste. 'Uncle Denis knows bloody well I don't care for boozing, I'd rather spend the money on painting materials, and he must have heard me say I don't know how many times I can't stand the way the Bittern's always full of tobacco smoke, you could cut it with a knife. When I told him what I thought about his orders, though, he didn't take any notice. He was shivering a little, as if he was cold. I could have been talking to a wall.

'He said as I didn't have any choice, that the fellows who wanted to see me wouldn't take no for an answer. When I asked what fellows, he told me to use my loaf, to be my father's son. He meant Danny Cardo's son, not Andy Doran's. They always do, when they talk about my father's son.'

'Yet you finally went along with him?'

'I had to.' The boy began to cry again. 'If I didn't turn up, he said, they'd take it out of him, and where would he be with a wife and seven, almost eight, kids to support?'

'You knew without being told who these people were?'

The boy lifted his head and said sombrely: 'I'm Irish. I wasn't born yesterday.' He took a deep breath before going on. 'When we got into the pub Uncle Denis took me behind the bar and through a door and down a long passage. There was another door where he knocked and told me to go in. Himself he scooted away like the banshees were after him — back to the bar, I suppose. He'd delivered the goods as ordered. He was in the clear.'

'Tell me what it was like in that room.'

'It was quite a small one, with a lot of chairs and a table at one end. I can't tell you much about it because the only light came from a lamp with a red shade on it at one end of the table, not much light at all. I could see that there were two men sitting at the table, but outside the lamplight. They were just shapes, I couldn't tell you how they looked or anything about them except that they didn't come from Donegal. They hadn't the voices for it. One of them had a very strong voice — Dublin, I shouldn't be surprised. He seemed to be in charge. The other fellow only spoke to agree with everything he said.

'When I came into the room, I stood there. I didn't know what to do. The man with the strong voice said, very chummy: "Well, here's our young hero! Congratulations, sonny!" I didn't know what to say, so I didn't say anything. The other one said: "And modest with it!" and the pair of them laughed. I'd have been really soft in the head not to know what they were on about, so I said: "If it's about blowing up that car, I had nothing to do with it." '

'What did they say to that?'

'They only laughed louder. They seemed to be in very good humour. Perhaps they'd been drinking, I don't know. The whole pub stinks of whiskey, so it was hard to tell. Then the hard voiced one said: "Just because you used up three times as much flour as you needed to, and even then caught the wrong rat in your trap, doesn't mean you have to apologize. You're among friends here. We all have to learn. It was still a fine first effort." '

'I said again that I hadn't had anything to do with the explosion, but they wouldn't take no for an answer. The strong voiced fellow told me to shut up. He said it in a good-humoured way, though. "The point is, laddie," he said, "you're elected, and that's the whole of it." '

The boy's voice broke. Jurnet tightened his hold and made soothing noises until a relative calm was restored. Presently he said gently: 'Tell me.'

'They told me I had to leave for Ireland — not in the morning, not any other day, but that very minute. When I said I'd promised the police that I wouldn't leave Angleby they laughed again and said: "So much the better." They said some good friends of theirs would drive me to Holyhead and hand me over to somebody else who would see me safely across the sea and all the way home to Donegal. A prince of the blood, they said, wouldn't be better looked after. I said I wasn't due to be going home till Christmas, I didn't know what else to say. But the strongvoiced one said, "Then you'll be giving your mother a fine surprise."

'They wouldn't even let me go back for

some luggage, not so much as a toothbrush. They didn't want the O'Driscolls to know I was off, though of course Uncle Denis would have guessed when I didn't come back that night. When I said I needed my clothes, that what I was wearing wasn't warm enough for a sea voyage and all I had at home was a few things I'd grown out of, I could tell by their voices and by the way they moved their bodies in their seats that they were beginning to lose patience with me. They said I wasn't behaving like my father's son. They said — ' the voice died away before resuming tremulously — 'they said that for every day I hung about in Angleby from then on they would pick off a young O'Driscoll. They didn't make it clear what they meant by "picking off", but those kids! They're a great bunch and my auntie would go bananas if anything happened to them.'

'So you went as ordered?'

'Fat lot of choice I had, hadn't I?' The tears flowed unrestrained. 'They could've killed them.'

Jurnet produced a handkerchief, mopped the wet cheeks with an impatient tenderness. 'So what d'you reckon it was all in aid of?'

The boy made an effort, got his act together.

'I've thought about it a lot. Laying a false

trail is what it has to be. They wanted to get the bloodhounds off the guy that really did the job. A big fish, someone they didn't want to get caught. Not, like me, what you would call expendable.'

'Hm. I suppose they never mentioned any name, or names, did they?'

Terry Doran shook his head. 'All they said was that now the pieces were in place they would be fools not to take advantage of every opportunity — not just in one or two big places like London or Birmingham but in every town of any size from Land's End to John o'Groat's. They were really going to set the mainland jumping and I'd got them off to a good start.'

The detective disengaged himself and stood up. Taken aback by the sudden withdrawal of support, the other leaned back on his hands, peering up uncertainly at the tall, lean figure. The boy's nose was running but he made no attempt to wipe the mucus away.

'Have a good blow, for Christ's sake.' Jurnet held out the handkerchief, spoke with a smiling exasperation. Then, urgently: 'Come back with me to England, Terry! What do you say?'

The boy shrank away.

'They'll put me in prison. They'll never believe me.'

'I do — why shouldn't they? I came to Shannon. I have to return the car there, and we can fly back together.'

'The fellows said I was never to cross to the mainland again unless and until they said so.'

'You surely aren't going to let a gang of yobbos ruin the rest of your life for you?'

'What about the O'Driscoll kids? I can't risk it.' But the voice was heavy with longing.

'*Because* of the O'Driscoll kids! What kind of a world will it be for them to grow up in if a bunch of thugs know they can get away with threats and murder? The police will make sure all the O'Driscolls — your uncle and auntie as well as the kids — have full police protection, and they'll make sure you don't come to any harm either.'

'You didn't hear them, Mr Jurnet.' The boy shivered again. 'They were laughing but they weren't funny . . .'

'And you want to throw in your lot with bastards like that? You want to be dragged down into that cesspit where there's only death at the bottom — not just your own death but that of a lot of innocent people beside? Is that what you want?' Jurnet dusted himself off deliberately. 'Because if it is, I've been wasting my time, and the sooner I get myself off this bloody Emerald Isle of yours and back to civilization the better I'll like it.'

He was more than half-way to the door before the boy was at his side.

'Tell me what to do.'

Jurnet looked down at the pale, resolute face, the boy become man, feeling the nearest to happiness he had felt since the morning Miriam had gone out of the flat leaving him sleeping.

'Be at that shrine at the top of the road tomorrow morning. I'll pick you up at nine thirty, near as I can manage. If you get there first, stay well back in the cave, just to be on the safe side. Are you sleeping here, or back at the bungalow?'

'The bungalow.'

'Right. Will you be able to get out of the house, d'you think, so that none of the neighbours see you?'

'No problem. There aren't any neighbours. They're all summer lets, all except ours.'

Stifling an admittedly mild pang of guilt at the thought of Mrs Doran left alone again among the empty bungalows — a woman, he reassured himself, well practised in coping with the twists and turns of fate — Jurnet inquired on a note of intentional sharpness: 'Are you proposing to tell your mother?'

To his relief, Terry Doran shook his head. Speaking out of his new maturity: 'Better she doesn't know. Then, if they come asking, she genuinely won't have anything to tell them, will she? Once she hears that you've gone too she'll probably put two and two together, but she won't know for certain.'

The two nodded at each other in grave agreement. Neither needed to define further who 'they' were.

'You'd better be on your way,' Terry Doran advised, 'or you'll run into her bringing my dinner.'

18

Jurnet walked slowly away from the boat-house, thinking that the Superintendent would be well pleased with him: mission accomplished, or on the verge of being so. As to whether he, Ben Jurnet, was equally pleased with himself, he was less sure. Time and the indeterminate outlines of the Irish landscape had altered his perspective. When it came to the point, did he really want to know who had killed Miriam, burden himself with a terrible knowledge requiring action which must contradict everything he had previously stood for?

He felt the aching indifference of grief descending upon him with every step he took, repossessing him utterly. Had he indeed run into Mrs Doran bringing her son's dinner, he could easily have sent back a message by her to the effect that the lad was not to bother going to the shrine after all or, if he went, let it be only to give thanks for deliverance from the devilish temptation to do something, anything at all.

Jurnet was suddenly struck by the amazing affinity between the Superintendent and the one-eyed giant who, at a blow, had made it possible for all who came after to reach the boat house and the sea: the same unbridled power, the same refusal to accept the world as anything other than an arrangement of molecules conformable to his wishes. Except that, in Balor's situation, the Superintendent would never have risked his beautiful manicure. He would never have needed to. One word of command from those aristocratic lips and the rocks would have parted even as the Red Sea had parted for the Children of Israel.

The grey Irish sky, so unlike the East Anglian ones to which Jurnet was accustomed, had once more lowered itself. Mist clung to the tops of the cliffs on either side of the road, or else abseiled down their weathered sides with practised ease. Feeling the damp in his bones, one more ache to add to that other which no change in the weather could ameliorate, Jurnet hunched his shoulders, quickened his pace until he was back at the junction, the car and the shrine a matter of yards away.

He made for the car, purposely averting

his eyes from the plaster madonna, though not before he had got the impression that the statue was balanced on its inadequate pedestal even more precariously than when he had first encountered it. The vibration caused by passing cars, he shouldn't wonder, or some small settlement of the rocks which walled her cubbyhole. He noted further, with a certain subliminal uneasiness, that one of the pots of dead chrysanthemums parked round the base lay on its side, black compost spilt on to the sandalled foot which peeped out from beneath the Virgin's robe. A further wondering as to whether he ought not, in charity, to pick up the pot, settle the statue more securely in its place, foundered on his diffidence, his reluctance to interfere with a ritual object alien to his upbringing and all his sensibilities. The statue was probably OK anyway, he told himself — had, most likely, stood tottering like that for donkey's years. Maybe the pose was even intentional, a ploy to make the faithful feel protective towards the Mother of God.

Such were the thoughts which drifted disconnectedly through Jurnet's mind as he went towards the hired car, feeling in his pocket for the car keys as he went. He had them in one hand, already stretching out the other towards the door handle, when it happened.

Without warning the Virgin pitched forward and fell against the car bonnet, breaking into two pieces at the waist. Neither the white dust which rose from the fracture, nor the clank with which the car bonnet responded to the impact altered the white face which, young and a little simpering, smiled up at Jurnet from the ground as if nothing had happened, God still in His heaven and all right with the world.

Aroused from his lethargy, the detective looked down aghast, in the same instant that the sum of his years in the police alerted him to a further interpretation of the statue's overbalancing. Reacting automatically, he flung away from the car, into the shallow depth of the Virgin's grotto, pressed himself against the rock, his hand shielding his eyes.

Scarcely had he done so than, with a roar like an angry bull, the car went up in smoke and flames. A spray of glass and metal fragments peppered the road surface. Some small pieces of stone detached themselves from the cave wall, one of them searing Jurnet's forehead and right cheek in transit. The cave itself vibrated like a plucked cello. Gobbets of soil, an ancient bird's nest, bits of moribund greenery rained down on the detective's head and shoulders. A wave of poisoned air momentarily wrapped him in a warm blanket which left him gasping until some other force unimaginable whipped it incontinently away.

When, trembling and feeling that his throat had been scoured with a lavatory brush, Jurnet brushed the detritus off his face and dared to look outside, the car was well alight, crackling cheerfully. The draperies which had covered the lower half of the Virgin had been reduced to the appearance of a mound of blancmange, brown where the white paint had taken fire. The upper half, which had fallen further away, was more or less intact, the image despite some bubbling blisters on forehead and chin smiling still.

Nobody came, that was the strange, the spooky thing. The flames had died down soon enough, leaving a column of smoke that rose to meet the low sky, a column which must have been visible from the adjacent village; yet nobody came running, either out of curiosity or a desire to help. Jurnet, keeping well back in the shadows, heard a car approaching from the direction of Larrakil; heard it stop with a screeching of brakes, reverse, and retreat by the way it had come.

Whoever had blown up the hired car had gone a good deal easier on the Semtex than the guy who had done for the Rover. A professional, conceivably — one who had used no more of the precious stuff than was needed to do the job. After his ministrations the car was still recognizable for what it was, even though the shattered remains of the driver's seat and steering wheel must have spelled curtains for anyone who had actually got the door open and himself inside before the balloon went up.

Jurnet contemplated the wreckage for several minutes before he went round to the passenger side of the vehicle and dragged the remaining half of the indomitably smiling Virgin back to the shelter of her grotto, where he propped her among the decayed chrysanthemums.

There was blood on her face. Jurnet looked at it in surprise until he realized that it was his, that he was bleeding, plentifully. He fished out the handkerchief that had staunched Terry Doran's tears and held it to his cheek, where it speedily turned red and redder, inadequate. Bored with the procedure, Jurnet muttered, 'The hell with it!' and threw the handkerchief away. The warm flowing blood reminded him that once again, Goddamit, he had escaped death, he had been rejected. At least, this time, no innocent victim had been roped in to die in his place.

Hardly was the thought in his mind than

his eye was caught by something in the road, something that shone emerald green amongst the shards of glass and metal. He had spoken too soon. A groan escaped him as he bent down and picked up the green eye of the Bingo bear. Uncertain as to why he had felt it essential to bring the toy with him to Ireland in the first place, and too shy actually to bring it into Larrakil Lodge for an inquisitive chambermaid to happen upon, he had left it on the floor in the back of the car, covered with the rug with which the hire company provided him. Now, he looked down at the shining eye in his hand and began to cry as he had scarcely cried for Miriam. Great sobs welled up inside him, escaping in a harsh discordance. Blood and tears mingled on his cheeks and dripped on to his sweater before he pulled himself together, slipped the eye carefully into a trouser pocket and set out for Larrakil.

'Jesus!' exclaimed Willie, consternation writ large on his face — or was it disappointment that a plan had miscarried? Jurnet was in no state to make a judgement as he stumbled up the front steps of Larrakil Lodge and into the hall.

The man came swiftly to the detective's side, took him by the arm and led him, muddied and soaking wet as he was, to an easy chair before running to fetch his mistress. Mrs Gibson came and hovered over her guest, her beautiful eyes wide with dismay — unless it was with annoyance at what he was doing to her upholstery. Unless it was chagrin that he had come back at all.

Jurnet, his head spinning too fast for him to distinguish between friend and foe, muttered that there had been an accident, somebody had blown up his car. He did not add that, for reasons which in retrospect appeared ridiculous, he had chosen to avoid roads and had made his way back to the hotel across country, discovering in the process that Ireland was a good deal less solid than it looked, a raft through which it was only too easy to put one's foot, if not one's leg up to the thigh, into the water which lurked immediately beneath.

'Blown up!' Mrs Gibson's eyes had positively blazed. 'This is the Republic, not the Province! Things like that don't happen here!' — a response which would have left Jurnet weak with laughter if his face, stiff with dried blood, had not demonstrated in the most practical way that, at that moment at any rate, mirth was not a reasonable option.

Greg Gibson arrived with more questions, more apparent concern, by which time

Jurnet's head had spun completely out of control, so that later he had only the haziest recollection of being helped up to his room, of being undressed, by whom he could not say; of the benison of soap and water and the warming comfort of a glass of Jamieson's held gently to his lips. He seemed to remember that by the time he no longer stank of bog and stagnant water somebody else — a doctor presumably — had arrived to dress his wounds, sew up his cheek as if it were a carrier bag of inferior manufacture whose seams had come apart at its first testing. The plaster Virgin, miraculously in one piece again, was what chiefly filled his thoughts — that and the Jesus of Willie's greeting. A fine pair to set up shop in the brain of a nearly-Jewish boy! What was the message the pair of them were intent on getting over? That if only he'd had the sense to turn RC instead of Jew it would never have happened?

Bemused and probably concussed, Jurnet fell asleep so completely that when he awoke it was night outside. Within, a small lamp left on by his bedside kept the dark at bay. Scarcely had he opened his eyes and reacquainted himself with his surroundings than Anthea Gibson came into the bedroom bearing a nourishing broth which, hoisting himself into a sitting position with a certain amount of difficulty, he accepted gratefully. He discovered that he was starving.

Mrs Gibson watched approvingly. Correctly interpreting his fingers searching the saucer for croutons or cracker, she said: 'The doctor said no solids tonight. Bully boys from over the Border,' she went on heatedly. 'Most likely safe home by now and toasting their feet in front of the fire where the Garda can't touch them. They'll be wanting a word with you in the morning, incidentally — the Garda, I mean. They were here already, but I told them the doctor had left orders you were not to be disturbed on any account. They said they'd traced the car from the number plates and got your name that way.'

Jurnet made no comment. He had awakened to find that his head was still spinning — no, not spinning, he decided, after a lightning analysis of his own condition: throbbing strongly but working with an efficiency which astonished him. Maybe a bang on the head was what everyone could do with once in a while to ginger up the old grey matter.

'Goodnight,' he said, hoping the woman would take the hint. He needed to be alone, urgently. He had things to think about.

However, Mrs Gibson had not yet finished with him. Out of her pocket she took a small folded paper with 'Telephone Message' printed on the uppermost side.

'Eleanor took it down,' she explained. 'She said you weren't available just then but she would see you got the message.' Her eyes bright with curiosity, she ended: 'It's from the hospital at Letterkenny. They wanted you to ring back as soon as possible.'

Jurnet felt sick, his newly supercharged mental apparatus having prompted him instantly as to what it had to mean, this call out of the blue. He took the paper, unfolded it and read the message for himself. The telephone number given was followed by another, presumably the relevant extension or some code prearranged with an ally on the switchboard.

'Actually,' Mrs Gibson said, 'the doctor said no phone calls either. But a hospital's different. Would you like me to get you the number? Are you sure you're feeling up to it?'

'I feel up to it. Please.'

Once the other had got through he took the receiver from her and waited, heart throbbing, not announcing himself. After a little a male voice, lilting and mysterious, inquired if it was indeed Detective Inspector Benjamin Jurnet he had the pleasure of addressing.

'Jurnet here,' he replied then, and listened

to what the voice had to say, listened as it articulated words for which he had already prepared himself. When the phone finally went dead he handed the receiver back to Anthea Gibson and announced without further preliminaries: 'They've knee-capped young Terry Doran.'

'God in heaven!' The woman put her hands to her face; took them away and stared at the detective distractedly: 'Why you? I don't understand. Why did they want to tell you?'

'The message was that the boy has already been operated on. He still hasn't come round from the anaesthetic.' Speaking with a brittle concern to omit nothing, Jurnet said: 'They said he won't be dancing any more jigs from now on.'

'Won't be dancing — Who are "they"?' Anthea Gibson cried out as if she truly did not know. 'And Frances, his mother — oh God! Is she at home or there at Letterkenny?'

'I've told you all that was said.'

'I must find out if she needs help. I must tell Greg.' Half out of the bedroom door, she turned and repeated wildly: 'Why you? What's going on?' Without waiting for an answer she was gone, only to return a moment later looking flushed and guilty.

'It's just that Frances Doran is a very

good friend of mine,' she attempted by way of explanation. With a pallid humour: 'Calmness, the doctor said. Whatever you do, keep him calm or I won't answer for the consequences. And here I go, winding you up like a clock.'

'Not to worry,' said Jurnet, sinking back on to his pillows. 'I couldn't be calmer.'

19

Jurnet lay in bed and calmly, his souped-up brain telling him to cool it, Buster, pondered what he knew and — this was Ireland after all! — what he knew and didn't know he knew. In his thoughts he went over the boathouse in every minute particular: the flaking wood of its exterior, the skylight, the window, the padlock on the door; and, within, the piled-up timber, the outsize sheet of plywood whereon were traced the lines that awaited transformation into the dreamboat that the Dorans, father and son, were going to translate into reality as soon as Dad's ship came home and it was once more OK to sweep up the wood shavings which littered the floor. After spending some time on these and other matters Jurnet heaved himself up again into a sitting position and then, aching with effort, swung his legs out of bed.

Outside, incredibly, the overcast had yielded to a young moon and a star-peppered sky of a heart-melting innocence. Making it determinedly to the window, Jurnet looked down on a landscape made up of silver and of velvet shadow, every twig, every blade of grass distinct from its neighbours, the whole as unreal in its pencilled precision as that other Ireland — the one of mist and drizzle he had become only too familiar with — was in its half-glimpsed blur.

Jurnet nodded, as if the silver and the shadow had made up his mind for him. He went to the wardrobe and rummaged in his bag until he found the black polo-necked sweater Miriam had brought back for him from a business trip to Italy, and the lean, dark jeans which went with them.

'You look like a mafioso,' she had exclaimed, delighted, when Jurnet had tried them on, only to be disappointed as time passed and he found yet another excuse for not actually sallying forth thus arrayed. Close as they had been her lover reflected, pulling the sweater over his throbbing head, she had never been able to accept that the dark Italianate features which were his personal cross were no more than an inappropriate covering beneath which the homespun heart of your common or garden Norfolk bumpkin beat regardless. He had only packed the sweater and jeans at all as some kind of cock-eyed salute to the operatic melodrama of his mission, never dreaming they would actually be called into use.

Having first located his torch and clipped it to his waistband, leaving his hands free, he checked that his pockets contained the small objects — bottle opener, cigar lighter, miniature tool kit — which he always made a point of transferring from suit to suit as insurance against the unfathomable demands which fate might spring on him. The cigar lighter had been a prize at a village fête, bowling for a pig. That is, he had actually won the animal — not the best-chosen reward for an apprentice Jew — and had been glad of an onlooker's offer to swap it for the cigar lighter, even though he had given up tobacco years before he had given up pork.

Now, thumbing the contraption to make sure it still worked, and reflecting on the strange workings of providence, he took pleasure in the tongue of flame it shot out viciously into the dark.

Jurnet unlatched the french window and stepped outside on to the small balcony. After the warmth of the bedroom he shivered in the frosty air, yet found himself pleased by the change in temperature: an affirmation of commitment, of reality as opposed to the cop-out of central heating. Only the moon and the stars watched as he reached for the convoluted main stem of the wistaria which filled the wall to one side; swung himself over the ornamental iron rail and, amid a spattering of leaf dust and desiccated bark, lowered himself gingerly to the ground.

A stiff breeze was already clattering the trees which dotted the lawns surrounding the hotel and nobody looked out to inquire what was amiss when the wistaria creaked in arthritic protest. Keeping to the shadows until he was well clear of the Lodge, Jurnet was soon on his way.

This time, having learned his lesson, he kept to the left of the road, to the high ground where though his heels jarring against the skeleton of rock barely covered by a skim of earth were an almost equivalent discomfort — at least there was no water to speak of, except in the dips between one hill and the next. The ache in his head had submerged itself in a thumping of heart that resounded in his ears, a pulsation that, demanding as it did all his attention, took his mind thankfully off that inner turbulence which had been swirling around inside him from the moment he had awakened from his long slumber.

He wondered whether he wasn't running a temperature and rather hoped he was, a built-in alibi. Otherwise what was he, Ben Jurnet, Detective Inspector Angleby CID, the law's very embodiment, as you might say, up to, jogging merrily under the moon on his way to perpetrate his own personal act of terrorism?

Deviating from the direct route to avoid a squelchy patch where reeds hung ragged and yellowing, he rejected his own definition. Not terrorism, justice. But wasn't that what they all said, the IRA, the Red Brigade, Old Uncle Tom Jihad and all? He was sweating, he *did* have a temperature, unless guilt always made you sweat, the way it turned all your values inside out and putrefied your soul with self-loathing.

The hell with it.

He owed it to Terry, to knee-capped Terry.

The bastards!

For all the throbbing head, the conflict and the confusion, Jurnet was pierced through with a thrill of childish glee to find himself looking down on Balor the Baleful's passage through the hills at precisely the point where he had planned to be. Walking back from his earlier visit to the boathouse, he had, with that inveterate habit of the police fraternity, that almost unconscious filing away of whatever facts — relevant or irrelevant, it made no difference — happened to be lying about in the vicinity, noted that in only one place was the sheer wall of cliff fronting the road breached — an old landslip, by the look of it, on the opposite side of the road from the boathouse and some twenty yards beyond it: a jumble of rock and scree descending to the sandy bottom in a slide which was definitely not for the kiddies but negotiable by any damn fool without climbing equipment prepared to break his neck on the way down.

Now, as he stood above it, the angle of descent looked even more horrific than when viewed from below. There must have been mica, or some such mineral, among the debris, for here and there, among the scattered stones, something glittered — unless they were falling stars, signalling *help!* to their mates riding free in the sky.

Across the way, the boathouse had lost its daytime banality and hovered fragile as a dream. In Jurnet's fevered imagination it seemed to sway slightly, to rise a little from the ground and then subside again, not a sound breaking the velvet quiet. The detective found it as hard to believe in its objective existence as in his own, present at that spot at that moment of time and come to do what he had come to do.

Suddenly afire to get it over and done with, he squatted down on his haunches and lowered himself over the edge of the fall, his legs shooting from under him sooner than he could have wished. Fast, faster, fastest, he slid down the ancient fault, the detritus dislodged by his scrabbling feet tumbling ahead of him like demented acrobats. Several of the small captive stars winked at him as he passed, but he was going too fast to identify them, let alone wink back. As he neared the bottom, the fault fanned out a little, the slope, in comparison with what had gone before, became almost gentle; so that it was completely unexpected that it should be here, all danger apparently past, his destination only steps away, that he was suddenly lanced by a pain such as might be made by a red-hot rivet dropped deftly into the join between foot and ankle.

Jurnet rolled over on to the sandy surface of the road, tried to stand and could not; lay there gasping, the boathouse, a mocking chimera, rising and falling, falling and rising. And as he lay there, the black gloom of failure shot through with an unimaginable joy that the matter, in the most practical way, had been taken out of his hands, the small door in the front of the boathouse opened and a figure came hurrying out, leaving the door ajar.

Something about Jurnet — perhaps the glass of the torch at his waist — must have caught the moonlight, for after a few steps the figure checked, peered in his direction and then came running. Eyes screwed up with pain, Jurnet managed to pull himself up into a sitting posture, awaiting her.

Mrs Doran, though dressed in black like himself, was more visible. Her blonde hair, tied back loosely, was turned silver by the moon.

'Get up!' she shouted, before she had even reached him. 'Run!'

Jurnet explained mildly: 'I've done something to my ankle — '

'Never mind about that!' she cried impatiently, grabbed at an arm and pulled. 'Get up — you have to get up! Run!'

On his feet somehow he hobbled a few steps that nearly made him faint, so intense was the pain. Between clenched teeth he got out: 'You go ahead. I'll follow — '

'No!' The woman grabbed at his arm afresh. 'I've set it for thirty minutes but I'm not sure. I've never set one before. So come on!'

He came. Her will was stronger than his agony, her complete lack of tenderness a challenge it was impossible to refuse. Even so, by the time they had reached the motor road and the shrine, which had been roughly boarded up, Jurnet was at the end of his endurance. Foolishly he wondered if whoever had done the boarding up had removed the Virgin first — or had they left her, in two pieces, abandoned in the darkness but still smiling away with that ineffable complacency which had got up his nose even as she had saved his life? If he knocked gently on the boards was it possible that, wounded as she was herself, she yet might rouse herself and give him strength?

'Come on!' Mrs Doran shouted.

The road in front of the shrine, churned and pitted as it was, shone with a particular radiance. It took Jurnet a little while to realize that he was looking at the last pulverized remains of the hired car — crushed glass, scraps of metal too small, presumably, for the authorities charged with the clearing up to bother about, reflected the stars and multiplied them. Rainbow patterns stretched themselves across skims of oil. A single warning lamp blinked foolishly off and on at the side of a pothole deeper than the generality.

Resisting the unrelenting pressure on his arm, Jurnet managed: 'Surely we're far enough away for it to be OK — '

'Oh!' cried Mrs Doran, her face twisted with annoyance at the need for explanation. 'The minute it goes up all the world'll be here — the emergency services, the Garda, the press. There's no way they won't pick you up.'

'What of it?' Jurnet discovered that by leaning back against the boards he could stand on one leg and there by ease the pain appreciably. 'In fact, from your point of view, what could be better? You safely home, tucked up in bed, and an obvious culprit wounded and waiting for them.'

'For Christ's sake, will you stop gassing and come on!' The woman's strength prevailed. Her hair had come untied and hung loose about her shoulders. In the moonlight its tousled silver made her look young and touchingly defenceless. *What a liar the moon was!* Jurnet thought, frowning; and found, to his confusion, that he had spoken the words aloud.

Frowning in her turn, the other demanded: 'What did you say?'

'Nothing . . .'

Somehow, with or without her help, he covered the remaining distance to the sad little crescent of bungalows marooned amidst the coarse grass. To his surprise, in so far as anything was capable any longer of surprising him, instead of making for her own home Mrs Doran, muttering something about bandages, led the way up the path to the nearest of the holiday lets, unlocking the front door with a key she took from her pocket and slid into its lock with the ease of long practice.

'Come along!' she snapped, opening the door no wider than was necessary to let them through, and shutting it the moment they were inside, cutting off the moon and stars and leaving Jurnet sagging against a wall in an abandonment of pain whilst she fumbled for the electric light switch. Even so, a copper *in extremis,* habit asserted itself so that, in those few moments of darkness and suffering, he was still able to identify a smell to the place that advertised it as having been lived in, or at least used, far more recently than the last summer letting.

In November, instead of the fungus-flavoured damp one might ordinarily have expected, Jurnet could smell cigarettes, crisps, beer, sausage that had contained garlic: he was still mentally separating out the constituents when the light came on to reveal a heavily curtained room which looked more like a small hospital ward than anything else. There were beds of white-painted iron with strictly utilitarian bedlinen, the blankets grey or red piled neatly folded on each, ready for the making: lockers between them, a somewhat battered television set with some rexine-covered chairs facing the blank screen . . .

Forcing his addled wits into an approximation of working order, Jurnet looked about him and inquired: 'Does the agent know you're using his desirable holiday residence out of season for the rest and recuperation of those bully boys of yours coming and going over the Border?' Not waiting for an answer: 'Of course he knows. The whole village must know.'

'None of your business! And not my bully boys. Not any longer.' Mrs Doran surveyed the room with cool grey eyes full of a hatred which contradicted the softness of her hair, loose about her face. 'You can't have heard what they did to Terry.'

'I heard. Why else d'you think I'm here?'

The woman turned to him, disbelieving. 'But he couldn't have told you what was hidden in the boathouse. Whatever else he told you he never told you that! He didn't know himself.'

'Give me a little credit. He didn't have to. Thinking it over, it wasn't all that difficult to figure out for oneself — that enormous sheet of plywood so conveniently covering up the best part of the floor, the timber piled up with such care in a place where otherwise the housekeeping was downright slatternly; the wood shavings which must on no account be swept up . . .' A wave of oblivion engulfing him, Jurnet tried unsuccessfully to reach the nearest chair. 'May I sit down? I'm afraid I feel . . .'

Even to his fainting senses the noise he made in falling was out of all proportion to his actual contact with the floor. All at once, the air in the room was insufficient for breathing and, almost immediately after more than a pair of human lungs could cope with. With a dull thud which seemed to have little to do with respiration but was somehow connected with it, two of the window panes fell out, sucking the curtains outside with them and allowing the nosy planets to peer in unhindered.

20

When Jurnet came to himself he was able to identify a new smell. Curtains back in place, the night sky once more excluded, Mrs Doran was bent over him, her hair in the electric light showing all its grey, holding a bottle containing sal volatile to his nose.

Taking deep restorative breaths he struggled to sit up.

'Sorry — '

'Be quiet, will you?' She swept his apology aside, together with his condition. 'Did you hear that?' she demanded exultantly, and again, as a staccato of exploding ammunition beat a distant tattoo, 'Did you hear that?'

Jurnet achieved a sitting position.

'You mean the boathouse has gone up?'

'Has it not! The sky's bright yellow. That'll be the sodium. It's also red, green, purple. It looks like there's fireworks down by the beach tonight, a great celebration anyhow.' The grey eyes, set shallow in her head, were

merry now, and bright with a girlish innocence. Congratulating herself on her own
cleverness: 'Half an hour to the minute! I'm
better than I thought.'

Despite the fact that he had himself set
out with the very same purpose in mind,
Jurnet found her jubilation repellent. A regrettable necessity maybe. No occasion for
rejoicing.

'Won't they guess it's you?' he inquired,
not without spite.

'How will they ever guess that?' The
woman laughed the suggestion out of court.
'It's that bloody Libyan stuff — that's what
they'll put it down to. They've had trouble
with it before. They've been talking I don't
know how long about using it up quickly
before it got completely out of control. Only
last month some of it went off too soon
outside Enniskillen and blew up the van and
the four fellows who were moving it. You
must have seen it in the papers and on TV.
Why should they think to pin it on me —
Danny Cardo's widow, Andy Doran's wife
and — ' the exhilaration draining away like
water into sand — 'the bitch so devoted to
the cause that she shopped her own son,
the way God did Jesus Christ? Suspect me?
I'm their Joan of Arc, their Mary Mother
of God, paragon among women!'

'How could you have shopped Terry? You couldn't have known I was going down to the boathouse after I called here this morning. I never knew it myself. I just thought I'd go and take a look at the sea. It was pure chance to find Terry down there.'

Frances Doran's eyes glinted with amusement.

'Not altogether convincing, Detective Inspector.' Revealing a strength he would not have thought her capable of, Mrs Doran half-dragged, half-lifted the detective on to a chair. 'I'm going to put a cold compress on that ankle.' She left the room and returned shortly with cloths and bandages and a basin of cold water. Kneeling then to remove his shoe, a manoeuvre causing pangs more exquisite than any he had experienced so far, she looked up from the floor still smiling. 'I'm a qualified nurse, in case you think I don't know what I'm doing.'

'I'd never think that,' Jurnet returned, willing himself to stay conscious. 'How did you know Terry had spoken to me at all? Did he tell you so?'

'In hospital, before they took him down to be operated on. Though he didn't have to — I knew already.' Head bent over the basin, concentrating on soaking the cloths for the compress, she added lightly: 'Did I mention to you that my late comrades in arms made such a mess of one of his legs it will probably have to come off?' Dry-eyed, with a twist of the lips that had nothing of humour in it, she commented: 'Typically Paddy, wouldn't you say? Can't even do a simple little thing like knee-capping without making a bloody balls of it.'

'I shouldn't have tried to speak to him,' Jurnet said, low. 'It's my fault as much as yours. I should never have come here.'

'Lucy wrote me about what happened to your girlfriend. You were entitled. Just as I was entitled, after you'd made your little social call and were out of sight, to turn back from visiting my old lady — to take the path over the hills that comes out at the rear of the boathouse. You can't get down that way but you have a fine view of anything happening below. I saw you go inside. And then, of course, like the good soldier I am, I ran back here to report what I'd seen.'

Jurnet snuffled the tobacco and other domestic smells again, only to find that the sal volatile had taken precedence over them.

'And I suppose you also told your mates who were dossing down here that I'd left my car parked at the shrine.'

'Naturally,' she agreed calmly, the while

her capable hands drew pain out of his foot. 'That was different. We have been fighting a war, after all.'

'OK, you mean, so long as it's some other mother's son at the receiving end?' A small clot of anger burst in Jurnet's brain. He jerked his foot away — no great gesture since she had finished her work on it. 'When it's your own, that's a different kettle of fish.'

'That's right. Just as it was a different kettle of fish when it was your girl.'

As they stared unforgivingly at each other, a riffle in the outside silence enlarged itself into the wail of a siren that reached a peak of triumphal ululation as it passed the crescent and receded into the distance.

'It's beginning,' Mrs Doran said. 'We'll have to be moving.'

'We?'

'You don't think you're going to make it back to the Lodge on your own like that, do you? How did you get out, anyhow, without anybody knowing?'

'There's a balcony outside my room. I climbed down.'

'That'll be Number 7,' she observed, the efficient receptionist. 'And what gives you the idea you're in any state to climb back up?'

Jurnet muttered: 'I'll manage somehow.'

The woman looked at him with more friendliness than she had shown hitherto.

'I shouldn't be surprised you would,' she commented. 'Fortunately, it won't be necessary. I have a set of the Lodge keys. They gave me the front door one for when I have to clock in early, but being who we are — who I used to be — ' she reinvented herself — 'we have keys to every door the way we have keys to every house of substance in our area. The front door'll be no use to you. They bolt it during the time I'm laid off, besides which it creaks loud enough to waken the dead, let alone the Gibsons who sleep directly above. But there'll be nobody else sleeping on your side of the house this time of year and there's a garden door just a bit along which they use during the season to bring in the flowers and vegetables for the house — '

'No bolts?'

'No bolts. We've seen to that. If you take the stair that leads out of the little vestibule up one floor, your room will be the second — no, the third — door on the right. Those stairs creak too but not to worry. Nobody will hear you.' The woman picked up the basin and the wet cloths, professionally neat. 'I'll just get rid of these, then we can go.'

'We?' Jurnet asked again.

'I told you, I'm a nurse. I'm also a midwife. There's a girl over at Sharney, only two miles on from Larrakil. She's expecting twins any day now and it's going to be tricky. I don't need any excuse, day or night, for looking in on her. You'll have to travel under a rug on the floor at the back, but I can drop you off. They all know me, the Garda. They'll let me through without asking questions.'

'Even though they must know it's your husband's boathouse?'

Mrs Doran shook her head.

'It isn't anybody's boathouse, anybody's in particular, that is. The old fellow that owned it died five years ago and it's just stood there ever since, going to the dogs. Nobody's ever claimed it. Oh, they'll find out in time that Andy was the one using it, I don't doubt, but it won't be tonight.'

'Once they do find out they'll be after him.'

Mrs Doran laughed at that.

'You don't know Andy! Quicksilver's the word for him. Anyway, he won't wait to be found. It's a Norwegian rig he's on. By the time they get through the formalities to fetch him back he'll be long gone — swallowed up in the US or wherever. One thing about the IRA, they look after their own, if they've served them well, and Andy has served them very well, over the years. He was Danny's best friend — did you know? They were at school together.' The laughter dying away, the smile persisting with a fixity which made Jurnet suddenly aware of the cold and the damp of the place: 'It's not only a knee-capped son that's happened to me this day, Detective Inspector. I've also mislaid a husband.'

'You'll find a way to join him. Wherever he is.'

The other shook her head.

'No. I shan't be doing that. You see, I only married the man at all on the promise that he'd let Terry grow up in his own way, his own time. I reckoned Danny was enough sacrifice for one woman, I wasn't called upon to offer up my child into the bargain. If the boy came to the cause of his own accord, I stipulated, I'd have to go along with that, it was his privilege, but no pressure of any kind. Andy only agreed because he was mad to have me at any price, but he's been a good father to the boy, I'll give him that. And Terry adores him. Even so . . .' Without change of expression she added: 'However well the two of them got on, however often Andy swears there's nothing he wouldn't do for me, if that husband of mine had been here today I know as well as if I'd heard the words drop from his lips that all the fathering and all the lovey-dovey would have counted for nothing. Sworn to that bloody Republic, he'd have voted for the knee-capping along with the rest.'

—— 21 ——

Jurnet lay on his bed again, his bed at Larrakil Lodge. He lay there sweating though the heating had long since gone off and the room was cold. He lay there, his head and his sprained ankle throbbing, not in unison — which for some reason he fancied might have been quite soothing — but in a syncopated rhythm which he seriously expected to end up by driving him crazy.

Could be, he pondered hazily, that was what Mrs Doran had had in mind when, supposedly bent on rescue, she had bundled him into the back of her car, on the floor under a pile of blankets, for a drive punctuated by several stops, by friendly voices that let her car through with comic commiseration once its driver had been identified. As a nurse, she must surely have known that the concussion was bound to catch up with him sooner rather than later, and that a journey folded in half like an airing mattress, every bump in the road resonating through the car floor into his damaged frame, must reduce him to gibbering insanity or the next thing to it.

As a final favour — ye gods! — once she had arrived at Larrakil and parked in the entrance to the Lodge drive, she had opened the rear door, removed the blankets, and, without prior explanation, prised off the shoe that had only been got on to the damaged foot at a price in pain not worth paying. In a swift, economical gesture she had ripped off the dressing which had brought such blessed relief, and whose summary removal added outrage to agony.

'It only occurred to me on the way,' she remarked briskly, rolling up the bandage at the double as if she had another patient clamouring for it. 'You can't possibly keep it on. They'll never believe you could have managed it yourself. When they put in an appearance in the morning, tell them you slipped and fell in the bathroom.' Regarding him with an air of cool, clinical assessment: 'You do understand, don't you, that you've got to get yourself out of that gear and stuff it away somewhere out of sight before you can call it a night? No flaking out on the bed for them to find you in the morning looking like the Phantom of the Opera.'

'I understand — '

'Right then!' Mrs Doran extended a hand into the car's interior, her expression one of impatient toleration. He might as well, Jurnet thought, have been a mum going slow on the bearing down routine, or a baby reluctant to exchange the security of the womb for the world outside and who could blame it? 'Make an effort, will you? You can't stay here. Anyone could come along at any minute, and I can't drive you up to the door in case I wake up Anthea and Greg.'

Somehow Jurnet got his legs out of the car and sat on the door sill panting. With an effort he reassembled his grey matter into an approximation of its former function. The thought that he was not yet ready to let this woman go, the knowledge that he might never have another chance to ask the ultimate question, took over powerfully.

'Miriam — ' he got out at last, each syllable lacerating his heart as if it carried its own built-in barb — '*did* the IRA kill her? did they do it or didn't they?'

'No good asking me.' Mrs Doran shrugged, irked at the further delay. She tugged at one of the detective's arms, urging him out of the car.

Resisting the pull, he persisted doggedly: 'Did they?'

'For Christ's sake! You haven't a clue, have you? None of us has a clue what goes on outside our own particular area. It's none of your business and if you aim to stay in one piece you'd better remember it.'

'Then why, if you and Terry weren't involved, and the IRA itself wasn't involved, would it matter to the point of knee-capping that the boy spoke to me?'

'Because you were police, stupid! Because they wanted to advertise to whoever it might concern that in IRA country nobody — but nobody — chats to the police and gets away with it. Because they thought Terry might well have let on to you that there were people he couldn't account for living in the holiday let.'

'As it happens he never said a word about them. Did he in fact know they were there?'

'He did not! The state that boy was in, the leprechauns could have taken it over and he wouldn't have noticed a blind thing. All he could think about was how he was going to get back to Angleby and architecture.'

Jurnet said: 'I hear what you say about separate cells. Just the same — ' returning to his overriding preoccupation — 'if you really wanted to, you can find out about Miriam for me.'

'Looks like it, doesn't it, after what's happened to Terry?' Breaking off: 'That reminds me, though. I've got something for you.'

She let go his arm while she fetched a small flat package from the front seat.

'You said you were interested in Terry's work. Well, here's something to remember him by. Stuff it up your sweater,' she instructed. 'You'll need both hands free to get yourself up to your room.'

He did as he was told whilst Mrs Doran took hold of his arm again. This time Jurnet offered no resistance; stood at last swaying in the driveway. The rain which had begun to fall did nothing to reduce the pounding heat which sought out every nook and cranny of his anatomy.

'Why?' he demanded nevertheless, determined not to let the woman go until he had an answer of some kind at least. 'Why are you going out of your way to help me get away?'

Mrs Doran got back into her car before replying. She started the engine, then leaned out of the car window to speak.

'Did I not tell you?' Her light, almost playful tone was worse than anything that had gone before. 'They've turned my boy — my bright, lovely boy — into a cripple for life. The wonder is, while they were about it, they didn't do for his hands as well. They might as well have. State of mind he's in, you'd better hang on to that drawing. It could become valuable. Scarcity value. Already he's saying he'll never paint again.'

The package contained a small sketch of Miriam: something done quickly on heavy cartridge paper using a sepia-coloured chalk which seemed to have been manufactured for the express purpose of catching to a T the wonderful hair, the warm skin tones of the dead girl. There was a touching amateurishness about the whole — Jurnet could see at a glance that it was no Rembrandt the IRA had nipped in the bud — but also a touching honesty; a giveaway of which, it could be, the artist himself had been unaware.

The detective smiled in affectionate understanding. In making a drawing of Miriam Courland, Terry Doran, in a sense, had drawn himself: portrait of a boy in love.

Under the soft glow of the bedside lamp Miriam turned on her lover the quick, eager look that had been at the core of her being — an exuberance for the next thing life had to offer, and the next, and the next. God knew not everything between them had been good — Jurnet was the first to know that and to flagellate himself with the knowledge — but neither failures nor disappointments had had the power to dim that remarkable inner light. It had taken a bomb to do that.

He had failed her. Disappointed her.

He could not bear it.

Miriam.

He forced himself off the bed, stumbled to the closet and the soft bag into which, obedient to Mrs Doran's instruction, he had already stuffed his Mafia jeans. He felt in the pocket, found what he was looking for, returned the jeans to hiding and came back to the bed again.

He put the eye of the Bingo bear down on the bedside table next to the sketch, nodding in satisfaction at the way its green glitter complemented and added meaning to the other's sepia.

Then he turned out the light and went to sleep, more or less. His heart bursting with sorrow, he went down into the dark like Orpheus seeking after Euridice, but even in dreams could not find her.

22

It was cold, far colder than in Ireland. Winter was much further advanced. In a wicked wind that sneaked along the pavements at ankle height the last of the fallen leaves scudded tiredly or else lay clustered like panic-stricken fugitives from some natural disaster, clogging the drains. Above the bare branches the orange street lamps shone without warmth.

Just the same, Jurnet breathed in the raw air with an involuntary lifting of the spirits. This, the Angleby Special, was, after all, his lungs' customary tipple. He paid off the cab and saw through the brightly-lit delicatessen window that Mario was busy slicing a boned roll of roast beef, lovingly transferring each slice to a large dish beside which sprigs of parsley and wedges of tomato waited ready to serve as garnish. At one of the small tables in the body of the store, a copy of the *Angleby Argus* spread out in front of him, the Superintendent sat waiting.

Suppressing the absurd conviction that the man had been sitting there ever since he had left for Ireland, Jurnet came into the shop trying unsuccessfully to suppress his limp and wishing he had managed to persuade the Irish doctor that he no longer needed the dressing the man had insisted on taping to the side of his head.

The Superintendent looked up from his paper and observed coolly: 'You look as if you've been in the wars.'

Before Jurnet could think of an appropriate rejoinder Mario put down his carving knife and came hurrying out from behind the counter, wiping his hands on the striped tea towel tied round his waist as he came. Even so, a scrap of the beef ended up attached to Jurnet's anorak sleeve as the other folded his arms about him in greeting, then drew back, alarmed.

'Mr Jurnet! You are wounded! What happened?'

'A small accident. Nothing to take on about.'

'You are sure? Thank God for that! Give me your bag. I will take it upstairs immediately. Sit down, take it easy after your journey. Here is the gentleman waiting to see you. I will bring two coffees.'

The Italian checked in his outpouring; removed the sliver of meat from the anorak, frowned at the spot of grease left behind.

'Maria will pop it into the machine together with anything else you have for washing. She will be so happy you are back. Every day she has prayed to the Virgin for your safe return from that wild place and kept your sheets aired. My friend,' he finished, the large Mediterranean eyes moist with emotion, 'I am very thankful to see you.'

With his back carefully to the boarded-up block of flats over the way, Jurnet returned in all sincerity: 'It's great to be home.'

It was even greater to be home when he turned back to the Superintendent and saw the unalloyed welcome on that patrician face. Not even the certainty that, sooner rather than later, inevitable as the turning of the tide, the irony would be back, the sardonic twist of the lips which proclaimed louder than words that, yet again, his subordinate had fallen short of expectations, could mar the sweetness, the bitter-sweetness, of that moment.

Perhaps testing the other's sincerity, Jurnet came to the table, sat down and spoke without preliminaries.

'Nothing proved, one way or the other. Only one boy, knee-capped and crippled, physically and psychologically. The sum total of my investigation.'

'Not quite the way I should have put it.' Amazingly, the lips did not twist, the kindness stayed undiluted. 'One Sergeant Mahaffey and I had a long talk. A good man. We could do with more like him on the Angleby complement.'

'Yes.' Jurnet nodded. He too had taken instantly to the keen-eyed, roly-poly Irishman who — both at Larrakil and in the less user-friendly ambience of Letterkenny police station — had treated him with such uncomplicated courtesy whilst at the same time making it crystal clear at the end of their conversation he was perfectly aware that he had been treated to only part of the story and had no intention of closing the file until he had uncovered the whole of it. 'He was very good to let me leave Ireland at all in the circumstances, with so much still outstanding — the insurance position on the car, apart from everything else. I promised to return any time he wanted me, of course, but just the same . . . If you've been on the line to him I suppose it's you I really have to thank for getting me home so promptly in one piece.'

'Not quite one piece,' the Superintendent contradicted. 'Slightly chipped at the corners, shall we say? And no — the Sergeant deserves all the credit. Heaven knows I don't envy him his job, out there on the frontier.'

'Maybe we ought to have taken a closer look at the map before making tracks for Donegal.'

The other shook his head.

'Not the kind of frontier I'm talking about. The one I mean is the one between civilization and criminal anarchy.' The Superintendent leaned forward in his seat, examined his subordinate's face as if just that moment making its acquaintance. 'The good Sergeant told me it was solely his intuitive assessment that, when it came to the crunch, you were constitutionally incapable of taking the law into your own hands which stopped him from holding you on charges ranging from arson to conspiracy to cause explosions.'

The irony back in place, and Jurnet perversely glad to see it, a signal that normal relations had been resumed: 'I, of course, for my part, took care to let not a syllable escape my lips to the effect that, whilst I held you in the highest esteem, I, alas, had no such perfect faith in the purity of your intentions.' The Superintendent leaned back to allow Mario to place two *cappuccinos* on the table. 'Incredible how anyone can actually acquire a taste for this perfidious broth,' he commented, drinking deeply with every appearance of enjoyment.

He put the cup down.

'According to Sergeant Mahaffey, bless him for saying so, you were quite genuinely out with concussion at the time, so that there couldn't have been anything more than a coincidental connection between the blowing up of your car and the destruction of the arms cache in that boathouse. He readily admitted that the Semtex the IRA has been getting its hands on is notoriously unstable and liable to go off without the help of any human agency. In their position, he said, he'd send the lot back to Gadaffi with love and detonators.' The Superintendent sipped some more of his *cappuccino*. 'He also said, somewhat to my surprise, I must confess, that you were concussed by rocks falling from the walls of a grotto containing a statue of the Virgin.'

'That's right. One of those wayside shrines they go in for, over there.'

'Ah. Hardly your scene, I should have thought.' Eyes bright with affectionate malice, the Superintendent took out a handkerchief of positively insulting whiteness and wiped the froth from his lips. 'It sounds a very Irish story to me.'

The malice faded, leaving only the affection. He reached across the table and touched Jurnet's hand lightly with his long fingers, a gesture whose significance was out of all proportion to its brief duration.

'Before we go any further,' the Superintendent said, 'I want to impress on you that you are not to feel guilty — that's an order! You have nothing to feel guilty about, neither for Miss Courland's death nor, now, for the savage treatment the IRA has seen fit to mete out to young Terry Doran. Guilt is for the guilty. For the innocent it is an unpardonable self-indulgence, paralysing the will and making a positive virtue of inaction. Do I make myself clear?'

Jurnet sat looking down at his hand. Never before had the man touched him. At last, his throat inexplicably constricted, he raised his head and asked: 'Am I to take this as a recall to active duty?'

'Mario!' called the Superintendent, twisting round in his place. 'That roast beef looks uncommonly good. Do you think you could rustle us up some sandwiches, a whole plateful of them? And two more of your frothy coffees? Mr Jurnet and I have a lot to talk about.'

'If only Mario had a licence,' observed the Superintendent when Jurnet, leaving out nothing, justifying nothing, had come to the end of his Irish adventures, 'I'd be ordering champagne to celebrate.' Smiling at the other's open-mouthed incomprehension: 'No need to look like that. It isn't every day one of my officers teeters on the edge of insanity and manages to recover his mental balance before it's too late.' Suiting the action to the word: 'As it is, in the unavoidable absence of the Widow, I raise this coffee-coloured substitute to toast that heaven-sent sprained ankle which not only prevented you from making a complete fool of yourself but also stopped you from implicating Angleby CID in a situation where heads would have undoubtedly rolled, in all likelihood mine the first of them.' With a familiar twist of the lip: 'All I could wish is that I shared that Irish Sergeant's faith in your utter in-corruptibility in all circumstances. What would you have done, I ask myself, had you in fact reached the bottom of that precipice unharmed, or if the boy's mother had not already done your dirty work for you?'

'I'd have done what I came for. Blown the bloody place up.'

Stung for the first time to defend himself, despite a belated flash of recognition that this might be exactly what the other had intended, Jurnet pointed out with some heat:

'Blowing up an IRA arms dump isn't in quite the same category as holding up a bank.'

'Agreed,' the Superintendent concurred readily. 'It's ten times worse. Robbing a bank, by a police officer of all people, is at least a vice on a human scale, motivated by nothing more elevated than personal greed. The criminal absurdity of taking the law into one's own hands, on the contrary, as in this matter of the IRA, is in a more serious category altogether, a playing of God, an arrogant assumption of judgement incompatible with an ordered society. There was after all, if I may dare to suggest it, nothing to stop you going to the Garda.'

Jurnet said nothing. His hand in his pocket closed over the green eye of the Bingo bear.

A further silence, at the end of which the Superintendent sighed, his face losing some of its finely chiselled detachment.

'But then again,' he admitted finally, the irony for once turned inward into self-mockery, 'who am I to talk, one in the fortunate position of never having been so consumed with love of a woman as to be heedless of the consequences?' Retreating to safer ground: 'Just the same we shall, as the Americans say, take a rain-check on that champagne, and not on account of that providential sprained ankle which we can thankfully consign to history. Here in Angleby our Anti-Terrorist hearties, having reduced the citizenry to a quivering jelly, are folding their tents and pulling out tomorrow. If that doesn't call for a celebration I don't know what does!

'Not that my heart doesn't bleed for the poor critters.' The broad smile briefly possessing the Superintendent's features was followed by a more appropriate expression of concern. 'Theirs has been an impossible task, as we could have told them, had they only thought to ask, before they ever set out for Angleby. Our local Paddies have drawn in their heads like tortoises, and who can blame them? I understand bar receipts at the Bittern have fallen off sixty per cent for fear of who might be leaning on the counter over a Guinness soaking up every casual word within earshot to report back to the proper or improper quarter.

'That O'Driscoll fellow, your erstwhile neighbour, still hasn't stopped trembling, the way they turned him inside out before letting him loose again. Not that our visitors haven't conducted themselves with absolute propriety — they've learned that lesson the hard way — and not that they weren't obliged to act as they did.' The Superintendent's face nevertheless framed a fastidious anger

Jurnet was only too familiar with. 'To speak frankly, it was their private conversation which got up my craw, their crass off-the-record confidences, their assumption that anybody who speaks with an Irish accent is automatically under suspicion. And yet,' he amended, with a reluctant but inescapable fairness which rekindled in his subordinate all the old affection and respect, 'what else could they have done? If they had, in fact, turned up something positive, wouldn't I have been the first to congratulate them with all my heart?' The Superintendent bit into one of the roast beef sandwiches Mario had brought to the table. 'This is good!'

'I suppose Jack hasn't turned up anyone or anything either?'

'I'm sorry, Ben.' The Superintendent shook his head. 'I wish I had better news for you. Batterby and our little Welshman have run themselves ragged. They've milked the computer for every villain you've been instrumental in putting away since the day you joined the Force — and drawn a complete blank.'

The Superintendent finished his sandwich and wiped his fingers on the linen napkin with which Mario had provided him. *Linen!* Well, natch. Jurnet's lips curved slightly as he fingered the paper one set by his own plate and waited for the great man to say the inevitable.

'You're going to have to come off the back burner, Ben, and get on with it.'

23

As if their conversation had cued in an actor waiting in the wings, Monty Bellman came through the delicatessen door and asked Mario for a cone, raspberry ripple with a double flake. While the order was being filled the man looked round the shop with his bright boot button eyes and spotted Jurnet.

'Mr Jurnet! Who'd 'a' thought it?' Approaching the table with every appearance of delight: 'Reckoned you must've died of a broken heart.' With an eye to the dressing on the detective's head: 'Bugger had another go, did he, an' missed again? Never mind — ' a grin displayed small, predatory teeth — 'third time lucky, tha's what they say, isn't it?'

'That's what they say,' Jurnet agreed levelly. 'You're a long way from home, Monty.'

'Not like you, eh, Mr Jurnet? Found somewhere convenient to kip, have you?'

'You can always reach me at Police Headquarters, should the need arise.'

The boot button eyes screwed themselves up in laughter, a small fan of wrinkles radiating from the outer corners.

'Cagey, aren't you? Can't say as I blame you in the circumstances. Can't be too careful.' The man jerked his head in the direction of Jurnet's old home, only too visible through the plate-glass window. 'Give it a few months, though, an' you'll be able to go back to your old love nest all done up, eh? Jacuzzi in every room, I shouldn't be surprised, *and* a brand-new dolly bird waiting to get in the water with you.'

Sunnily ignoring the detective's suddenly clamped jaw as well as, on the face of his companion, an upper-crust distaste of nostrils assailed by a bad smell, the safe-breaker continued: 'From all I hear over the grapevine that bugger Hepton'll have to make do with a refit. The word is that with his record he hasn't a hope in hell of getting permission to rebuild. One thing at least — ' brightly innocent, he ended — 'you've prob'ly noticed he's got rid of that ruddy great hole where your lady friend copped it.'

Under the Superintendent's speculative eye waiting to see what he would make of the provocation, Jurnet took a deep breath: relaxed.

'As I said, Monty — a long way from home.'

'I thought I tole you, this is one of our favourite walks, Billy an' me — 'cept it isn't walk any longer, or won't be, once Billy gets the hang of his new buggy, which won't be long now. Didn' I tell you he was a genius with anything mechanical? Could have been another Henry Ford or a Nigel Mansell if you hadn't done for him. Another coupla practices an' he'll be off like Formula 1 and me breaking the three-minute mile to catch up. I might even send him out on his ownsome and sit home with me tatting. Hear that?' A low electrical whirr sounded through the delicatessen window. 'Music, in't it? A BMW don't sound no sweeter.'

Monty Bellman went back to the counter, accepted the completed cone from Mario, and handed over the money.

'Whyn't you come outside, Inspector,' he called back across the store, 'an' take a gander for yourself? See what I do with my ill-gotten gains?'

Sensing that the Superintendent would not be best pleased to have one of his men dancing to a villain's tune, Jurnet rose nevertheless, murmured something vaguely placatory to the stony face across the table, and followed the safe-breaker out on to the pavement where Billy, his face a mess of chocolate and raspberry ripple, was devouring in great slurps the ice cream his big brother held up to his mouth. The boy was strapped into what was evidently a state-of-the-art invalid carriage, a long low contraption of metal and gleaming paintwork which looked more the brain-child of a bored motor-bike designer looking for something new to try out his hand on than equipment geared to the limitations of a disabled driver.

'Take it easy, Jaws!' Monty Bellman protested affectionately, stuffing the last bit of cone into the slavering maw. 'How you think I'm goin' to ply me trade, earn the bread to keep you in ice cream an' this little beauty in working order, if you take off me bloody fingers?' The man wiped the boy's face with a tissue, and then turned to Jurnet, his eyes brighter than ever. 'What you reckon then, Mr Jurnet? In't she a little beauty?'

Jurnet looked at Billy; at the head sunk down on the chest now that there was no more ice cream to be had, at the large-knuckled hands purposelessly plucking at the air. He said kindly enough: 'I'm sure you mean well, Monty, but there's no way Billy can safely control a gizmo like that.'

'Tha's all you know!' The man leaned across the resplendent gadget, captured the boy's wandering hands and clamped them firmly over the controls. 'Head up, Billy! Head up an' hold tight! Down to the nex' lamp-post — we'll show his fucking lordship, won't we? — turn yerself round and then back here, to this very spot — OK?'

Billy gave no indication of having heard the instructions, let alone of having taken them in. Concerned for the damaged boy's safety, Jurnet moved forward with intent: not fast enough. The whirr moving up a few well-bred tones, the apparatus was on the move, warily at first, then with more assurance, keeping a safe distance from the circles of earth round the trees set at intervals along the way; slowing down for the lamp-post, rounding it smoothly before accelerating back to its starting point. Arrived there and stationary once more, Billy's hands resumed their aerial explorations. His chin sank down to his chest, his eyes closed, everything the same as before save for an almost palpable air of self-satisfaction that enclosed him in a bubble shot through with all the colours of the rainbow.

'What you say to that then?' Monty Bellman crowed, proud as an owner whose horse has just won the Derby. 'What you say to that?'

Jurnet felt in his pocket and pulled out some change.

'Go and get the boy another ice cream,

on me. He deserves it.'

Jurnet had not intended going to the synagogue. He had nothing to tell Rabbi Schnellman save that Miriam was as dead as ever and as unavenged. Up in the flat above the delicatessen, the crucifix above the bed, he had fleetingly wondered whether Father Culvey's might not be a more sensible address at which to call and pay his respects. He could always use the excuse of wanting to tell the priest what had happened to Terry Doran, in case he hadn't heard.

Maybe — he wouldn't want to bet on it but you never knew — the Father's Roman Catholic God would be able to pull off something of which the Jewish one, on past form and with the best will in the world, was incapable.

Jurnet looked questioningly at the suffering figure on the cross and, after a moment, shook his head. On second thoughts, probably not. A God who couldn't even save His own son had troubles enough of his own, poor bugger.

Conducting him upstairs, suitcase under one arm, a bottle of brandy under the other, Mario had entertained no such doubts as to where his guest should best look for an answer to prayer.

'Not too much, mind,' he had stipulated, setting the bottle down on the bedside table and fetching a glass from the kitchen. 'Medical. Because of the head, you understand, it would be wise to go a little carefully. But equally, because of the heart, not too carefully. You are tired from your journey and your wounds and it is a sad homecoming. Drink and sleep.' On his way out the Italian paused, his hand on the knob to the outer door, his eyes liquid with earnestness. 'My dear Mr Jurnet, remember you are among friends.'

24

Jurnet did not drink any of the brandy. It would have been too easy a way out. Instead, waiting for the sounds from below which would tell him that Mario had locked up and gone for the night, he steeled himself: went to the bedroom window and stared squarely at the block of flats across the road.

In the orange light from the street lamps, one wall bulging, its entrance and many windows boarded up, it no longer looked like anybody's home; more like a sinking ship from which the rats had long since prudently departed. Most alienating of all was the complete absence of the overflowing black plastic bags whose invariable presence on the forecourt had always spoken reassuringly of used condoms, expired tea-bags, a detritus of Chinese takeaways, all the rich tapestry of the consuming life.

Only half-mocking his own foolish fancies, Jurnet stared long and hard, willing the bags, the golden days, to return: but nothing. Hard as it was to believe, the dustmen had actually put in an appearance, made a final collection and slipped silently away. It could only mean that the end of the world was nigh.

Steeling himself further, Jurnet picked up the telephone directory, located Jolly Jim Hepton's number, and dialled. The voice that came through the receiver was as fruity as ever.

'Jim Hepton speaking. What can I do you for?'

'Jurnet here.' The detective kept his voice carefully colourless. 'I thought I should let you know that I propose making use of that key you left with me, the one to the back door of the flats. There are some things of mine I want to get hold of.'

'Oh dear, oh dear!' mourned Jolly Jim Hepton in his jolly way. 'That key! You'll never get in with that, Inspector. We've boarded up all the doors now and fitted new padlocks. Security, what you and your play-mates are always on about, eh? Can't have every Tom, Dick and Harry getting in and helping themselves now, can we?'

'I need to have access.'

'Besides which — ' the man continued as though there had been no interpolation — 'can't let the movers in under any circumstances. Danger to life and limb. Our insurers would have fits.'

'No one's talking about movers. I just need to pick up some clothes, a few personal things. I'll send you a letter absolving you from all responsibility, if it'll make you feel better. How early in the morning can you send somebody over to let me in?'

' "How early in the morning — " ' Jolly Jim Hepton repeated. 'Typical!' In the laughter which exploded from the receiver Jurnet could envision the rosy cheeks wobbling, the blue eyes reduced to slits in the surrounding fat. 'Mr Jurnet says jump, we all jump — right?' Hamming it up in a mockery of regret: 'I'd love to accommodate you, Inspector, I truly would, old friend and all that, but no can do. We're snowed under. Earliest I could get somebody over there would be — let me see, what's today, Monday? — the earliest would be Thursday A.M. Can't be more definite than that.'

'I'll be there.'

'Don't ring off, Mr Jurnet!' Jolly as ever: 'Since, by a happy chance, I've got you on the blower, I just wondered whether you'd happened to hear anything about my planning permission for the flats.'

'I've been out of touch.' Jurnet's tone was brusque.

'I heard about that. Change of surroundings, very sensible. Not the same though, is it, a holiday without the little woman? I could have told you that, as you know. Like I say, I just wondered. Something might have been said. You know how it is when you're all rarin' to go, everything in place except for that bloody bit of paper. Thursday A.M. then. Take care!'

Jurnet replaced the receiver, shrugged on his anorak and left the flat. During his exchange with Hepton he had heard the gates to the yard being opened, Mario's van moving out: a pause while the gates were re-shut and then the van moving off smartly, the delicatessen owner eager to get home to his Maria, either to her pasta or her body warm and comfortable in the bed beside him.

Or could be both. One thing at least, Jurnet determinedly reminded himself, he didn't have to look back to with grieving nostalgia. About Miriam's cooking — if you could dignify by that name her impatient opening of whatever can or packet happened to be to hand, whatever pre-cooked chemical mess was uppermost in the freezer — the less said the better.

Nothing like looking on the bright side.

The sudden paroxysm of pain which shot through him as he gave himself this good advice, he unfairly put down to too many *cappuccinos* before accepting it for what it was — a memorial celebration of all the bouts of indigestion he had suffered at his beloved's hands, God bless her.

The detective went downstairs, out to the yard where Miriam's red Renault awaited him polished and eager, straining at the leash, one might almost have said, to be out on the road again. Jurnet deliberately did not do the sensible thing — shine his torch on the underside before getting in: and was obscurely troubled to find himself relieved when the engine started sweetly at the first try.

Over the road, as Monty Bellman had pointed out with pointed malice, workmen had filled in the hole where the bomb had exploded. From the bedroom window over the shop Jurnet had been able to trace the irregular outline of the new tarmac. The hole in the universe occasioned by the irreparable absence of Miriam was less susceptible of repair. Edging the Renault out on to the road, loneliness drove Jurnet through an Angleby grown immeasurably remote, to the flat above the synagogue, seeking, not exactly solace, but the warmth of the tribe, that Jewish intensity of concern for each fellow-member's well-being from which he had previously retreated in some alarm. 'A pack of nosy parkers!' he had complained to Miriam who had stared at him, uncomprehending.

Now, wounded in body and spirit, never had he felt so much a Jew and never so close to understanding a God, poor sod, who, forever vaunting his one-ness, as if it were something to be proud of, must be very nearly as lonely as Ben Jurnet.

If that was possible.

To his surprise it was Rafi Galil who opened the door to him, the man's scarred face seaming in a smile of welcome and concern.

'My dear Benjamin!' Drawing the detective with both hands into the little hall at the foot of the stairs: 'You are hurt. You are limping. What has happened? Are you all right?'

'A small accident. Nothing of consequence.'

'Thank God! We heard you were in Ireland and we worried for you. A nation of poets but alas, at the same time barbarians. The Rabbi will be so relieved you are back safe, if not quite sound.'

'As near as makes no difference.' With an effort Jurnet managed the polite inquiry: 'Everything OK at the workshop?'

'What shall I say?' Galil shrugged his shoulders humorously, his mop of white hair rising a little in harmony with the movement before flopping back into place. 'Not easy. You cannot lose a presiding genius and expect to go on as if nothing has happened. But we are managing, one step at a time. As must you likewise, I am sure, Benjamin — sometimes the step so small, eh, it is hardly to move at all, but still it must be taken, day by day.'

'So they tell me.'

'No wonder you are here to see the Rabbi!' the other exclaimed. 'Not a moment too soon, from the sound of it! And here we are, Pnina and I, getting in the way. But don't worry, I have an appointment, I would be gone already except that the dear man insists on making tea to go with the cookies we have brought, which is why I answer the door bell while he is busy in the kitchen.

'Pnina too, she will not stay long, she is going swimming. Can you imagine, swimming at this time of year, in this weather, at this time of night? But she says the water is heated and tonight is late closing at the Baths.' The man's voice softened. 'I think, poor girl, she prefers to go when there are less people.'

'Oh? How's she getting on?'

'Invaluable! I do not know what we would do without her. Always knows better than anybody else, of course, but there! Isn't that what it is to be young? I am only here because I gave her a lift with her box of cookies. Mrs Levine, where she lodges, makes the best *kiklach* in Angleby, in the world, but requiring careful transportation. You will be able to test at once if I am not speaking the simple truth. Let us go up. The tea will be ready.'

The warmth of the tribe, Jurnet thought again, gratefully, as he hoisted himself up the narrow stairs to more concern, more hor- rified exclamations over his limp and his damaged head: reassurance, however, which, whilst it made him cry inwardly, a healing haemorrhage, at the same time only activated an added burden of guilt.

'Another cup, Pnina!' the Rabbi ordered joyfully. 'Good and strong, the way the In- spector likes it!'

The girl — who looked tired, Jurnet thought in a brief, not over-interested in- spection: pale and ugly, the shadows dark beneath her dark eyes — went into the kitchen and came back with the tea in one of the fussy cups which had been the late Mrs Schnellman's pride and joy. Handing it over, she spoke a little tentatively: 'I hope it's strong enough.'

Jurnet didn't say it was, he didn't say it

wasn't. Aware of the Rabbi watching him with loving eyes that missed nothing, he said: 'I've arranged to get into the flat Thursday morning to pick up one or two things, personal stuff. There's some clothes of Miriam's — I don't suppose her mother will want them. It would only upset her. I thought, Rabbi, your Ladies' Guild might have some ideas what to do about them.'

'I'm sure they will. Either to sell for charity or to give to somebody in need.' Rabbi Schnellman straightened his tiny black *yarmulke*. He suddenly looked much happier. 'You are beginning to accept what has to be.'

'Am I? I'll fetch them over.' Jurnet finished his tea and set the cup and saucer down on the hand-crocheted cloth, Mrs Schnellman's handiwork, which, as always, was draped catercornerwise on the curly-legged table. He could not understand how the Rabbi could bear to see it there, day after day; bear the memory of fingers wielding the crochet hook, the ecru-coloured thread unwinding, the Greek-key pattern growing until one day complete. If Miriam, he thought, had ever crocheted a table-cloth he would have wrapped what remained of her body in it as a winding cloth, buried it with her, anything to get it out of his daily sight.

On the other hand, what had he himself, beside his aching heart, to remind him of his lost love? Jurnet put his hand in his pocket and fingered the green eye of the Bingo bear. Not much, but something.

Rafi Galil put in a casual inquiry: 'I don't suppose there was anything in your flat related to the business?'

Jurnet took his hand out of his pocket, shook his head.

'Miriam always said there was quite enough paper at the office. She was hanged if she was going to drown in it at home into the bargain. Just the same — ' able, to his surprise, to contrive a smile at the inconsistency — 'you couldn't sit down on a chair or pull out a drawer without finding it full of balls of wool, swatches of yarn, all kinds of samples. She was always on the look-out for something better than what she had.' *Something better than me?* Self-pity rose like bile in his throat, to be hatefully swallowed. 'I'll take a carrier bag along with me and fill it full of the stuff if it's of any use to you.'

'Please!' Pnina Benvista intervened, with an eagerness which, for no discernible reason, made Jurnet sorry he'd offered. 'Miriam was already working on the designs for next autumn. They might help us to understand better what she had in mind.'

'If it's not too much trouble,' Rafi Galil put in, sensing a need for diplomacy. 'And if, despite what she said, anything of her paper should turn up — '

'Not a chance. All she kept at the flat was her personal file.'

'And that contained nothing relative to the business?'

'Her personal file,' Jurnet repeated repressively. 'I'll see that Mrs Courland gets it. You can always ask her what's in it.'

The Israeli burst out laughing, the scar crinkling his face into the appearance of a garden gnome.

'There I go again!' Laughter remaining bright in his eyes: 'Do I need to remind you one more time that I am not an Englishman? Of course you did not pry into Miriam's personal file — how could I ever have imagined such a thing, even after what has happened?' At the sight of the detective's closed face, the man quietened. 'My dear sir, I apologize. I would like you to think well of me. I am only trying, if that is possible, to keep Miriam's business alive — for her mother's sake, and even more, for those poor souls at Tel Tzevaim. Even with the indispensable help of Pnina here, it is not easy.'

The Israeli girl seemed not to know how to handle praise, took it as an awkwardness of a piece with her awkward body. She picked up a holdall from the Louis Seize sofa where, not so long before, Jurnet had lain drowned in sorrow, and announced: 'I have to go. The pool will be closing.'

Galil excused himself: 'It is out of my way and I am late for my appointment, otherwise I would gladly take you . . .'

With the lack of grace which characterized her the girl returned: 'I can walk it.'

Jurnet surprised himself by suggesting: 'I'm in no hurry. I can drop you off if you like.'

'All right.'

Jurnet turned to Galil in sudden recollection: 'The Renault. Headquarters is laying on another car for me. I'll bring it back to the workshop, shall I, unless you want it left somewhere else?'

'No hurry, and the workshop will be fine.'

'Thanks for letting me have the use of it.'

'A pleasure to be of help.'

Pnina Benvista spoke up bad-temperedly: 'Are you coming, then, or aren't you?'

25

Jurnet sat under a palm tree, grudgingly breathing in the chlorinated miasma that, under the glass dome of the municipal swimming pool, passed for air. The mug of coffee on the small table by the poolside tasted of the same mixture made viscous.

Outside, across the expanse of lawn stretching away from the windows, he could see the lights of cars and buses moving along the road, a tracery from another world. The calls which resonated from the sparsely tenanted pool, the occasional splash and thrash of disturbed water, reached him each encased in a ghostly echo.

What the hell was he doing on this alien planet where the vegetation was plastic and the oxygen had turned it in for the night?

Jurnet knew damn well what he was doing. Anything to put off his return to the flat over the delicatessen with its suffering god on the wall and its ringside view of freshly laid tarmac. A man in minimal trunks on his way to the pool steps, carrying his pale belly before him like Salome the head of John the Baptist, paused in his progress to cast a humorous eye, first at the dressing on the side of Jurnet's head and then up at the improbable fronds moving languidly in a breeze undetectable at ground level.

'Got to watch out for them coconuts.'

Pnina Benvista came out of the women's changing rooms barefoot, her hair hidden under a cap that gleamed silver in the overhead lighting. She made towards the pool, not looking to see where Jurnet was, or indeed whether he were there at all; clip-clopping along, her deformity made explicit in the simple grey swimsuit she wore with an air of defiance, her head held high, eyes fixed straight ahead.

Wracked anew as he was by his return to an Angleby without Miriam, Jurnet could not afford the luxury of compassion. He shut his eyes so as not to have the girl in his sights, only to find the pitiful image, inescapable, etched on the darkness behind his lids. When, after an interval, he opened them again, reluctantly, hoping to find her no more than a bare arm, a silver cap showing above the surface, nothing to frighten the horses or disturb the exquisite sensibilities of a bereaved copper, aversion changed to alarm. With a concentration semaphored by every line in her body, Pnina Benvista was hauling herself up the steps to the diving board — to the highest board, what was more.

Jurnet pushed back his chair aghast and sprang up, wanting to cry out to the girl to go back for Christ's sake, yet afraid the very warning might precipitate what he most feared. It might have been his imagination but it seemed to the detective that the noises in the pool had died away, a collective holding of breath pending the inevitable catastrophe.

Pnina Benvista hobbled the length of the diving board. Higher still, piercing the upper blackness, a single star hung remote and indifferent. Even at that height, when one might have expected the slender figure on its lofty perch to have taken on at least the grace of distance, the watchers below were aware beyond anything else of its lopsidedness, its fatal disproportion.

Reminding himself afresh that he could not afford the luxury of compassion, Jurnet allowed the anger which, since Miriam's death, seemed to be ever lurking below the surface, to rise, mingle itself with his concern. The stupid bint! What did she think she was doing, showing off for his benefit, for the benefit of anyone with two good legs who might be looking? For a moment he savoured the satisfaction, hateful but therapeutic, that he was not the only one suffering.

He turned away deliberately, to the trails of light moving along the road, the headlamps that flared momentarily before subsiding as the cars threaded a bend and melted into the night. Useless. Ashamed, he raised his head to the domed roof again.

In the brief interval something had happened. Arms raised in invocation, the Israeli girl stood poised at the end of the board. She looked like a silver bird, and like a bird she took off, rose in a graceful arch and seemed to hang there motionless for an instant before cleaving the air in an ecstatic descent to water which opened silver to receive her silver body.

It was a beauty to bring tears to the eyes. The deformed body, transformed, flashed through the water like a dolphin, tumbling and cavorting out of sheer joy at being made whole at last. The other swimmers in the pool made way, shouting encouragement. The glass dome filled anew with noise, with laughter, with love.

Jurnet resumed his seat feeling suddenly light-headed, purged of grief and envy alike. When the girl at last climbed out of the pool and made her way towards him, pulling off her bathing cap as she came, he greeted her smilingly: 'You ought to be a mermaid.'

Immediately the limp worsened, the dark hair cascading on to her shoulders framed a face from which the light drained like water out of a cracked vessel. Her voice harsh and unforgiving, Pnina Benvista returned: 'Unfortunately, I don't have a tail.'

In the car, on the way back to her lodgings — a lift accepted without demur but without thanks either — he roused himself to say the right things. *Are you comfortable in your digs, are you settling down OK in Angleby, how's the work going?* Remote after her liberation in the pool, she returned conventional answers which seemed to the detective to mask a newly refurbished despair at what it was to live a cripple on dry land.

He tried again.

'Where did you learn to swim like that?'

'My mother and my father.' Unwittingly he had touched the right chord. A smile, bleak but loving, lit up the face which had reflected closed and dreary in the windscreen. 'They too, I think, dreamed that one day I might grow a tail, sit on a rock with a comb and a glass in my hand. Make for myself

291

an element where I was the equal of everybody else.'

'You *are* the equal of everybody else.'

'Yes.' Next to him he felt the squaring of her shoulders, the uplifting of her head. Only the slight tremble in her voice still gave her away. 'Twenty times a day that is what I tell myself.'

'Well, then — '

'Unfortunately,' she said, the tremble gone and in its place a touch of mischief for which, absurdly, he took a pleased credit, 'it is only eight or nine times out of that twenty that I convince myself.' He could not remember having heard her laugh before. It was a laugh that did not last long but fell pleasantly on the ear. 'You ask, am I settling down in Angleby. The answer is yes and no. Everyone is kind — too kind. That is the trouble. They are always making allowances for me.'

Jurnet changed gear, gave a nod of understanding. 'Must be maddening.'

'Worse than that.' Winding through the medieval streets of the city centre, Jurnet sensed, rather than saw, that the girl had turned her face towards him, the eyes huge and troubled. 'It makes it impossible for me to do what Miriam sent for me to do. The whole reason I am in England at all.'

'To set up the new computers, wasn't it?'

'Not only that. It was to learn the whole business, everything from A to Z. Miriam was going to brief me, as she said, on the journey back from the airport.' After a silence which Jurnet did not feel able to break, the girl went on: 'I have thought about it so many times, what she was going to say to me, what instructions.' Pnina Benvista hesitated, but only for a moment: hesitation was not her way. 'I have already told you she wanted to arrange things so that she did not have to come into work so much. So that she could stay home and have your child.'

They were rounding the castle mound. High above them the floodlit keep, brutish by day, glittered against the velvet sky like a confection of spun sugar. My city, thought Jurnet, my beloved city. Ashes without Miriam. A vision of a child — his and Miriam's — shouting with glee as he scrambled up the castle mound, his parents in laughing pursuit, had him suddenly doubled up with pain over the steering wheel.

The girl, noticing his contorted face, demanded: 'Are you feeling all right?'

'Yes.' Jurnet took a deep breath, relaxed his grip on the wheel. 'How are people too kind? Mr Galil at any rate has more sense than to patronize you with kindness.'

'Uncle Rafi most of all.' Pnina Benvista slapped the flat of her palm hard against the dashboard. 'This car, for instance, Miriam's, but belonging to the company, you understand. You are bringing it back. You didn't hear him saying I ought to have it instead, did you? Of course you didn't, even though all the time I am running to and from the outworkers like an errand boy — that's the kind of work he finds for me to do. At least, with a car, I could do it in a quarter of the time. But always if the subject of a car comes up, Uncle Rafi says it is too risky with my legs. To hear him, you'd never think I hold an ordinary driving licence and an international one, that I drove in Israel where everyone drives like crazy and never had an accident.'

'Was it, perhaps, a specially adapted car?'

'What if it was?' Pnina Benvista demanded. 'That is not the point. Though not specially, as it happens — only automatic, instead of gears you have to change. It did not cost all that much more than a regulation model. Uncle Rafi could easily change this car for one of those — the cheapest kind would do, or second-hand, I wouldn't care, so long as it went. If only he would stop being so kind and worried about me that he doesn't let me do anything.'

'You could speak to Mrs Courland, perhaps.'

'She's as bad as he is — about business, I mean. Both of them, they don't understand the first thing, they are little children. I am sure Miriam only took on Uncle Rafi out of kindness because of all the bad things that had happened to him, and because he was a relation. Well, I understand that, I am all for families. She gave him a title — Financial Director — so that at Tel Tzevaim he would sound like somebody. Everybody there likes him but, to be truthful, all he did was dodder about. Really he was nothing. Computers! What did he know? He was always saying his fingers and thumbs came before machinery, can you believe it? He just about knew how to use an abacus.

'It didn't matter. Miriam had arranged things so that he was accorded his respect, you understand? That was what was important. But here in Angleby, without Miriam to guide him, and not knowing her plans to give me responsibility in the running of the business, I am afraid he will run it into the ground altogether, and then what will they do — him and Mrs Courland and the cripples at Tel Tzevaim?' The girl glowered at Jurnet as if he too was to be included in the general blame. 'It isn't fair to Miriam.'

Jurnet said: 'I'll try to put in a word about the car.'

Mrs O'Driscoll, back to manageable proportions and humming a tuneless little song that sounded more like bees in spring than a fitting accompaniment to autumnal damps, was tucking her latest offspring into a fine new pram parked on the grass when Jurnet unlatched the garden gate and came towards her smiling.

Despite the weather, it was difficult not to smile at Mrs O'Driscoll, such a picture of maternal contentment did she present, rosy and fulfilled and casting an occasional loving eye over two more young O'Driscolls, the ones on the next rungs of the domestic ladder, who, wellied and waterproofed, were squatting in an improvised sand-pit, fashioning sand pies with the absorbed dedication of a chef piping mayonnaise round a salmon mousse.

When the woman saw who her visitor was, the humming swelled into triumphal song before being extinguished. She gave a last pat to the small helmeted head showing above the pram quilt, then held out both hands in greeting.

'Mr Jurnet — your head! What have you done to your head, then? I heard you were in Ireland. "No good'll come of it," I said to O'Driscoll, and I see it did not. Did they take a shot at you then, the uncivilized trash?'

Without waiting to hear the truth of it, she wheeled about.

'Eileen! Patrick!' The children kept their heads down, preferring not to hear. 'Did you ever see anything like it?' their mother cried delightedly, before rounding on the pair. Everything seemed to please her. 'How can I go indoors and make Mr Jurnet a cup of tea if you don't stop what you're doing and come inside as well where I can keep an eye on you while the kettle's hotting?' No answer and she finished: 'Not that there mayn't be a biscuit in it for each of you for the dear obedient kids you are.'

'A choclet biscuit?' demanded Eileen, settling down, from the look of it, to an enjoyable session of bargaining.

'If you wipe your feet properly on the mat, a chocolate one. Two if you rinse your hands under the tap first and remember not to leave the water running.'

The children scrambled out of their hole and made for the house, shouting. Jurnet asked: 'Is Mr O'Driscoll about?'

At that the Irishwoman's contentment with life, if that were possible, intensified even further.

'Mr O'Driscoll is not about. I'm surprised you'd not have heard. Mr O'Driscoll is not about any more, never. Not about here, that is. I'm sure I wish the man no harm in the world so long as he stays that way, away from my door. And if you please, Mr Jurnet, would you kindly note that from now on, so far as me and the kids are concerned, we've dropped that bloody O, drowned it dead in the Irish Sea. From now on it's Mrs Driscoll an' all the little Driscolls. I've spoken to Father Culvey, was there anything in the Church or the Law against it, and he couldn't say as there was.'

'Of course.' Jurnet looked a little bemused. 'If that's what you want.'

'That's what I want, Mr Jurnet,' the woman said firmly, leading the way to her front door. 'British. The kids were all born here and Angleby is where they're going to grow up, British by birth the way the Lord and the British Government made them.'

Some of the happiness leaching out of her voice: 'You heard what happened to Terry?' Jurnet nodded. 'Well, then! What kind of a country is it where things like that can happen to children? Not one where I can take the chance of it happening to mine.'

Mrs Driscoll's bosom, comfortably maternal, rose and fell with emotion.

'British by birth and British by name. No fancy O's and commas to make folks over here afraid I'm going about with a bomb in me shopping bag, hidden under the taties and the soda bread. No O's either to make us afraid that one dark night some great gawping hooligan will slide in through the door without waiting to be invited, an' for the sake of not waking up dead in the morning we'll be forced to put up with his company for weeks on end, let him eat us out of house an' home without forking out a penny to pay for it, and then, when he finally takes himself off, make us swear to say nothing or he'll be back with some pals who don't have his good manners.'

Making a ceremony of it, Jurnet said: 'Mrs Driscoll.'

'Thank you.' Mrs Driscoll inclined her head in regal acknowledgement. They came into the house, into a hall bright with shining linoleum. 'I know I shouldn't rightly say it to you after what happened to your young lady, the lovely girl she was — ' a haze of genuine sympathy invested the woman's soft Irish features — 'but I can't say too much how fine it is here, enough rooms for us all and no ole banger rusting out front for the kids to cut themselves on an' get gangrene — '

'And no Mr O'Driscoll . . .'

'And no Mr O'Driscoll.' Mrs Driscoll's face was a glory to see. 'Eight little nippers, Mr Jurnet. It was all he was good at, and he was good at that, I'll give him that much — each one healthy and bright with it, God bless them. I won't say I didn't get some enjoyment myself in the making of them, but enough is enough I always say, and eight is already a whole lot more than that.'

'And that's why you sent him away?'

'I never did!' Mrs Driscoll looked shocked. 'And don't you go letting Father Culvey think I'd ever do a thing like that. 'Tisn't *my* doing he's off into the wide blue yonder — more your lot, really. The police kept coming round and coming round, they wouldn't let him alone, and I reckon those others — the ones down at the Bittern, whoever they are — must've begun to worry what it was all in aid of. Nights he'd been working behind the bar he'd come home the colour of an ole dishrag.

' "I can't make 'em believe I never told the buggers nothing," he used to say to me, tears in his eyes. If they'd known him the way I do, they'd have known he was speaking the Gospel truth. My husband, Mr Jurnet, was born shitting himself with fright at the world he'd come into — one of nature's

300

cowards, bless him. It was the best thing about him and I only hope the kids take after their pa, grow up with the same sense to keep their heads down instead of going looking for trouble.'

Following Mrs Driscoll into the kitchen Jurnet demanded urgently: 'So what happened to him? Did they come and take him away?'

Mrs Driscoll filled the electric kettle at the sink, plugged it in with a conscious delight in her mastery of modern technology.

'Wait for them like a sitting duck! What do you think! I saw how it was, how the man was half out of his mind with the worry of it. I cashed the week's Giro, give it him, and off he went, out of the house like a rocket, didn't even wait till the kids got home from school to say goodbye.'

'Went where?'

'That I couldn't tell you,' Mrs Driscoll returned composedly, spooning tea into a brown earthenware teapot meticulously warmed for its reception. 'I don't know and I don't want to know, except it would have to be Ireland. Anywhere else he wouldn't only not know what day of the week it was, poor juggins, he wouldn't know what century. I don't know and I don't want to know, but since, to hear him tell it, there's barely a soul in

County Cavan that isn't related to him by blood or marriage, I should think all you have to do is stand there at the nearest convenient crossroads and call out his name. Somebody's bound to be passing who knows where you can find the poor innocent.'

The woman frowned, paused in her preparations.

'Not that I hope you'll be doing any such thing, Mr Jurnet. You're a sensible man and by the look of you you've already had enough of Ireland to last you the rest of your life. Sure, 'tis a lovely country, I always say, but never lovelier than when you're looking at it from a long way off, with no intention of going back.'

Over tea that was as brown and nearly as thick as the pot out of which it came, and Rich Tea biscuits served on a plate covered with a lace doily, Jurnet ventured with a certain diffidence: 'You called your husband a poor innocent? Thinking it over, are you sure about that? There could have been pressure put upon him, pressure he couldn't withstand. You said yourself he was a coward. Fear can make a man do terrible things, completely out of his usual character.'

Mrs Driscoll poured herself a cup of tea, sugared it with three lumps and sat down at the kitchen table across from the detective.

'No need to be shy, Mr Jurnet,' she assured him, stirring the resultant goo vigorously. 'Don't think I haven't thought about exactly that, many times, in bed at night. Since O'Driscoll's gone I've had time to think lying lovely and quiet, the whole bed to myself. You have to be married, Mr Jurnet, and the damage done to appreciate what a blessing it is to be a virgin. I often used to think how lucky Our Lady was, to have Jesus with none of that sweaty business to go through, just an angel coming to tell her like it might be the man from the football pools.'

'You haven't answered my question.'

'I'm trying. Sometimes I've thought to myself, he would never have set off an explosion so close to our own place an' risk hurting the children, but then I remember how mad he was when I bought those net curtains, he never could stand them, so perhaps he did. He said they were a criminal extravagance. But then I thought again — ' idly dunking a Rich Tea in her cup before sucking it into her mouth with a pleasure it was a pleasure to see — 'and it couldn't have been him, because if it had been, it wouldn't have happened. Either he'd have wired it up wrong, or the Semtex would have been damp or something and wouldn't have worked.

There'd have been bound to be something. There always was. That was the kind of man he was. Is.' The woman looked across the table with calm assurance. 'You can take my word for it, Mr Jurnet. You can always rely on O'Driscoll to be unreliable.'

26

It was more than flesh and blood could stand.

Even those few select buggers who couldn't stand him — and after years at Headquarters he knew who they were, he didn't have to be formally introduced — came up to him slimy with solicitude. In the canteen, Doris on the urn handed over his cup of tea without, for once, slopping a single drop in the saucer. Young bobbies blushed to the roots of their hair as they mumbled something about how great it was to see him back.

Now Jurnet understood exactly how it must feel to be Pnina Benvista. Everyone was too bloody kind. It was all he could do not to throw up.

Most sickening of all, they had even tidied up his desk. It actually smelled of lavender, for Christ's sake, some meagre paperwork disposed about its shining surface like a bit of minimalist art newly arrived at the Tate. A grey plastic holder bristling with freshly sharpened pencils added a finishing touch.

Whilst his mates stood around, modestly awaiting his word of appreciation, Jurnet sat down shakily. He wanted to laugh and cry. He should have known that coming back to this world which had once fitted him like a glove was a ghastly mistake. Miriam alive hadn't been able to stop him being a copper: Miriam dead was making it impossible for him to continue to be one.

Tinker, tailor, soldier, sailor, security guard, deliverer of red-hot pizzas — a list of alternative ways of keeping a roof over his head was filing forlornly through his consciousness when a manicured hand reached over his shoulder and, with a strength he would not have thought it capable of, snapped the poncy points off the pencils, every last one of them.

In acid tones that made Jurnet's heart lurch with love the Superintendent demanded: 'Am I to take it I'm the only one that's come to work today?'

After that it had been a day much like any other. Out on the ring road an articulated vehicle had shed its load of chemicals, which would have been routine except that a held-up motorist, for want of something better to do, had lit up a cigarette and, with it, a liberated, lethal vapour, dying along with three others before the resulting fire could be brought under control. A defectively braked buggy, its year-old passenger still strapped inside, had trundled quietly down a slope and ended up in the river, moving so quietly over the grass that its minder, pleasuring herself nearby with an airman on leave from Mildenhall, had noticed nothing until it was too late to do anything except scream her head off. One of the largest firms in the county had just woken up to the fact that its chief executive wasn't coming back from his vacation in South America and neither was the three-quarters of a million missing from the company coffers. A young man with a history of schizophrenia had donned his mother's kimono, samurai fashion, before disembowelling himself with the electric carving knife.

The day passed quickly in pursuit of these normal events. There were times when Jurnet all but forgot that Miriam was dead. At lunch in the canteen Doris, to her credit, sloshed tea about with all the abandon of the days of old. Jurnet's desk — though the whiff of lavender persisted — began to accumulate a homely clutter. Jack Ellers, with the air of a woman thankfully unhooking a tight girdle, told a dirty story.

Altogether a better day than Jurnet had anticipated.

If only the Superintendent, God rot his aristocratic guts, hadn't seen fit to throw a spanner in the works.

Serene behind his antique desk, his gold pen in front of him as it might be the mace to indicate that the House was in session, the Superintendent had summoned Jurnet to inform him — gently enough, but with that underlying exasperation which, with him, always accompanied any admission of failure — that, so far as Angleby CID was concerned, the murder of Miriam Courland was not so much to be put on the back burner as taken off the stove altogether, to be handed over to the skills or the incompetence of a different bunch of cooks. Never mind what the Superintendent might have said privately in the past on the subject of that puffed-up elite, from now on the Anti-Terrorist Branch would be taking over the pursuit, if indeed there was any more anything or anyone to pursue, which was increasingly doubtful. But there it was, an operational decision had been made. There was no more to be said.

Nevertheless, when Jurnet received this intelligence in the requisite silence, the Superintendent's face became progressively darker, the splendid eyebrows drew closer together. In a voice of ice, each syllable crackling, the man enunciated: 'I would be glad to have your observations.'

'I can't say as I have any — sir. If that's all, sir . . .' Jurnet half-turned, politely, awaiting his dismissal.

'All!' The other exploded. His hand reached unconsciously for his pen, taking strength from its classic perfection. 'Damn it, Ben! You know I'm only doing what has to be done. You're back here, fine — but I've been watching you. You've still got that look on your face — not here, or only partly here, the rest of you obsessed, chasing the illusion that finding the villain who killed your girl and bringing him to justice will somehow make her death easier to bear. Rubbish! Time's the only thing that will help you do that, if anything can. And if it can't you'll either have to find yourself a new love or else make do with your memories. At least you've got some to be grateful for, which is more than you can say for most of us.'

The Superintendent regarded his subordinate with a smile which put the world to rights between them.

'None of which, of course, is to say it's any business of mine what you get up to in your free time.'

The days were drawing in — good! Pity they couldn't reduce themselves to the pin-point of light left on the turned-off telly. Another second and that too was gone: peace, perfect peace. So far as Jurnet was concerned, the fewer the daylight hours to be got through the better. As for the nights, they couldn't possibly be longer than they were already.

The one to hand had his permission to go on for ever. That way, there would be no Thursday, no necessity of going back to his flat for the last time, of slipping off their hangers the clothes that had moulded themselves lovingly to Miriam's lovely form and stuffing them, together with her shoes and underwear, into carrier bags for the syna-gogue ladies to dispose of charitably.

Christ! No wonder the ancient Egyptians had buried household goods in the grave along with the corpse. An end to memory along with everything else.

An operational decision had been taken. There was no more to be said.

At least the day, amidst all its crowding negatives, had yielded one plus: one human being made happier through his intervention. *Be kind to cripples day* — the corners of Jurnet's mouth turned down in self-disparagement even as he took wry pleasure in the thought of Pnina Benvista's dark eyes aglow with excitement, the uncompromising planes of her face dissolving in delighted astonishment as she heard from Rafi Galil the news that she was after all to have for her own exclusive use a company car with automatic gear change and all. For a moment he regretted that he had impressed upon the Israeli that the girl was not to be told he had had any hand in the decision: it would have been gratifying to see those eyes lighting up on his account.

Instantly, with the thought, the corners of Jurnet's mouth turned down more than ever. Other people's gratitude was not for the likes of either of them.

He had brought Miriam's car back to The Courland Collection that morning before going to work, to find Rafi Galil standing in the drive at the rear of his own car engaged in mortal combat with a pile of outsize cardboard boxes collapsed flat for transit but apparently reluctant to exchange the comfort of the car boot for the dubious advantages of getting out into the world.

Jurnet braked, jumped out of the Renault and came across to help.

'Here! Let me take some of those . . .'

Thankfully, the Israeli had let him take the lot. The man was still panting from his exertions, his rosy face too red, when, the detective following, he led the way round to the front of the workshop and unlocked the door. In the lobby, for all his heaving chest, he stood smiling as if, even *in extremis,* a smile was the arrangement of features which came most naturally to him.

'What it is to be young and strong as a giant!' The smile widened in recognition that it, meaning life, was all a joke, youth and strength included. 'When I was young I thought that brains were the most important thing. Only now that I am old do I realize that all the brains in the world cannot make up for muscles and a good back.'

As Jurnet stood without saying anything, waiting to be told where to deposit his burden: 'Drop them where you stand, my dear Mr Detective. We have a young man, his head solid bone, whom we pay money to pick things up from one place and put them down again in another. Not always the right place, but there! You can't have everything. I should have left the boxes in the car for him to bring in, in the first place, only I am too vain to admit, even to myself, that I am, as you say, past it.'

For the first time that morning the man looked at Jurnet directly, a long, searching examination at the end of which he gave a little nod, as if he had satisfied himself of something or other. When he spoke again his voice was gentle. 'You shouldn't have brought back the car, Detective Inspector. As I told you, we have no need of it here and it is part of Miriam. You should hold on to what little of her there still remains to hold on to.'

'No thanks.' With an effort Jurnet held ill temper at bay. Everyone in the world bar himself knew what he ought to do. 'Appreciate your suggesting it, though — ' an answer which, albeit clumsily, provided him with the opening he needed. If The Courland Collection had no further use for the little red car, how about turning it in against an automatic for Pnina? With legs like hers it must be hell having to get along on Shanks's pony.

'Figure of speech,' he finished, embarrassed by the look of incomprehension on the other's face. 'Colloquial way of saying walking.'

'Your English language!' The Israeli shook his head humorously, a movement which expanded itself into a good-natured shrug. 'A car for Pnina — why not, if you say so?

You know that she has already asked?' Jurnet nodded. 'And that I have said no?' Jurnet nodded a second time. 'Not for the money it will cost, although that is, naturally, a consideration, but because she is here on a temporary visa only. We cannot officially give her anything, use company funds for that purpose, however much we might wish to. Even as it is — ' a mischievous grin crumpled the scar on his cheek — 'I must be careful, mustn't I, not to let the police know that she has no business to be working for us at all without a work permit — '

Jurnet commented, straight-faced: 'That's right. Don't let the police know whatever you do. What surprises me is that Miriam didn't get everything settled in the first place.'

Rafi Galil frowned slightly.

'I couldn't say why not. Miriam never told me what was in her mind. I think myself all she intended for the girl was a short visit, more a kind of prize for her hard work at Tel Tzevaim than anything else. Who was to know how things would turn out?'

'Yes.' After a moment Jurnet returned to his effort on Pnina Benvista's behalf. 'But as it is, she could certainly do with a car.'

The mischievous look, wonderfully like-able, back in place, the Israeli inquired: 'I'm to take it, I gather, that she has already told you she drove in Israel?'

'So she said.'

'She drove!' The other shook his head again, this time in comic horror. 'You may thank God you were never her passenger. In every other respect a completely sensible woman — but behind the wheel, I tell you, a she-devil! I have never been more frightened in my life.' Softening his own harsh judgement: 'Not a bad driver in the technical sense, let me say — in fact, very good. Too good. She takes it for granted that everybody else out on the road is as quick-witted as herself, as well able to make decisions in the split second before disaster strikes.

'I think — ' the voice was gentle now, warm with understanding — 'I think perhaps it is that, in a car, she can forget her legs, she is the same as other people, better than they are, even.'

The Israeli had reached out then, put a friendly hand on Jurnet's arm. 'You teach me a lesson, Inspector. One I should know without being taught. Pnina shall have her car.'

27

Mario had been keeping watch. He waylaid Jurnet as the detective came out of the yard and before he could take himself unnoticed up to the flat by the side door. Gently, without asking, the delicatessen owner ushered his quarry into the shop and to a table where he set in front of him a steaming plateful of spaghetti bolognaise.

'But I'm not — ' Jurnet began.

'Eat!'

And Jurnet did eat, chasing the last delicious thread of pasta round the dish and discovering to his guilty astonishment that he had been ravenously hungry. Released then with his host's approval, he went upstairs, stripped and took a shower, reflecting that Pontius Pilate, faced equally with an operational decision, had made do with a mere washing of hands. Had the Procurator of Judaea, he wondered, felt cleansed after that limited catlick? All he could say was that the all-over hadn't done a bloody thing for Detective Inspector Benjamin Jurnet, Angleby CID.

Naked and damp, he lay down on top of the bedclothes and fell into a doze from which he awakened to find the room brighter than one might have expected from the street lamps alone — bright with a capricious glow which alternatively faltered and blazed forth brashly triumphant. Even with the window shut Jurnet could smell smoke and a familiar sourness of crumbling bricks and rotting wood. Fully awake, feeling fragile but excited, he swung his legs off the bed, crossed the floor and peered out.

Just as on that fatal day never to be forgotten, the pavements and roadway were full, people and vehicles still arriving. Thankfully, no crevasse had opened up in the forecourt like last time. Instead, a column of water alive with jewelled reflections soared up and over, arching itself towards flames that reared upward in challenge.

The block of flats was on fire. Jurnet wanted to cheer.

None of Miriam's things to sort out after all, none of her wools and papers to retrieve, no furniture to wonder what on earth to do with . . . Suddenly anxious lest the fire was only in the front of the building,

317

that the rear still stood intact, Miriam's clothes hanging pristine in the closet, Jurnet hurriedly pulled on jeans and sweater, thrust his feet into trainers and ran downstairs, willing the Fire Brigade to let well alone, let the bloody place burn down to the last substandard brick.

The pavement outside the delicatessen had been cleared, except for a motorized invalid chair where Billy Bellman sat hunched making uncouth noises and waving his hands about. PC Bly, one of the constables engaged in keeping spectators at a safe distance, recognized Jurnet as he emerged from the flat door; hurried over thankfully.

'Can't get him to move, sir. Whenever we go near to get the brake off the perisher works himself into such a lather we're afraid it'll bring on a seizure.'

'Leave him to me. I'll have a go.'

Jurnet went into the shop where Mario, on the tried and true principle that nothing stimulated the appetite more than a really good disaster, was busy slicing up an outsize cabbage for coleslaw.

Jurnet jerked his head over his shoulder.

'What's the kind of ice cream the bloke buys for that kid?'

'The imbecile, you mean?' Mario looked up in the direction of the shop window.

'Raspberry ripple with a chocolate flake.'

'Let me have one, will you? I'll settle up with you later.'

The Italian put down the cabbage, wiped his hands on a cloth and went over to the freezer. 'What's the fellow doing, leaving him out there, alone? He could get hurt.'

'Busy committing a bit of arson, I shouldn't be surprised.'

'So that's what he does for a living!' The Italian paused in his labours, looked up with a smile. 'Only, in that case, would he leave the imbecile here in full view as an advertisement?'

'Wouldn't put it past him. He's a weird bugger.'

Jurnet went outside again, noting with satisfaction as he went that flames were now shooting out from the side of the building as well as from the front. With luck, his time-expired love nest would be well on its way to ashes, like his time-expired love. Everyone, the Rabbi included, had taken care not to let him know that Miriam was not only dead but buried; but it stood to reason. The inquest had been completed, the body therefore released, the *yahrzeit* candle in its glass burning for twenty-four hours to light the freed soul safely home to eternity.

Jurnet watched the tongues of flame reaching out for the ragged hedge which marked the boundary of the property. Some of the hawthorn twigs were already spitting out sparks to ignite the rest of the moribund greenery. In the old days, didn't they, women in India used to fling themselves on their husband's funeral pyre. Feeling deeply guilty that, despite everything, he could discover in himself no compulsion to dash across the road and immolate himself, Jurnet wrenched his gaze away from the spectacle and took Billy Bellman his ice cream.

The boy seemed tremendously agitated. Whether it was rage or anxiety which activated the alternate growls and falsetto keening issuing from the slobbering mouth Jurnet had no means of knowing. On the chance that it was anger at the non-arrival of his customary treat which had inspired the blood-curdling performance, Jurnet proffered his gift, only to have it dashed to the ground with a sweep of the hand the detective could not think to be anything but deliberate, such directed force was behind the gesture, such malevolence to the head swaying on its stalk of neck like a seeding puffball.

At a loss Jurnet retreated, mumbling something about going to find out where Monty had got to. PC Bly, who had been monitoring the encounter with lively interest, approached not without satisfaction that his superior officer had had no greater success with the idiot boy than he himself.

Jurnet ordered: 'Leave him be. I'll find his brother.'

Across the road the air quivered with heat, an oasis in the evening chill. For the first and the last time in its life and death the block of flats looked magnificent, red and gold swirling at every window, the firemen's spouting hoses seeming to perform no other function than that of adding to the spectacle. Just the same, Ted Gorman from the Postlegate station, his yellow coat filthy, his kindly face blackened, took time out to assure the Detective Inspector that they had got on top of it. 'Another half-hour, it'll be guttering out like a spent squib.'

Jurnet, doing his best not to flinch from the good man's transparent signalling that he had not forgotten his earlier attendance at that address, took avoiding action.

'Any idea how it started?'

'Plenty of ideas.' The fireman passed a hand over his face. 'You know, though, how it has to be — leave it to the experts, suspend judgement till the big white chiefs have spoken. You got all your stuff out, I hope.'

'All I wanted.'

'That's all right, then.' The man moved away, bracing his tired shoulders as he went. 'Arson,' he offered, by way of farewell. 'Plain as the nose on your face.'

Jolly Jim Hepton had another word for it.

'Serendipity, Inspector — ' arriving at Jurnet's side with a big smile on his face. ' "The facility of making happy and unexpected discoveries by accident." Remember?'

'How could I forget?' Jurnet faced the man squarely, the view of that unrelentingly jolly mug bringing him no joy. 'I also remember something about your wanting planning permission to rebuild.'

'Meaning, I suppose, to suggest I started this little rave-up?'

'Or paid someone to do it for you.'

'Cra-zee!' The man's good humour was unwavering. 'Some mothers do have 'em! Why on earth should I bother to do such a thing with the place a ruin already? Waste of a good box of matches. All I have to do is wait for the forms to go through.'

Jurnet shook his head.

'Not a ruin, and not all cut and dried. The committee could well decide the place isn't a complete write-off at all. Put it in repair and go on as before — that could easily be their attitude.'

'Who knows? Not for me to contradict a police officer! Water under the bridge now, either way. Like our little arrangement, eh? You won't be expecting someone along with the keys now.'

'No.'

The other nodded his head benignly. 'I have to say, Mr Jurnet, it's a great comfort to me to know your household goods have gone up in smoke. More serendipity! Lovely word — I'd have it put on my tombstone except I wouldn't want Mary to get confused. I've got my plot in the cemetery reserved next to hers, and I can just see her looking across and wondering what on earth I was on about. "Who's this Serena something or other?" I can hear her calling out. "What you been up to, you old devil, once me back's turned?" ' Jolly Jim Hepton broke into a fat gurgle of laughter and turned his eyes upward to the November dark. 'I'll tell you one thing, Inspector. However much you an' City Hall got it in for me, somebody up there loves me.'

Jurnet purposely did not go looking for Monty Bellman. Sooner or later the safe-breaker would be putting in an appearance, seeking his little bit of fun. Why else would he have left Billy marooned in full view, if not to make explicit his own presence in the neighbourhood — to tease, to titillate, to give rise to such questions as: had or had not Monty B. set the block on fire, and if so, why? For cash out of Jolly Jim's pocket, or simply for the fun of destroying the Detective Inspector's possessions as he had already destroyed the Detective Inspector's girl — or was it simply an additional nudge to remind the bloody copper that revenge for Billy did not come cheap?

Sure enough, it wasn't many minutes before the man himself materialized, neat as ever in a belted raincoat with a Paisley cravat, reflections of the flames trapped in the shining toecaps of his snazzy brogues. Only the fronds of hair which were usually lacquered into place over his bald patch had lost their cool, sticking up like spectators anxious not to miss anything that might be going on.

'What you reckon, then?' Bellman greeted the detective with the easy familiarity of an old friend. 'Couple of winos fixing themselves eggs on toast an' got carried away; or dirty work at the crossroads?'

'You tell me.'

'Me!' The peterman spread out his hands, the hands of an artist. 'What do *I* know? All I done is bring Billy his usual walk.

Didn't expect the floor show.'

'You oughtn't to leave the lad alone like that. It's not safe and he's in a mood. I bought him an ice cream and he threw it away.'

'What flavour?'

'Raspberry ripple with a — What's flavour got to do with it?'

'That accounts for it. He's gone right off raspberry ripple. Chocolate mint's the flavour of the month.'

'Then I suggest you go right over and buy him one. He's in quite a state, I can tell you.'

'What you know about Billy,' the other demanded mildly, ' 'cept how to muck him up for life?'

Jurnet, unanswering, kept his eyes on the burning building which, he now saw, was indeed, as Ted Gorman had predicted, slowly running out of steam. Not long before it became a steaming mess of cinders, a bloody bore.

Bellman, on an exaggerated note of disappointment, exclaimed: 'Don't tell me you're not going to pull me in to help with your inquiries! Only came over to let you know as how I was available.'

'We know where to find you if we want you. In the mean time, get young Billy home before he either freezes or blows his top.'

'Don't you tell me what to do with Billy!' Monty Bellman snarled. The next moment, the mocking humour back in place so speedily as to make Jurnet wonder if he wasn't imagining things: 'Cutting down at the nick, are you? Recession affecting you lot like everyone else? An' there was I, looking forward to a nice hot cuppa on a cold night an' a dear little WPC to hold me hand. Still, whatever you say, guv . . .'

One of the fire engines was making preparations to leave, sure sign that the party was over. Across the road, at the sight of his brother on the further kerb, poised to cross, Billy Bellman stopped waving his arms about and set the electric wheelchair in motion. It bumped down the slight incline of the paving stones and into the roadway.

'Wait there, you silly git!' Galvanized into action, Monty Bellman ran out into the road. 'Get back on the pavement, for Christ's sake!'

Unheeding, Billy came steadily on, steering towards his target and only altering the course of the invalid chair to left or to right as the other — realizing too late what his little brother was up to — frantically changed direction.

'What you playing at, Billy?' Monty Bellman screamed. 'Put a sock in it! Get back!'

Nothing doing.

With a pin-point precision which, in different circumstances, would, in one of the boy's impaired abilities, have been a matter for congratulation, Billy struck his brother square on the shins with a force which toppled him unerringly into the path of the departing fire engine. Before the driver could slam on the brakes Monty Bellman was under the front wheels, justice done.

Nobody could say Billy Bellman didn't know how to manage that wheelchair. Within an ace of disaster himself, he turned the chair through a hundred and eighty degrees with the coolness of a Concorde pilot avoiding a near miss, and, straight as a die, made for the pavement from which he had sallied forth, completing a further turn before coming to rest, as before, parked outside the window of the delicatessen.

Leaving others to attend to what was left of the best peterman in the business, Jurnet ran across to the boy. Heartsick, he looked down at the waving arms, the slobbering mouth out of which came a noise to freeze the blood.

It took him a little while to realize that Billy Bellman was laughing.

28

'If you're here to say how upset you are, you can save your breath.' Mrs Bellman stood at her door, barring entry. 'You want to show you're sorry, you can turn yourself round and go get him, bring him back home where he belongs, otherwise don't bloody stand there using up my air.'

Jurnet began: 'I only wanted to let you know, in case you hadn't heard, they're taking Monty off intensive care this morning — '

'Not Monty, yer silly prick! Monty'll be all right — always falls on his feet that one. Billy! They got him shut up in that loony bin, they'll never let him go. Where's them human rights they keep on about? You want to do something useful, you get the kid out an' fetch him home!'

'Not the loony bin,' Jurnet corrected gently, moved less by the woman's pain than by her evident inability to find any outlet for it other than anger. 'The hospital.'

'Oh yeah?' Mrs Bellman responded sardonically. 'An' I'm the Queen of Sheba. Don't give me that. I can remember, not all that long ago either, when they called it the lunatic asylum. Wha's in a name, eh? Won't be long they'll be calling it the sodding Ritz.' She came away from the door on to the narrow path and caught hold of the detective's sleeve with a hand that was like a claw. Tiny, wrinkled and red-eyed, she looked, thought Jurnet, like a vulture deprived of her young. 'Wha's Billy done they have to lug him down there, 'stead of charging him at the station like anyone else with all their marbles?'

Jurnet intervened.

'There's no question of charging Billy with anything — '

'An' why not? In't he good enough fer your lordships?' Mrs Bellman's voice rose to a screech. 'Jest because he's handicapped don't mean he's mental. It's bloody discrimination, tha's what it is, treating him any different from the rest!'

With difficulty Jurnet disengaged the claw and retreated out of range of the strong odour of rum which pervaded Mrs Bellman's particular brand of air. He looked at Billy's mother incredulously.

'You can't be saying you actually want to

see the boy charged with attempted murder!'

'You haven't a clue.' Mrs Bellman calmed down. She joined her skinny hands together and wrung them, a gesture from which Jurnet averted his eyes as being too private for observation.

'You don't bloody begin to understand. Billy's got to have his pride, his self-respect — it's all he's got left, poor bugger. What he done, I allus knew he'd do it, sooner or later. The way Monty went on and on about it all being your fault and he'd have you for it didn't convince anybody — didn't convince Monty neither, which maybe was why he went on sayin' it over an' over, trying to convince himself. He knew bloody well he should never have taken Billy along with him on that job, never mind how much the kid begged to go.

'It didn't convince Billy; that's for sure. He knew who he had to thank for going through that glass roof and who was going to have to pay for it one of these days. Many a time I seen it in his eyes, the way he looked at Monty, his big brother what been the livin' death of him, biding his time. An' now that it's come and it's happened, those clever bastards who think they know everything are saying he's out of his mind, he didn't know what he was doing. Balls!

It's an insult, Mr Jurnet! It in't human. You got to do something about it!'

'I'll do my best,' Jurnet said.

'You and the boy,' said the Superintendent, picking up his gold pen from in front of him, and fondling it as symbolic proof that, despite appearances, law and order still prevailed in the kingdom, 'I don't know which of the two of you is the more out of his mind.' Eyeing his subordinate officer in a way which betokened that, notwithstanding the comment, he had in fact long ago made up his mind on that score: 'One minute of rational thought should be more than enough to convince even you that we can no more bring Billy Bellman to court than we can the Man in the Moon. Even accepting for a moment the preposterous fantasy that the DPP went along with the suggestion, can you imagine what the media'll make of it — just one more instance of police brutality?'

Jurnet persisted, knowing the cause already lost: 'His mother says the boy's sane; that he knew what he was doing and did it deliberately. And I believe her.'

'His mother!' The Superintendent's glower of disapproval yielded to a look of pained resignation. 'Here we go again! How many times do I have to spell out that it isn't the job of the police to get involved in the sub-text, only in what's printed in black and white, visible to the naked eye? Though this, I have to admit, is a new one for the book — being urged to see that an idiot is charged with a serious offence on the ground that it will damage his self-esteem if he's treated as the moron he is, not fit to plead!'

Because — as Jurnet, who reluctantly loved the man, well knew — the Superintendent was an honourable man, that was not, however, quite the end of the matter. Expressionless now, the Superintendent opened the folder which lay on the desk within reach, and extracted a document. 'That said,' he continued, 'I am bound to tell you that the psychiatric report on the boy lends some support to your sentimental maunderings. Having gone on for most of the page about the brain damage which has reduced Bellman to his present state, it nevertheless ends up by concluding that, despite everything — and I quote — "amazingly, to the extent that we are able to make a judgement, there remain unmistakable intimations of a lively intelligence, albeit hedged round and frustrated by the terrible reality of his physical condition." ' The Superintendent raised his head, his patrician features transformed by a smile which bound Jurnet to him anew.

'In the circumstances, don't you agree, the least and the most we can do for him is get him safely home to Mummy.'

The pool, heaven be praised, was sinfully warm. Jurnet, whose attitude to swimming was forever mediated by memories of himself as a skinny kid blue with cold being yelled at by well-larded PE teachers additionally layered in a carapace of sweaters, turned on to his back and floated, serene. Strangely, ever since his flat had gone up in smoke he had felt better about Miriam — or, if not better, better able to cope with her loss — and had decided there must be something intrinsically purgatorial about fire, an ancient ritual which, in appeasing the gods, left one at peace with oneself.

And now one more of the basic things, water. Was water an even more primitive remembering, an unconscious recollection of those blessed months when the unborn child had floated in the amniotic fluid, proof against sorrow?

That night, the night of the fire, he had cried off his date to go swimming with Pnina Benvista. Tonight he had been glad to come. Uncompetitive as he was by nature, no envy had sullied his admiration of the crippled girl in her persona of silver bird, planing down from heights the mere sight of which gave him vertigo; whilst the sheer joy of her gambols in the water seemed to have communicated itself to the very element which slapped him playfully whenever she came near, diving and surfacing, free.

There had been a moment, when he himself had emerged from the dressing room and the Israeli girl had seen for the first time his bare torso with its tally of scars, mementoes of past encounters with persons whose concept of the law differed in vital particulars from his own, that her dark eyes had clouded with a sudden unhappiness.

'What has happened to you? Have you been in an accident?'

'You could call it that.' The accident of making up your mind to be a cop when there was every other trade and profession to choose from. The accident of obstinacy which had kept you true to your commitment even as the record wrote itself redly across your flesh.

'I thought, in England, such things do not happen. Or not often.'

'They don't, as a general rule, and then mostly to policemen. Occupational hazard.' He had smiled down at her in reassurance, wishing she'd get a move on into the water, become a silver bird again instead of the pitiful travesty she was on land. 'No need for you to worry.'

'Who said I worry?' The girl had bristled with outraged pride. Too touchy by half, Jurnet had decided, but excusable in one so handicapped. 'I can take care of myself.' Her eyes, still intent on the other's battle honours, brightened again as she commented rudely: 'You cannot be such a marvellous policeman or you would have learned to dodge.'

'Quite right. I need more practice.'

Diving, swimming, she became another person, out of temper only when they raced the length of the pool and Jurnet let her win and she sensed it.

'If you make allowances for me once more I shall never ask you to come swimming again.'

Jurnet had apologized. They had raced again, and again he had won, but a winning he had had to fight for; a close-run thing that had left him panting and her triumphant at having put up such a good showing.

Afterwards, when they sat at one of the poolside tables drinking coffee, she was still crowing over her near-victory.

Jurnet asked: 'Why does it matter so much to you?'

Pnina Benvista replied: 'Everything matters

to me. No!' Laughing she corrected herself, throwing back her head so that her damp hair fell back from her face, leaving it touchingly young and vulnerable. 'Nothing matters to me except my car.'

They had driven away from the pool, as Pnina Benvista had phrased it, 'in procession'. Herself first, Jurnet following in the Rover under strict orders to note how expertly she drove, with what dedicated attention to lights, pedestrian crossings, to each and every other traffic hazard encountered on the way.

'I know I owe it to you. Uncle Rafi said so. I want to show that your faith in me is justified.'

They drove back to Mrs Levine's, Jurnet suppressing the impulse to surge ahead, get back in the shortest possible time to the flat above the delicatessen to test out whether the serenity of water, as opposed to the purgation of fire, was something that stayed with you, at night in an empty bed.

Outside her landlady's house was a space into which the girl drove her car, to-ing and fro-ing until satisfied that the wheels of the Ford Escort were in perfect alignment with the kerb. She got out, locked up with enormous satisfaction in the doing of it, and stood waiting for Jurnet who had parked a little further along the street.

'Well?' she greeted him. Flushed with her achievement, the face which could be so nearly ugly was for the moment nearly beautiful. 'How did I do?'

Jurnet said truthfully: 'You shouldn't have driven in like that. You ought to have backed in.' Annoyed with himself for having occasioned the instant fading of her beauty, he added: 'Not that I wouldn't have done the same myself, given all that room.'

'You mean it, truly?'

'Truly,' echoed Jurnet, with great firmness.

'Just think! Tomorrow I shall be able to give Mrs Levine a lift. Every morning we will drive to work together.'

'She'll be glad of that.' Jurnet looked up and down the modest little street. 'Not all that many car owners, by the look of it. You shouldn't have much trouble finding a daily parking space.'

'Which I shall take care to back into, even if I am the only car for miles around! Oh — I am so happy!' Pnina Benvista hobbled forward on her crippled legs and flung her arms round the detective, a gauche reaching out which touched him as no smoothly executed manoeuvre could ever have done. 'Thank you! Thank you!'

'I told you — I didn't do anything.'

'I know what I know.' The girl looked up shyly, the beauty for once explicit. 'Would you permit me to kiss you as a thank you for the car? In Israel we kiss each other all the time.' Stumbling towards the end of what she had to say: 'It does not mean anything. That is — it does mean, but not anything serious.'

Jurnet laughed and bent down to the glowing face; careful, however, to proffer a cheek, not lips, to her own. Pnina Benvista seemed perfectly satisfied.

Jurnet said, using a phrase he had got from Miriam, 'Use it in good health.'

Back home above the delicatessen, Jurnet dithered about, making himself a salami sandwich he did not want, and a cup of cocoa he wanted even less. After the salami it tasted even more horrible than usual. He undressed, took a shower although he had already taken one at the pool. Anything to put off the moment of going to bed, of surrender to the demons of the dark.

He fixed his mind grimly on the plus things of the past day. The Israeli girl had got her car — good! Better still, Billy Bellman would soon be home again with his ma. Best of all, in their exchange about the Bellmans, the Superintendent had permitted a rare glimpse to escape of what lay beneath the ritualized hostility of their ceremonial joustings: momentarily lifted the visor of that armour each donned against the admission of their mutual love.

Christ! Jurnet thought, as the warm glow engendered by this last faded, and the remains of the cocoa grew a skin which rendered it disgusting beyond belief; anyone misunderstanding the nature of a relationship he himself only imperfectly understood might think they fancied each other!

Which brought him back again to Miriam and the abyss of loss at the bottom of which he was trapped for eternity like Dante's Judas in the lowest pit of hell.

It came as no surprise that, put to the test, the remembrance of water, of the serenity of swimming, provided no comfort. The telephone woke him up as he was going down for the third time. Disoriented at the interruption, he reached for the receiver, automatically noting the time — 4.15 — as he did so. The voice at the other end — one he could not identify — sounded distraught, mouthing words that were unintelligible, conveying no other message than its desperation.

Jurnet came fully awake.

'Who's calling? Calm down. Speak slowly and begin again from the beginning — '

The voice began again, a mounting hysteria pouring out of the mouthpiece until cut short in midstream by the intervention of a second, a voice blessedly familiar: that of Detective Sergeant Ellers.

'Ben? Jack here. Mrs Levine's a bit upset. We didn't intend getting you up, only she took it on herself — '

'Mrs Levine!' At the name of Pnina Benvista's landlady Jurnet pushed back the bed covers and swung his bare legs down to the floor. More than the chill air of the bedroom was making him shiver. 'What's happened?'

'Take it easy, Ben,' said Jack Ellers, in a voice he should have known better than to use on his mate. 'Nothing to take on about. Everything's under control. Only, so long as you're up, it might be as well if you came over instead of waiting till morning — '

'For Christ's sake!' Jurnet shouted down the phone. 'Will somebody tell me what the hell's going on?'

'Nothing's going on right now. Only, there's been an explosion.'

29

At the top end of Mrs Levine's street Jurnet pulled in to give way to an emerging ambulance. Lights flashing, siren screaming, it disappeared into the night trailing its deadly unease and leaving Jurnet, outwardly cool, inwardly on the brink of desperation. *Not again!*

Further along the street and there was no doubt of it. Like it or not, he was in for a rerun. All the tried and trusted ingredients were in place — fire engines, police officers, people pressing forward for a better view. The only immediate difference he could see from last time was that the spectators — as, given the hour, was to be expected — looked a hastily assembled bunch, anoraks and scarves bundled on over nightgowns and pyjamas, women with their hair in curlers, dogs running around distractedly, barking and bewildered.

So far as Jurnet could tell, peering through

the windscreen of the Rover at all the comings and goings, there was, this time, a good deal less damage to property. That was something, he reassured himself, as if it made a blind bit of difference. So far as he could see, a couple of low garden walls were down, the bricks lying shattered about the pavement, there was some destruction of garden gnomes; not all that many windows broken. A small explosion, its force apparently concentrated on the pile of metallic junk which cluttered the kerbside outside Number 23, Rosedene, Mrs Levine's modest villa, and which had once been Pnina Benvista's new car.

At least, going off in the dead of night with people tucked up safely in their beds, the bomb was unlikely to have harmed anybody. Yet why, in that case, the hurrying ambulance? Miriam could not die twice, that was one doubtful consolation, but what if the Israeli girl, transported with her new plaything, had crept down in the middle of the night to have another go at it, a little drive round the sleeping houses?

Convinced he had hit upon the answer, Jurnet pulled in to the kerb, switched off the engine and sat. Sat. He simply could not take any more.

Sergeant Ellers opened the Rover door, slipped into the passenger seat and touched his superior officer gently on the arm.

'Ben. It's all right. All right.'

Jurnet turned his face towards his friend, not really seeing him.

'Then why the ambulance? What was that all about?'

'Well . . .' His chubby cheeks pale, the other amended his earlier statement. 'Not actually all right, but the girl's OK. She was in bed asleep at the time.'

Thankfulness flooded through Jurnet, followed by instant shame. It was not actually all right.

'Who was it in the ambulance, then?'

'Two kids. A boy and a girl. Seems they'd been to a party and didn't fancy the walk home.'

'What happened to them?'

'The boy's dead. The girl — I don't know. She was breathing, just about. They don't give much for her chances.' Startled as he saw Jurnet's hand move towards the ignition switch: 'Now you're here, Ben, you can't just leave! The Super's here, he knows you've been told. Besides, there's the girl. That's why her landlady got on to you. For some reason she thinks you'll be able to calm her down. The poor kid seems to think it's all her fault for wanting the car in the first place.'

'*Her* fault!' Jurnet set the engine going purposefully. 'You can tell Miss Benvista from me, the less she has to do with me from now on, the healthier for her. Tell her she ought to be thankful, not sorry, those kids copped it. If they hadn't tried to take the car away it would have been there waiting, bomb and all, for her to drive off in, in the morning — her and Mrs Levine and anybody else she felt like offering a lift to. Tell her, just because we went swimming together, somebody must have taken it into their head to think she and I had something going, and they aimed to do to her what they did to Miriam. Tell her I'm poison. Tell her, for Christ's sake, if she knows what's good for her, to keep away from me.'

'OK, if you say so.' His face etched in grim lines which sat incongruously on his inbuilt cheerfulness, the little Welshman got out of the car without further argument. 'I'll tell her.' On the pavement, he spoke through the wound-down window: 'So long as, at the same time, you tell me what to say to the Super.'

The Superintendent's face was dark with anger, the nostrils of the fine-chiselled nose pinched, the lips set in an unforgiving line. Confronted with this forbidding aspect, Jurnet felt neither worse nor better than before. He knew only too well his superior officer's invariable reaction to violent death. He had seen it too many times not to recognize the ill-controlled fury at the waste of a precious life.

In this particular instance, two lives: young, foolish, and perhaps, for those very reasons, all the more precious. Apparently, the names of the two joy-riding kids were already known to the police. A third kid had been found sicking his heart out a few yards along the road, a kid who, more cowardly than virtuous, had hung back from breaking into the car; had said goodnight and set off for home, the taunts of his companions ringing in his ears until a louder noise had overwhelmed them. When Jurnet came into Mrs Levine's kitchen — at the rear of the house and consequently little damaged — this third youngster was still there, looking ashen and old and being fed hot sweet tea, spoonful by spoonful, by Pnina Benvista.

The Israeli girl, purple rings under her eyes, looked little better than her charge. So engrossed was she in her task she barely acknowledged Jurnet's arrival; the merest nod before turning again to the stricken boy.

'Just one more spoon . . . and another . . .'

The Superintendent, on the other hand,

had relaxed a little at the sight of him, even if a mite embarrassed that, once again, the mysteries of his subordinate's private life looked set to spill over into the limelight of police business.

'They must have thought you were staying the night.'

Jurnet shook his head, rejecting alike the statement and its implications.

'This is the first time I've even been inside the house. If they were watching at the pool they'd have seen that I left in my own car.'

'That's the Irish for you.' The Superintendent shrugged his shoulders. 'Staffwork leaving something to be desired.'

'I think they knew what they were doing, whoever they are. I think they knew exactly. I think they saw, last time how . . .' Jurnet fumbled for a viable word, discarding any that came within a mile of encapsulating his continuing agony, '. . . how upset I was about Miriam, and they thought, looks like he's got another girl, let's have another go.'

The Superintendent, his eyes on the crippled girl, her legs, her bony face, inquired austerely: 'And had you?'

'No. Defective staffwork again.'

The Superintendent took a deep breath, as if Jurnet had had him worried for a moment. His mood was improving by the minute.

'We'll leave it to the Anti-Terrorist Branch,' he said, almost jauntily. 'A continuation of the earlier incident. Looks like Semtex again, only difference much less of it than before. Either they're running short or — since, if you're right, the prime object was to harm Miss Benvista, not the surrounding property — they reckoned they could get away with using a good deal less than last time.' He inclined his lean height a little, bringing his face closer to the other's. 'You understand what I'm saying, Ben?'

'I understand. You're telling me to stay clear.'

'Got it in one.'

'At least Monty Bellman's out of the frame, the poor bugger.'

'So far as you're concerned, Bellman and everyone else. I hope I've made that clear. We've been on to London already, the big boys are on their way. What, after all, do we pay them for? By the way, though, and purely as a matter of interest — ' the chattiness gone, the distance between the two of them re-established, unbridgeable — 'have you heard that that Irish boy's mother — what's his, or rather, what's her name? — is here in Angleby, staying with her cousin, your ex-neighbour? Small world, isn't it?'

The Rabbi had the coffee ready when Jurnet arrived, later than the time he had agreed over the telephone. The Rabbi's other visitor was already seated, sipping from one of the delicate cups set out on the lace tablecloth. Steam rose from another cup, cooling while the Rabbi had gone downstairs to let the detective in.

'Rafi you know,' Rabbi Schnellman said. He looked sad but undefeated. 'Troubles,' he pronounced with a sigh which did not preclude a tender indulgence for the unfathomable ways of the Maker of the Universe. 'The world and its troubles.' Making for the kitchen door: 'I fetch you some coffee, then we talk.'

'Not for me, thanks. I've just had some. Sit down and finish yours before it gets cold. I can't stay long.' Jurnet determinedly turned up the corners of his mouth in token that everything was all right, car blown up, two kids dead or dying, all in the day's work, no need to worry. He looked across the table at Rafi Galil, at the features whose prevailing good nature not even that fearsome scar could disguise.

Two good men. What did they want of him?

He knew it must have something to do with Pnina Benvista. 'What do you think?' exclaimed Rafi Galil, his voice resonant with paternal pride. 'After all that happened, she was back in the workroom this morning as if nothing was out of the ordinary. Both of them together, though Mrs Levine, poor soul, was shaking so much she couldn't thread her machine. I called a mini-cab and sent her home. But such spirit!' He shook his mane of white hair in wonder. 'Pnina, though — she looked very pale, you could see it had been a shock — I said to her, "You go home as well, my dear. You too need a rest to get over a bad experience," but would she go?' The man spread out his fingers in humorous bafflement. 'She sat down at her computer and her files and her floppy discs and goodness knows what else she arranges all about her like a toyshop and said she was quite all right, thank you, and she had work to do. What can you do with such a girl?'

Jurnet suggested: 'It was probably the best thing for her, keeping herself occupied — '

'You think?' Rafi Galil finished the last of his coffee, then shook his head doubtfully. The man looked very neat and trim in his dark suit with a camel-hair weskit, formal but not too formal, a business man with a human heart. 'I have been worried before that she is overdoing it — but now!'

Rabbi Schnellman nodded assent. 'The poor girl has been looking very washed out.' Looking at Jurnet: 'Rafi thinks you are the one to persuade her to take a rest.'

'Why me? I've no special influence with her. Besides which, after last night, you must see that the best thing I can do for her just now is keep well away.'

'That is the other thing.' The Israeli opened his eyes wide. 'The danger! As if the poor girl hasn't enough to worry about without that. Which makes it doubly important that you back us up in what we say, the Rabbi and I. You are wrong in saying you have no influence. She knows, quite rightly, that you are a good friend to her and that therefore whatever you recommend will be for her best good.'

'Only because she insists on giving me the credit for getting you to buy her the car. A good buy that turned out to be in every sense of the word!' Jurnet got up to leave. 'I have to go. Even if I did have a word with that young lady she'd most likely tell me to mind my own business and say if she needs a rest she can wait till the weekend like everybody else.'

Rabbi Schnellman put in: 'Rafi doesn't

mean a day or two. He wants her to go back to Israel.'

Jurnet came back to the table.

'The warmth. The sunshine,' Rafi Galil expatiated. 'A climate to put the roses back in her cheeks. Back among old friends.' The man spoke with a pleasing delicacy, anxious not to be misunderstood. 'Back among disabled friends, if you understand me, a place where she is not a solitary cripple on her own in a land where everybody else walks on two good legs.'

Jurnet frowned.

'What about The Courland Collection? It's my understanding she's here because that's what Miriam specifically wanted. Is what you really mean that she isn't pulling her weight?'

'On the contrary!' The other raised his hands, pushing away the very idea. 'I don't know how we will manage without her, except that we must manage if it is a question of her safety and her happiness.'

'While I understand your concerns, I don't think Pnina'll be all that happy to be shipped back to Tel Tzevaim just now, however much safer it is, however brightly the sun's shining. Far as I can make out, she feels she has a sacred responsibility to get the computer on stream, bring the plant really up to date — '

351

'The computer!' Rafi Galil exclaimed indulgently. 'She and Miriam both! Child's toys! We are in the business of knitwear, Mr Jurnet, not computers.'

'Doubt that's the way Pnina sees it.' Jurnet pulled himself up, unsure why he felt impelled to take up the cudgels for a spiky female who, if it came to the crunch, was perfectly capable of taking care of herself. He turned to Rabbi Schnellman. 'What do *you* think, Rabbi? Do *you* think she ought to be made to go?'

'*Made,* no.' The Rabbi looked unhappy. He fiddled in his trouser pocket, produced a bobby pin which he used quite unnecessarily to anchor his *yarmulke* to his bald patch. The accomplishing of this unlikely feat did not appear to raise his spirits notably. 'But go — ' his voice firming with his resolution — 'certainly, if she can be persuaded, while there is still time.'

'None of my business, of course. Only said anything because you asked.' This time Jurnet really was going. 'Just the same . . .' In the doorway he paused, turned towards the Rabbi, uncertain that, in his haste to be gone, he had heard aright. 'What did you mean, while there's still time?'

'Time for her to stop falling too much in love with you.'

30

At Mrs Driscoll's a young man was standing on the crumbling concrete which surrounded the house, painting her downstairs window frames. Only half-done, still their glossy white, catching the fitful sun, already gave a lift to the nondescript facade, encouraged the tired grass of the front garden to grow a little greener.

The young man worked with a smile on his face, as if he enjoyed what he was doing. He was amazingly handsome, black-haired, blue-eyed, slender and straight of build, but with it all the touching diffidence of one who had not yet perceived the power such advantages placed within his grasp.

At the sight of Jurnet pushing open the gate he looked up from his work and said, with the politeness of a well-brought-up child addressing an elder, 'I'm sorry, you just missed Mrs O'Driscoll. She's gone off with the kids to pick the others up from school.'

Since Jurnet had been lurking in a van parked a little further along the street, awaiting Mrs Driscoll's departure (the detective, even in thought, fastidiously observing that lady's expressed preference for dropping the O) he made only a perfunctory pretence of being sorry to have missed her. The Anti-Terrorist bloke who, judging from the pong, had been staked out in the van for days, if not years, had been bored out of his mind and sorry to see the local copper go. He had been glad to impart the information that the Paddy with the paint pot was called Dennis Nelligan; that he had arrived at the house with the woman, and nothing was known against him except that his old man had been shot dead by Loyalists years ago when the son was just a lad.

'With a background like that you can never tell which way they'll go. Some grow up single-minded, lusting for revenge, others get frightened off for life, go to Mass every day, marry and settle down to a kid a year as long as the spunk holds out.'

The lad was now, if records were correct, coming up to his seventeenth birthday, too early to tell which way he'd turn out. A lot would depend on the company he fell in with. As to which — if Jurnet wanted his, the ATB man's personal opinion — the woman, who

354

was quite a looker but, God knew, no chicken, ought to be run in for cradle-snatching.

The front door of the council house opened and Mrs Doran came out. She carried a tray on which was a mug of tea and a plate with some chocolate biscuits on it. She looked at Jurnet with no sign of recognition.

'Mrs O'Driscoll is not at home.'

Crossing the strip of grass between the improvised sand-pit and a detritus of abandoned toys, she set the tray down carefully on an upturned crate. Jurnet gazed at her in some surprise. The ash-blonde hair he remembered as strained back uncompromisingly from the face had been cut short and peroxided to a buttercup yellow. Her skirt was too tight and her sweater too low cut for the time of year and her time of life. Still she looked good in a tarty way, and young too, so long as one stayed at ten paces. In a clinch one would have been bound to realize that the goods on offer were not precisely as advertised, by which time it would probably have been too late to matter anyway.

'Don't leave it to get cold, now,' Mrs Doran admonished. She went close to the young man, rubbed the back of his neck affectionately. 'I hope you take note I've brought you chocolate fingers this time. No more boring old digestives.'

The young man put down his paint and brush. He had blushed bright red. Taking pity, Jurnet said: 'Actually, it was Mrs Doran I wanted to have a word with.'

'I am Mrs Doran,' the woman admitted coldly.

'Oh! Well, Father Culvey, over at St John's, asked me, as I was passing, to call by and inquire about young Terry, when he's expected back. I gather he's in the Father's catechism class or something — you'll know about that — and he needs his book back. Terry didn't turn it in and he's one short.'

The woman frowned.

'As you're here, you'd better come in and I'll have a look around. Maybe Mrs O'Driscoll fetched it over with his other things.' Turning to the young man called Nelligan, she said fondly: 'Give me a yell if you want some more.'

Nose buried in mug, the blush unfading below the long black lashes that framed the blue eyes, very beautiful, the young man mumbled: 'Ta. I will.'

'No more biscuits, though, or you'll be getting fat.' Reluctantly, as if she found it hard to take leave, even for a matter of minutes: 'I'll be back for the tray.'

Indoors, in the cluttered little living-room,

Mrs Doran remarked accusingly: 'You're still limping.'

'Only a little. It's fine really. Thanks to you.' Jurnet found it hard to speak to this woman who looked so different from the one who had tended his wounds. He said as much: 'I scarcely recognized you.'

'That', she returned matter-of-factly, 'is because I've got my toy boy to think of. My cousin Lucy thinks it's shocking. She's going to take it up with that priest you mentioned — what's his name? What do *you* think?'

'I don't, since you ask. All I wonder is why.'

'Why am I doing it, you mean?' Jurnet nodded. Mrs Doran went to the window and looked out to where Dennis Nelligan sat cross-legged on the concrete eating chocolate fingers, licking off the chocolate coating before biting into the underlying biscuit. 'I'll tell you why.' Turning back to the room: 'Because my son sits all day in front of the television, he won't eat, he won't talk. Because Denny Nelligan's father was killed by the Prods and he was brought up over the Border by some cousins who I think are the ones who killed Terry.'

'Killed?'

'That's right, killed. Worse than killed.

357

Unfortunately they left him still breathing. If only I had the guts I'd finish him off myself.' She spoke without emotion. 'Denny's the only one of the family I could get at. School holidays for the last few years he's been coming across the Border to get odd jobs from the summer people. Ever since he was a kid he used to follow Terry about like a dog. When I offered him a trip to England he was over the moon.'

'What's your idea — to pick them off one at a time?'

The woman shrugged her shoulders impatiently. 'You've seen the boy. Can you see any evil in him? No,' she said, not needing a reply, 'I'm as sure as it's possible to be sure he had no hand in it, that he's no idea what kind of men his cousins are. What I'm counting on is that when, as I'm doing at every opportunity, I ask him about his life before we got together, he'll let out something without knowing it, something that will tell me all I need to know. I'm not a butcher, Mr Jurnet, the way most of them are. I have to be certain.'

'If that happens, I can only hope you'll have the sense to share that knowledge with the CID and leave it to them, or the Garda, to take action.'

Mrs Doran looked at the detective with

more kindness than she had shown hitherto.

'You're thinking about that girl of yours, aren't you? It's understandable. I think of her myself, a lot. If she hadn't been killed and you come over to Ireland, Terry would still have his legs in one piece.' Her voice hardening: 'I suppose you know they had to take off one leg above the knee.'

'I hadn't heard. I'm sorry.'

Mrs Doran took another look out of the window. The young Irishman was on the last chocolate finger, eating it in tiny bites to make it last as long as possible. She turned back to Jurnet, searched the detective's face for something, he couldn't think what, any more than, at the end of it, he could have told whether she had found what she was looking for.

'I don't know what it is about you — ' She broke off and began again. 'Do people always tell you the truth?'

'Far from it, I'm sorry to say.'

The woman shook her head, her buttercup curls jiggling.

'You're not doing yourself justice.' She added, offhandedly, as if it hardly needed saying: 'I haven't told you everything.'

'I didn't think you had.' It was Jurnet's turn to look out of the window. 'The boy,' he said.

'The boy,' Mrs Doran repeated. 'At first I hated him, because he was whole and beautiful and my own boy was maimed for life. I wanted to make him suffer for what had happened to Terry. I wanted to make everybody suffer.'

She paused and considered what she had just said.

'No,' she went on then, rejecting it. 'The one I really wanted to suffer was that one who was never there when we — I needed him; the husband who was never there when I needed a man in my bed; the father who was never on hand to protect his son when he needed protecting.' A malicious enjoyment infusing her words: 'So what did I do? I seduced that lovely child out there — to get even with that bastard and to hell with the rest of the world. Oh, I didn't admit it, even to myself. I told myself the only way to get information out of a man was to sleep with him — real Mata Hari stuff! — so I slept with the kid.

'*Slept with him!*' A small laugh of affectionate reminiscence. 'I taught him what it means to sleep with a woman. The only thing I hadn't counted on — ' she finished with a deliberate coarseness, punishing herself — 'was falling for him myself like a ton of bricks.'

Jurnet stayed silent for a little, then said: 'Another car was blown up in the city last night. I thought you might have heard about it.'

'No, I never — ' Her eyes suddenly wild, the woman came towards him, took him by the sleeve. 'He was with me all night, if that's what you want to know. All night long!'

Disengaging the clutching hand not ungently, Jurnet moved a little further away. 'This is an unofficial call. It's the Anti-Terrorist Branch's pigeon, actually. When they come asking, they're the ones to tell.'

'Was — was anyone hurt?'

'Two kids who intended going joy-riding. Teenagers. A girl and a boy. Boy dead, girl critical.'

'Dear God!' the woman whispered.

'Dear God indeed. But the reason I'm here is that, if the two of them hadn't chanced to break into that particular car when they did, the bomb wouldn't have gone off until its rightful owner got in to drive off next morning. A young woman. A young woman I happen to know. One that some of your friends from over the water, with their playful habit of getting the wrong end of the stick, may have got the idea was the new love of my life. If it worked once, why not twice? Teach the bugger a double lesson.'

The young Irishman tapped on the window pane, holding up the tray, white teeth showing in a smile. He was indeed a beautiful man.

Mrs Doran repeated chokingly: 'He was with me all night. All night long!'

—— 31 ——

It was the time of year when people went about complaining there was no afternoon. By the time you'd had a midday bite to eat, the day had had it. Down in the Market Place the first intimations of Christmas were making a tentative appearance, testing the water: collapsed swags of paper chains, tree ornaments with the lids still on the boxes, bright red panties and bras still virginal in cellophane. Mr Marcantonio, his ice cream cart long gone into hibernation, his little monkey face blue with cold, was selling roast chestnuts, the glow of his portable stove the only warm note in the prevailing grey, insufficient to warm his Mediterranean blood.

Jurnet, peering out with a morose pleasure at a scene which accorded so well with his inner dissatisfactions, was seized with a sudden fierce longing for roast chestnuts the way only Mr Marcantonio knew how to do them — cooked right through, the outer

skin artfully burnt to a crisp but, underneath, the flesh golden and mealy. Only some
residual sense of duty, reminder of a distant
time when a copper had seemed a good thing
to be, kept him at his desk and at work
under the fluorescent lights which knew no
season. He stopped looking out of the window
and instantly, to his vague regret, lost the
hunger for roast chestnuts along with the
hunger for everything else. It had been quite
a bonus to want anything.

Jack Ellers came across the room overflowing with an anxious enthusiasm which,
so far as his superior officer was concerned
at any rate, seemed nowadays to dampen
down his natural cheeriness.

'Ben, you haven't forgotten about tonight?
Rosie's expecting you.' Apprised by Jurnet's
expression that the invitation had indeed been
forgotten: 'She's making all your favourites,
boyo — onion soup, boeuf Wellington, crème
brûlée — ' the menu delivered on a note
of rising desperation. 'She even managed to
get some of that Caboc cheese you were so
gone on.'

'Not me, Jack. Miriam.' Jurnet smiled
fondly at his side-kick, the gloom momentarily
lifting. 'Tell Rosie I love her almost as much
as I love her cooking, but she'll have to forgive me. I honestly can't manage tonight.'

'She worries about you, Ben.'

'Tell her there's no need. I'm living over a delicatessen, for Christ's sake!'

'That's what she says. All that manufactured stuff, might as well be silicon chips as French fries, she says, they all come out of the same machine.'

'Don't let Mario hear you say that! Tell her he's looking after me marvellously, everything home-made. Nowhere near up to her standard, of course, but you can tell her yourself how well I'm looking.'

'She knows without being told. Says she caught sight of you out in the street the other day modelling for one of Lowry's matchstick men.'

'Mario sees I have everything I need.'

Jack Ellers shook his head. He took a deep breath; got out what he was evidently under orders to say. 'Rosie says what you need is a girl.'

Jurnet drove home, inwardly raging against friends who could read you like a book. Feelings of guilt and disloyalty stirred up the lees of grief the way, along the gutters, the wind of the Rover's passing stirred up the dead leaves that had escaped the street cleaner's shovel and broom. Waiting at the traffic lights he allowed his thoughts to race out of control, to linger in explicit detail on Mrs Doran instructing her pretty Irish boy in the arts of love. He felt himself breaking out in a sweat of lust and envy.

Maybe he should have taken up Mario's offer of the Italian girl. Italians understood such things. They understood that love was a hoot — which was why, in grand opera, they bellowed love at each other till they fell down on the bed too exhausted to do a damn thing about it. What was the girl's name — Carmela? Sounded sweet and chewy, not good for the teeth but otherwise just what the doctor ordered.

He sure as hell could do with a girl.

Jolly Jim Hepton was waiting for him in the café, spinning out a coffee, the evening paper folded ready so that the picture of Pnina Benvista's wrecked car showed uppermost.

'Serendipity!' he called out, as Jurnet came into the shop. 'Hail Serendipity! What did I tell you?'

Mario came out frowning from behind his counter.

'You want more coffee?' One at whose door Jolly Jim's happiness banged unavailingly, he demanded: 'What this serendipity?'

'For that you must ask the Detective Inspector here — eh, Mr Jurnet? I'll tell you this much — a new brand of pasta it isn't.' Opening the paper to its full extent, the happy man pushed it across the table towards the detective. 'Read it. Wonderful what they put in the papers these days. The girl died this afternoon, had you heard? Two healthy kids instead of a cripple who should've been returned at birth for a refund. The ways of the Lord are serendipitous and no mistake. Not for us to question, you may say, but who can help it?' Brimful of smiles: 'Will you join me in a coffee and a bite, Inspector? If they had a licence here I'd make it champagne. It's a dangerous thing, in case you haven't noticed, being your little bit on the side. Those floozies of yours, they deserve to be toasted in champers, they deserve a medal for bravery. As it is — ' the man raised his empty cup, pretended to drink — 'to serendipity! May its shadow never grow less!'

Mario, not fully understanding the point of the exchange but his face dark with dislike, turned his back on his unwelcome customer and spoke to Jurnet, his voice strongly vibrant.

'I thought, tonight, you must be tired, you would rather eat upstairs. I have a tray ready. Only the coffee is to be added.' Moving back towards the espresso machine: 'In one moment I have it ready.'

'I don't mind — ' Taken aback by this departure from what had become their normal routine, Jurnet began, and stopped. Come to think of it, he did mind having to eat with Jolly Jim for company. 'It's very good of you.'

'Is nothing.' The delicatessen owner re-emerged from behind his counter bearing a large tray, draped over with a small cloth. The outline of a coffee pot could be discerned poking up the material.

'What's this?' Jurnet took the tray, feeling the weight of it. 'Feels like you've given me enough for six.' Balancing the load on one hand, he went to raise the cloth.

Mario imperiously intervened.

'Leave in place, please, till you sit down to eat! It is hot, it will get cold.' He held open the door to the flat, waiting there until Jurnet was half-way up the stairs. Then he called up softly, *'Mangiare bene,'* before returning to the shop and to the table where Jolly Jim Hepton sat folding his paper. 'You want something more?'

'That's all, ta. What do I owe you?'

'One pound eighty.'

'Hey!' The happy bloke looked appreciably

less happy. 'That's a bit steep for a cup of coffee — '

'You not satisfied, you don't come here again.'

The flat was warm, almost welcoming, if any place could have been welcoming to Jurnet, ever again. Mario must have been in, turned the heat up, drawn the curtains, shutting out the ruin across the road. The delicatessen owner had even put a table-cloth on the small dining-table along with what, at a brief glance, looked like a quite unnecessary abundance of cutlery. Jurnet put the tray, still shrouded, down on the table and went through to the bedroom to take off his coat and his shoes, to go through all the habitual gestures of being at home when, as ever nowadays when he was alone with his thoughts, what he wanted to do was scream, wail, hammer the heavens in protest at the desolation which was his life.

He switched on the light and there in his bed, beneath the crucifix, only her head showing above the duvet, was Pnina Benvista, her black hair spread over the pillow, her eyes huge but unafraid. On the bedside table the green eye of the Bingo bear gleamed knowingly.

Somehow, Jurnet did not feel surprised,

he did not feel anything. Without speaking, he took off his coat and jacket and threw them down on a chair, sat down and unlaced his shoes; poked his feet into the moccasins he used as slippers. He went into the bathroom and sluiced his face and hands.

When he came back the girl was sitting up in bed naked, her skin golden in the light. Her slender neck and pointed breasts were very beautiful.

She said: 'They want to send me back to Israel.'

Jurnet said: 'I know.'

She said: 'I love you. Do you know that too?'

'I didn't know. I'm sorry.'

'Don't be sorry,' she admonished. 'I personally am very happy about it.' She settled the duvet about her waist. 'This flat', she remarked, as if it explained her unclothed condition, 'is lovely and warm.' Going on to the next thing: 'There are two reasons why I don't want to go back to Tel Tzevaim. The first is I'm sure Miriam wouldn't have wanted it and the second is because if I go back I shall probably never see you again.'

When Jurnet vouchsafed no comment on either observation she added kindly: 'Don't think you have to be sorry that you don't love me back. I have lived long enough to know that I am not lovable. Do you remember the night when I first came to Angleby, the night we slept together, very proper with all our clothes on? I knew then, as early as that, that I loved you but that you had Miriam — even if she was dead you still had her — and could never love anybody else.'

His throat dry, Jurnet contradicted, louder than he had intended, 'I don't still have her. I don't have anybody.'

'You could always have me,' Pnina Benvista pointed out with an air of sweet reasonableness. 'Not to love — I quite understand that is not possible — but to be loved by. To be loved by anybody, that must be better than nothing.' She added, in reassurance: 'I am not a virgin, in case that is what is bothering you. Don't look surprised — it is not very complimentary. At Tel Tzevaim we had a young man, an airman who had crashed and his body was all twisted. He was going to die. He was going to die, he said, and he had never had a woman and it was not fair. If he had been an Arab he could have waited for the houris Mohammed promises in heaven to those who believe in him, but he was a Jew and Jews do not know what God has in store, or if He has anything at all.

'And so I slept with the airman, many

times, until he got too ill to worry about such things and he died, very quietly and sure that whatever God had in store for him was good.' She leaned forward a little, smiling. Her breasts were very beautiful. 'It was not an easy sleeping together, as you can understand. For him to move at all was difficult and, as for me, I had to be very gentle.'

The dark eyes regarded Jurnet with a tender calm.

'I want you to know that what I did, I did not do out of pity. I enjoyed it very much, for my own sake as well as his. Chiefly, I learned from the experience that I am not frigid, which is a good thing to know. Because of that experience I can be sure that if you will sleep with me I shall respond with love and passion, which must, I think, be better for your enjoyment and certainly more healthy than going with a prostitute — '

Her breasts were very beautiful. Jurnet could not stand the sight of them.

'What are you saying?' he threw at her harshly. 'There's supper on the table. It'll be getting cold.' Beside himself with desire and self-loathing, he grabbed at the duvet and flung it to the floor. 'For Christ's sake get up, make yourself decent and come and eat!'

The girl lay back in the bed unmoving,

looking at him with eyes still unafraid: two women in one, the loveliness above the waist and, below, the distorted hip, the legs of a cripple. Inside Jurnet's head the anger burst like a bubble, its place taken by an overwhelming admiration for a courage and acceptance of life which put his own self-pitying retreat from it to shame.

He bent over the girl and kissed her gently, not on the lips nor the breasts but on the bony protuberance which had made Pnina Benvista the miracle she was. He began to undress, not raddled with lust but calmly, without guilt.

'Not out of pity?' she demanded, as he came into the bed, his body between her and the light.

'Not out of pity.'

'Good.'

32

The Superintendent could not have been more co-operative. The three newcomers from the Anti-Terrorist Branch were welcomed with the deference due to experts in the field; seated comfortably, regaled with coffee whose aroma advertised that it had not come out of the machine on the landing. It took someone like Jurnet, who both loved and hated the man, to read the signs indecipherable to outsiders: the subtle tightening at the corners of the mouth, the tinge of sardonic mirth which underlay the voicing of sentiments entirely proper to the occasion. Every now and again, when the tension became all but impossible to contain, his subordinate was unsurprised to see the elegant, manicured hands reaching out to touch the gold pen displayed on the desk in front of him, and moving the bauble, his personal mace, an inch or two, this way or that.

As to the visitors, well used to coming

up against the blank wall of local pride, they couldn't have been happier. They were, all three of them, dark-visaged men with blue eyes, broad-shouldered above a comfortable stockiness — Irishmen all, one would have sworn, except that not one of them spoke with an Irish accent. Perhaps, however, they could put one on when circumstances made it desirable, just as maybe, by the same token, the IRA, when out and about on business, could move over to Cockney or Scouse at the drop of a bomb.

Each the mirror image of the other, could either be trusted? Was it possible, Jurnet wondered, but expecting no enlightenment, to confront absolute evil without some of it rubbing off on the confronter?

One thing nearer home Jurnet noticed during his silent observation of the conference: he himself was actually *seeing* the new arrivals, the outlines precise, the detail explicit, as opposed to the way, ever since Miriam's death, his eyes had tended to slide off their objective — the art of taking stock, like everything else in the greyness of mourning, too much bloody fag. Whatever else Pnina Benvista had or had not done for him, she had returned him to a world of three dimensions.

Trying conscientiously, among the give and

take of matters of presumed moment, not to think of the Israeli girl, he thought about her all the more. He wished she had felt able to stay longer in the flat over the delicatessen. It would have been good to feel that indomitable body nestled against his own through the entire night, but if she wasn't back by midnight Mrs Levine, as she had rightly pointed out, would be running to the police to find out what had happened to her lodger. As it was, he had got out the Rover again, driven her home, and parted from her with the kind of kiss he might have given a maiden aunt.

'Don't worry!' The girl had chided him in parting, patting his face as she might have patted that of a baby or a pet dog. 'You worry too much!'

One of the Anti-Terrorists was talking about Dennis Nelligan.

'Youngest of the family. Nothing on record so far,' he admitted. 'But one of that devil's brood — he's bound to be up to something.'

Painting Mrs Driscoll's windows, Jurnet thought, but didn't say so. Bringing Mrs Doran a little joy.

'In that case,' the Superintendent suggested with exquisite courtesy, 'might it not be a good idea to take him in and send him packing, back to where he came from? Nip the infernal enterprise, whatever it may be, in the bud?'

The other, all condescension to the backwoods boys in the sticks, shook his head. 'He'll have had his instructions. We need to wait and see who he teams up with. That way, with luck, we'll collar the whole shoot.'

'Even at the risk of leaving it too late?'

The man returned sententiously: 'One of the risks we have to take, sir.'

Jurnet wanted to puke. One of the risks *who* had to take?

He said, less good at dissembling than his superior officer: 'Those children who blew themselves up here a few days ago — have you spoken to their parents yet?'

'Not our pigeon, Inspector.' The Anti-Terrorist man looked quite amused at the implication it might be. 'We've had the report on the explosive, though. I can let you have a copy. Less than half the Semtex used in your earlier incident. Hardly enough, one would have thought, to kill one, let alone two.' On a note of severity, dissatisfaction with poor workmanship: 'That's part of the trouble with the IRA — though the Loyalists aren't much better, come to that. You never know where you are with either of 'em . . .' Addressing himself to Jurnet in particular: 'That attempt to get you . . . Enough explosive to make a whole block of flats un-inhabitable, all to blow up a single copper — incredible! Not to mention putting paid to his own home in the course of it.'

Jurnet said in his most neutral voice: '*And* I'm still here.'

'My point exactly! Hitting the wrong target after all that preparation! That's exactly the kind of balls-up we're coming up against, time after time.' With a jolly smile: 'Not that, in the circumstances, you'll be the one to complain.'

The Superintendent, after a swift glance at his subordinate, intervened with: 'You've definitely fixed on O'Driscoll then, have you?'

The Anti-Terrorist sucked in his cheeks judicially. 'Let's just say, pity you let him go when you had him in your hands. But there — we all make mistakes some time, don't we?'

The Superintendent put his hand on his gold pen: kept it there.

'Don't take it to heart,' the Anti-Terrorist advised kindly. 'The bastard's back in the Republic, we know that, not gone to ground in some banana republic. We're keeping tabs on him. One way or another, we'll get him sooner or later.' This time he laughed out-right, the rumbling belly laugh of a man

378

well pleased with the world. 'It's a bloody game, sir, isn't it? What a bloody game!'

After the visitors had gone and he was safely back in his own quarters, Jurnet dialled The Courland Collection. Waiting for the phone to be picked up he almost returned his own receiver to its cradle. He had no idea what to say to Pnina Benvista.

He needed to hear her voice.

The operator at the other end of the line said: 'I'm sorry. Miss Benvista is out of town today.'

Why hadn't she told him, even if it was none of his bloody business? He'd be hanged if he'd ask where she was, what time she would be back.

He asked: 'Where has she gone? What time will she be back?'

The operator said: 'She's gone up to London, to the show at Earls Court. I'm sorry, I can't say when she'll be back. Probably late.' She finished, envy in her voice: 'She said she might try to get in a bit of shopping, after. She said it was late night opening at Harrods.'

'You don't happen to know what train she's catching?'

'She didn't go by train. She took the bus. Ever so much cheaper and practically as quick now the bypass is open.'

'You don't happen to know what time bus either?'

'Haven't a clue.' The operator's tone had taken on a touch of malice. Harrods plus an eager boyfriend was too much. 'Bound to be late, though. With her figure she'll be lucky to find anything to fit!'

Jurnet put down the phone between disappointment and relief at having been spared embarrassment. Jack Ellers and Sid Hale were out on a new case, one to whose paper ramifications he now settled down with model concentration. A lady bountiful, mellowing in a Palladian mansion stuffed to the rafters with pictures and silver, had been forcibly divested not only of her objects of virtue but of virtue of a more intrinsic kind into the bargain — indeed there were indications that the horrific rape had been the prime object of the exercise, not an optional extra. The lady was a Lady with a capital L and there were intriguing possibilities: a Sans-Culotte rapist out to wreak vengeance on the *aristos,* or a criminal psycho-snob turned on by a title?

Jurnet closed the file, its contents half-read. Bugger the Lady, with or without the capital letter. He wished Pnina Benvista had been there to answer his call.

She would be coming back to Angleby on the bus. Jurnet weighed up the pros and cons of hanging round the bus terminal on the chance of running into her. At the very least he would be able, tired as she was bound to be after her day in town, to give her a lift back to her lodgings. Alternately, assuming she approved, he might bring her back to the flat above the delicatessen. Mario would be pleased.

Not only Mario.

He remembered the way, in bed, the Israeli girl's deformed hip had thrust itself into his side, not disagreeably: more like a calf nuzzling its mother. The recollection made him feel maternal, paternal. He doodled a suckling calf on his desk pad; tore the sheet out and threw it, crumpled up, into the waste-paper basket.

After that, he spent some time wondering how late Harrods stayed open, and if it would be worth while ringing up to find out. He also wondered how frequently the buses ran, taking advantage of the new bypass. The bypass struck a chord somewhere, vaguely. He thought some more about Miriam, about Miriam and Pnina Benvista both. Chalk and cheese. One nothing to do with the other.

Jurnet sat and drowsed, not exactly asleep, not exactly awake either, his thoughts swirling randomly like the pieces in a shaken kaleidoscope, until, without warning, they settled in a new pattern.

Abruptly he straightened up in his chair, awake and appalled at what had suddenly been revealed to him. Appalled at his past inability to make sense of what had happened, his failure to understand.

Christ!

The last bus pulled into the yard and Pnina Benvista was not on it. Jurnet waited until the last passenger had moved off into the darkness beyond the parking bay and the driver climbed tiredly down from the driving seat *en route* to the staff canteen.

No, the man replied to Jurnet's query, he had not taken on any disabled young woman at Victoria, nor anywhere else along the way. He confirmed that no further bus would be coming in from London before morning. Clasping his clipboard to his chest he had turned thankfully towards the lights beckoning in the distance, towards baked beans and a mug of cocoa, only — moved by the fellowship of the night and something in his inquirer's face — to turn back again.

'Disabled, you say? Maybe she got to Victoria too late. We start on the minute and you'd be surprised how many of that kind miscalculate how long it's going to take them through bloody London traffic and the crowds. Not used to it, y' see. Tonight alone we had three reserved seats not taken up. Any one o' them could be hers — it happens all the time. Phone up the terminal, why don't yer?' he ended kindly. 'They got a woman there takes care of handicaps and lost kids.'

'Thanks.'

Jurnet did not phone up Victoria. He felt instinctively that Pnina Benvista was not a girl to miss a bus under any circumstances; that even to make a phone call would be an indirect insult. Chilled by the November cold, he got back into the Rover: sat briefly pondering his options before once more setting the car in motion.

Ordinarily, Jurnet loved Angleby best of all by night, even though, as a copper, he knew too much about the place not to take the sacramental quietude of the city centre under the stars with a sacramental pinch of salt. Tonight, pierced through with anxieties, he found its emptiness full of threat, the full moon flooding the winding streets with torrents of light and shadow that washed against the medieval ramparts and the windows of Boots the Chemist with impartial menace.

The river, when he reached it, flowed black and silver. Quiet enshrouded the quayside like a disaster waiting to happen until, sure enough, as he looked for somewhere to park, the door to the building housing Miriam's flat suddenly burst open and a slab of light fell across the tarmac as two figures projected themselves across the road towards the low wall which edged the strip of green fringing the river bank. Half-way across the road the leading figure twisted round and, with an insulting ease, pushed its pursuer to the ground, itself barely losing a step in the doing of it.

By the time Jurnet had stopped the car, got out and run towards Pnina Benvista, the crippled girl had regained her feet and renewed the pursuit, limping on to the grass verge and heaving herself painfully over the low wall and into the river.

Jurnet, following, nearly stumbled over the shoes she had kicked off before diving in. In front of him the river flowed moonlit and full, each separate ripple touched with a silver scale, the stream turned into some fantastic marine creature rolling with calm certainty down to the distant sea.

In the seconds it took the detective to get rid of his own shoes, fling off his anorak, he could see no sign of the two he was looking for; but once in the river itself, its cold enfolding him in a baleful embrace, he shook the wet and the moonlight out of his eyes and struck out for the two figures struggling in the water.

If Pnina had gone to the rescue of the man who had run away from her it was quickly evident that the man did not choose to be rescued. Worse: the arms that foiled all her attempts at lifesaving did not thresh the surface in the panic of a drowning man. Instead, they moved in and out of the water with deadly intent: a double drowning, not only of himself, but of the crippled girl equally.

Even so, mustering all her remaining strength, Pnina Benvista hung on grimly, panting for air whenever she managed to evade the writhing tentacles dragging her down. The river was flowing strongly, sweeping the struggling pair downstream, the man so determinedly bent on a double destruction smiling ever more widely, the scar across his cheek puckered silver.

Jurnet shouted: 'Hold on, Pnina! I'm coming!'

That she heard him was unlikely. The river had taken over, singing its own song, going its own uncaring way as the Israeli girl fought for her life against a killer bent on depriving her for ever of the light. As Jurnet caught up at last and Rafi Galil, still smiling, was forced to let his captive go, the girl, in the unbelieving ecstasy of being free, rose half out of the water before gasping, 'Don't let him get away!'

Down below the moonlight Jurnet dived, into the blackness of the deep river. He felt its power, felt himself powerless to counteract it; surrendered to its cold and its strangeness. It was only by fate or blind chance that, near the limit of his endurance, his groping hands found a body, his fingers attached themselves to a waistband as he thrust madly for the air and the moon. Even so the man, in love with death, made a last effort to pull away.

Jurnet disengaged one hand. Using all his remaining strength he hit Rafi Galil on the jaw.

33

'Rafi Galil IRA! What do you think of that for a title, Inspector? Only the accent is a little wrong, eh? No begorrahs, certainly no Hail Marys. You cannot know how many times I have smothered my laughter, turned it into a cough, buried my face in my handkerchief, at all the talk I hear about bloody Irishmen, the harm they do, the bombs, the dead people. All the searchings, the security checks, your own chasings about the bogs of Ireland.

'And all for nothing!

'If I may say so, Inspector, you do the IRA less than justice. They too have their place in the scheme of things. A pity, I often think, that we do not have them in Erez Yisroel to vary the eternal conflict of Jew and Arab. How useful it would be to have such a perfect scapegoat ready to hand, recipient of blame from either side! Here in England, if only they had the sense, your policemen, so far from hunting them, should put them on the payroll as perfect alibis.

'I verily believe that if, in this country of yours, a baby falls out of his cot and breaks his head on the floor, you say IRA automatically. And if a policeman's car is primed with Semtex to go off when a foot is pressed down on the accelerator, how can it be anyone else but the IRA which is responsible?

'When I think of Miriam, I must confess, I sometimes have to laugh outright. I can't help it. Can you imagine how angry that darling girl, so hot for women's rights and female equality in all things, would be to know that, so far as I can make out, never once, in all your conferences and investigations, did it occur to anyone in the police to wonder if the real target of the bomb that blew up your car might not be the policeman after all but the woman?

'I laugh, Inspector, but I also cry. I loved Miriam. I did not want her dead.

'I see your eyebrows come together in disbelief. Patience, my friend.

'It is a long story, a travelogue, as you might say, with stops at places like Auschwitz and Buchenwald, and death, death, death punctuating the journey — the deaths of golden people who did not deserve to die.

I have spoken of this to you before, I think. I do not wish to repeat myself, only to say the important thing, which is that I am a child of the Holocaust. I am a survivor, a word whose meaning only another survivor can wholly understand.

'If, just the same, I try to convey to you something of what that word means, understand, please, that it is not because I seek to justify my killing of Miriam, but simply to make it clear that no justification is called for. To have survived what I survived in those days — to have lived like a beast, killed like a beast, to have put aside every instinct that marks the human race as human in the overriding interest of staying alive — is to have discharged once and for all any obligation I may once have held to that terrible God who put us on Earth in the first place.

'You may even say that, despite everything, I was not wronged by this horrific Creator of ours: I was blessed. By my sufferings I have earned my freedom from all the petty taboos and hypocritical evasions with which society seeks to hedge the unregenerate passions at its core. Henceforth, the world existed for me and for me alone, the survivor.

'How romantic it sounds, doesn't it?

'So what did Rafi Galil do with this boundless freedom which he had won by his own heroic efforts? What Everests did he scale, what kingdoms conquer?

'Now, Inspector, it is your turn to laugh. He went on living, this splendid survivor, one day after the other, sometimes honestly, more often dishonestly, sometimes up, more often down, until the lovely Miriam came to Israel, set up her workshop at Tel Tzevaim, and out of the goodness of her heart gave her poor old relative who had suffered such dreadful things the job of Financial Director of The Courland Collection.

'So! I had security, good wages, the respect that goes with a title on the office door: but I was a survivor, that is the thing to hold on to. My life was tuned to a different key from that of others who had never had to hang by their fingertips over the abyss. Inevitably, sooner rather than later, I began to dip my fingers in the till, small sums at first I could easily cover up, larger amounts as I grew bolder. Let me say that I did not steal from the company with any particular purpose in mind. I did not take drugs, nor keep expensive mistresses. At this stage of the game I really could not tell you what I did with all the money I stole. Gambled a little, gave a lot of it away, making myself doubly loved by all who came into contact with me. Good old Uncle Rafi! Such a soft touch!

'Only then, alas, like the rumblings of fate, along came the computers, those infernal machines whose mechanical guts had never been programmed to take on board the agony of six million dead, or the peculiar compulsions of those who have escaped the gas chambers. Did Miriam begin to suspect that I was fiddling the books, or did she not? I honestly don't know, only that she announced one day that, moving with the times, we were going to be computerized. The plan was for the system to be installed at the English headquarters initially, and then to be linked up with Tel Tzevaim. Pnina Benvista, that clever little cripple who understood all about these new monsters, would go from Israel to Angleby and stay there as long as it took to oversee the change-over.

'One thing I have to say. Whether Miriam had found me out or not, she continued to treat me with the same loving courtesy as ever. Still, I felt in my bones that it was only a matter of time before my little adventures were laid bare for all to see. And it was only then, funnily enough, with discovery staring me in the face, that I suddenly awoke to how much I stood to lose. Call it vanity if you like, I had grown into my role of dear old Uncle Rafi, the sage who had gone through the crucible of suffering and emerged purged and perfected. Besides, I wasn't getting any younger. Was I really, in my old age, going to let that unspeakable God who had tumbled me into the depths of hell in the first place, prepare an even deeper pit for me to fall into?

'You are a fair man, Mr Jurnet. You will understand that I could not stay still and let that happen.

'When Miriam insisted I should take a week or two off from work, spend it in London, her mother was feeling depressed and would welcome my cheery company, I did not need to be told that something was in the air. It had to be that she wanted to get me out of the way whilst an independent firm of auditors went over the accounts — with the regular ones I had long ago made an accommodation, to our mutual advantage. However, I of course accepted the suggestion with a proper gratitude and left for London within a day or so. If Miriam needed time to make her preparations, so did I.

'Over the years — I wonder whether you policemen have any inkling — we survivors have formed our own freemasonry, our own network of mutual help. You would be surprised how easy it is for someone like me to procure a few kilos of Semtex if you know where to go. So when, after I'd been in London no more than a week, Miriam telephoned me at her mother's house to say she was planning to come up to town from Angleby next day, I was already, literally, well primed. She needed to speak to me, she said. It was important. She still did not say what it was about, but everything — the sadness of her voice especially — proclaimed that she had found me out, the denouement was at hand.

'Worst of all, from my point of view, she informed me that Pnina Benvista would be arriving at Heathrow that same afternoon. So far, she said, letting the cat well and truly out of the bag, she had said nothing to the crippled girl, but once she arrived she would, for the sake of all the people at Tel Tzevaim, be forced to put her in the picture as to what had been going on.

'*What was going on?* Naturally I expressed complete ignorance. Miriam's voice grew even sadder. "Oh dear!" she said. Nothing more but Oh dear.

'A little later in the day she telephoned again, very put out, to say that something was the matter with her car, the wrong part had been sent from the makers, and consequently she would have to come up to town by train. We rearranged our appointment accordingly. She gave me the train times, emphasizing that I must be at our rendezvous — a café near Marble Arch — punctually, so that she could still get to Heathrow in good time to meet Pnina. She mentioned, quite by the way, that, as her car was out of action, she would get you, Mr Jurnet, to run her to the station.

'Put like that, my dear sir, what choice did I have?

'That evening I took the Semtex and drove down to Angleby and back — a tiring journey each way what with the dark, the autumn mists, the hold-ups where they were making the bypass, besides which I was upset. Believe me, Mr Jurnet, it takes a lot to make a survivor give way to tears, yet all the way to Angleby my cheeks were wet with them. If there had been any other way out I would have taken it.

'At least, I consoled myself, Miriam would not be alone at that supreme moment which, as you must by now understand, was unavoidable. I had to stop her mouth for ever before she could let Pnina, and therefore the whole world, know what manner of man I was.

'I knew with that inner certainty which is part of the working equipment of survivors that your car as on the last time I had been in Angleby, would be parked outside your block of flats, easily available to my small readjustments. And so it proved. To put the Semtex in place was a matter of minutes.

'I felt no guilt. What better end could one wish for a woman passionately in love than to depart this life in a flash, without pain, in company with her lover? For that matter, what better end could you, Inspector, have wished for yourself? Can you honestly say it has been better to live on, as you have been condemned to live on, endlessly grieving?

'How, above all, could you have been so crass as to sleep late that morning of all mornings — so late that Miriam had to die alone, leaving you in bed?

'It was inexcusable.

'Inexcusable, equally, that you presently took up with Pnina — or rather, that she took up with you. It was no mystery to see the light of love which came into her eyes when she looked at you. In other circumstances I would have said *charming!* Such kindness to a poor cripple! Such consolation for a bereft lover! Only now I had to worry, what secrets is that cripple prying out of that accursed computer whilst you, Inspector, were away chasing leprechauns?

'You may say I became a little paranoid. I admit it. It was so lovely to be at last in sole charge of The Courland Collection, no one to give me orders, to tolerate me with good-humoured exasperation, no one to value me at less than I valued myself. Didn't you yourself put me down as a sweet-natured old gentleman when you suggested that the girl should have a car of her own and I gave in with barely a demur?

'Who could have expected such an act of kindness to have such an unforeseen outcome? Certainly not I, the Semtex in place ready for Pnina to drive away in the morning, before those two foolish children tried to steal a ride and it was all to do again.

'I think, looking back, that it was that second explosion which was the turning point, the moment when God decided once again to take an interest in my plans. When Pnina announced her intention of going up to London for the Earls Court fair I recognized the warning for what it was. There was nothing in the exhibition to take our interest. Our merchandise was in a totally different category from what was on show there, and besides, the poor girl was not a good liar. She blushed as she spoke, she twisted those terrible legs of hers into knots.

'Waiting in Miriam's flat by the river for her return — for I knew she would come, I had no doubt of it — I reviewed my options. Florida was what of late I had been planning for myself, a slow winding down of the business which everybody knew I had done my best to save, nobody could have done more — and then palm trees and sunshine, visits to Disneyland, a child again, preferably with one of those American widows on my arm, blue-rinsed and rich as Croesus. Such pleasures were surely worth the elimination of one of nature's mistakes. Indeed you could say I was doing the poor girl an act of kindness.

'Let me tell you how Pnina Benvista must have spent her day in town. She would have found her way to two addresses which her computer had spewed out for her — one just off the City Road, the other on an industrial estate in the wilds of Acton. According to our records, the City Road people, V.V. Yarns, were suppliers of substantial quantities of yarn to Tel Tzevaim, the Acton firm, Olgar Importers, one of the company's best customers for finished goods.

'*According to our records.* What the girl would in fact have found, with some difficulty and even more astonishment once she had got there, was that City Road was a mere accommodation address, whilst out at Acton, Olgar Importers consisted of a large shed and a concrete standing for a couple of lorries.

'Not that the two firms did not exist, far from it. On the contrary, each could be said to exist twice over — once in the accounts of The Courland Collection, once in the little book in which I noted my own private transactions. Each did substantial business with Tel Tzevaim, everything above board except that the invoices relating to these matters seldom, if ever, coincided with the reality of the merchandise received or delivered.

'How did I manage it, you ask? The answer is, with an almost shaming simplicity. One could, if only for one's self-respect, have wished for more challenge — but there! I am not complaining. There are always, if you know where to look for them, corrupt people waiting to be used, and foolish ones as well — for I am afraid, my dear Inspector, that for all her beauty and her generosity of spirit, one thing your Miriam was not: she was not a business woman. She did not have the first idea! It was like depriving a baby of its milk. She gave me the title of Financial Director out of the goodness of her heart, never for a moment understanding that mine was the intelligence which sent the company's money moving — chiefly, I have to say, in my direction.

'Do you remember when you happened to mention a personal file of hers still in your flat? I asked you about it, I should have kept my mouth shut. As a result, to be on the safe side, I decided I must break in and take a look at it myself, the evening before you were due to return there to collect the rest of your possessions. I need not have troubled. Your Miriam, bless her, hadn't a clue, as they say. Virtually every reference to me in her file remarked on my childish inability to add two and two together, how I had no idea how a business works. I could not decide, in the circumstances, whether to take what she said as an insult or a compliment!

'Childish, I thought. Childish she calls me — right! And childishly then (as also to cover my tracks) before leaving I set your whole block of flats on fire and enjoyed its burning enormously. Childishly.

'To be fair to Miriam, though, in this time of an end to deception, it could be that she knew me better than I knew myself. Childish is what I am, what I have always been — despite the wrinkles, never grown up to a man. And sooner or later, as always happens, a child tires of its games. Time to put the pieces away. Waiting for Pnina to arrive back from London I found myself tired of the whole business, especially when I considered what I would be forced to do to the girl in view of the knowledge she would be bringing back with her.

'Despite its obvious necessity I found myself with little stomach for the task. I felt, illogical though it might be, that her earlier escape from death had earned her a reprieve. Besides which, I discovered in myself for the first time that, even with its rich old women and its Mickey Mouses, I was not really all that keen to go to Florida. Without realizing it, I had grown used to the damps and dews of Norfolk, its mighty skies and the cold wind that, looking out of the window as I waited, I could see riffling the waters of the river.

'If you know your Bible, Mr Jurnet, as you probably do, studying as you are to become a Jew, you will know that in the beginning the earth was without form and void, and darkness was upon the face of the deep. The Bible certainly does not say that, on that first day of creation, there were street lamps alight and, every now and again, a car passing. And yet, as I stood looking out at the road waiting for the girl to come, it seemed to me that the spirit of God moved

400

on the face of the waters as in the beginning of things.

'Well, as you know, she came, the crippled Pnina. The bell rang and I went down to answer it. I opened the street door and there she was, pale and twisted, her eyes burning. But if you think I have some dramatic confrontation to report, Inspector, I have to disappoint you. Nothing was said, not a word. There was no need: only the cold wind on my face through the open door and, across the road, summoning me, the spirit of God moving on the face of the waters.

'I doubt, Mr Jurnet, that you, who have never been a survivor, will be able to enter into the relief I felt at that moment when we two stood face to face in the hallway: no more secrets, instead a great peace, the sense of time as a burden slipping thankfully from one's shoulders. How, time's slave, had I previously been deluded, imagining myself free! Almost I could hear Him, the Master of the Universe, splitting His sides laughing.

'I pushed the girl aside and ran towards the river and that laughter just out of earshot. When she followed after me I turned and knocked the little fool to the ground, only she picked herself up and persisted in the pursuit.

'She followed me across the road and the

grass and over the wall, scrambling over it in her clumsy way. And when at last I was in the water she still would not let me alone. Sinking into its depths I opened my mouth and my eyes wide, allowing the spirit of God to penetrate my entire being — a moment of supreme joy if only I had been left to enjoy it undisturbed. Instead, the girl butted me like some tormenting fish, trying to drag me back to the surface until, in self-defence, I was forced to take her down with me to the quiet below. I had no alternative.

'Did you finally appear from nowhere, Inspector, like the Fifth Cavalry in the movies? Did I finally let her go? I don't remember. They tell me you knocked me unconscious and so saved her life. If that is how it happened I wish you had not, in the process, found it necessary to save mine also. I had not thought you could be so cruel.

'Perhaps you were paying me out for killing your Miriam. If so, I suppose I must not complain. But honestly, my dear friend — yes, I dare to call you by that name in spite of everything — are you any happier for knowing at last how and why she died, and that, in place of the fairy stories, there is nothing left you but to face that ultimate lie, the truth?'

34

Jurnet sneezed. The Superintendent frowned and touched his gold pen, his talisman against evil. Ill-temper distorting his fine-etched features, he observed tartly: 'A pity you sat about in those wet clothes.'

'Yes, sir.'

'A cold night,' the other conceded, disarmed, as always, by agreement, 'and a very wet river. Still, at least you came out of it better than Galil. Pneumonia. Just as well you managed to get his statement first. They still don't know if he's going to pull through.'

Deeply troubled, Jurnet said: 'He seemed perfectly OK at the time — and then, a sudden collapse. Almost as if he'd organized it that way.'

'He didn't take anything, if that's what you're hinting.' The Superintendent fiddled with the report on the desk in front of him. 'Absolutely no question of that.'

'I didn't mean . . .' Jurnet fell silent,

unsure of what he did mean.

'Apparently the girl's all right, that's something. No ill effects at all. Strange the way the halt and the lame have unsuspected strengths hidden away for an emergency.' When his subordinate had no comment to make on this sharp piece of observation on an alien species, even had the gall to sneeze again without apology, the Superintendent — it was an old ploy to put the other in the wrong — blossomed in all his charm.

'I still haven't figured out how you managed to turn up in the nick of time.'

'It was something Galil said when we first met, except that it didn't register at the time.'

'What didn't register?'

'The bypass. He'd mentioned that when he drove Mrs Courland down to Angleby after the news of Miriam's death came through he was relieved to find the bypass open. There'd been none of the previous hold-ups, that was the gist of what he said. But Miriam died on the very day that the bypass was opened, so how was he, a stranger from a foreign country, in a position to know anything about prior conditions one way or another, unless he had in fact already travelled over that road? Once you thought about it — as I certainly ought to have thought before

404

I started chasing Irish moonbeams — there could only be one answer. He'd been that way before.'

'Yes.' After an interval the Superintendent added gently, 'Easy to miss, though. And even if you had picked it up earlier, Miss Courland was already dead. It wouldn't have saved her.'

'Could have saved those two young joy-riders,' Jurnet retorted savagely. Defences down: 'I made a right muck-up of that one.'

'Occupational hazard.' For a precious moment the love in which the two held each other was permitted to shine through the ritual belittlement with which they habitually fenced it round. 'At least — ' delicately feeling his way — 'it's over now. Now that you know the truth about how your Miriam came to die you can begin, little by little, to come to terms with it.'

'The truth — ' Jurnet scowled at his superior officer, even as his heart noted with a leap of joy that the man had for the first time spoken of Miriam by name. 'What did Galil call it — the ultimate lie?' His voice held steady. With effort he announced: 'It's the truth I can't stand, if you want to know, the bloody triviality of it — that she had to be wiped out all on account of a few pounds out of the till.'

'Well, well!' The Superintendent's withdrawal from intimacy more than matched that of his subordinate. The patrician features grew remote and contemptuous. 'Do I detect a certain regret that it isn't the IRA after all — madmen, scum of the earth but still, some would say, idealists acting for a cause? Is what you're saying, in effect, that there are different social levels of murder, from Economy Class all the way up to Concorde, and there isn't all that much cachet in one predicated on the price of sweaters? That if, let us say instead, it had been a case of somebody making off with the Crown Jewels, you'd have found the whole dreadful business that much more bearable? I'd never taken you for a snob, Inspector, but there! You live and learn.'

Jurnet, head hanging, muttered 'Justice — ' a word which appeared only to fuel the other's impatience.

'For heaven's sake, let's keep a sense of proportion! Since when was justice on a copper's agenda? Justice is for the courts, not the likes of us. We are merely the day labour.' The Superintendent, as was his custom when roused, got up from his chair and went to look out of the window at the people below in the Market Place. 'What precisely is the nature of your complaint?' he demanded, turning back calmer and apparently reassured by his sight of the real world. 'That Galil isn't a fitting enough villain to have killed your splendid fiancée; or that, in his way, he too is a victim?'

'Victim!' Jurnet's head came up abruptly. In a tone he had never before used in any of their exchanges, he observed sourly: 'You've changed your tune!'

Ignoring the insolence, the Superintendent sat down again, his fingers momentarily touching his gold pen.

'If,' he said, 'you really believe I could ever, in any circumstances, condone murder, in whatever shape it presents itself, we've wasted all our years together. But think of it, man! In the same circumstances, what would a thief who wasn't called Rafi Galil have done? Taken the money and run — to Spain, to Brazil, even to Disneyland. From what I've gathered of Miss Courland I don't suppose for a moment she would have pursued him there, any more than, without the other's history, he would have thought the money worth killing for. As it is, a child of the Holocaust, Galil had forgotten — if he had ever had time to learn, poor soul — the common language of humanity, that perception of the sacredness of human life which is basic to a civilized society — '

Not caring whether he interrupted, Jurnet said: 'Being preached at doesn't make it any easier — '

'No.' After a moment — not a moment too soon — the monosyllable was followed by another. 'Ben — '

Sergeant Ellers came in and nodded to the Superintendent as at some prearranged signal.

'We've got her downstairs, sir. They're still operating on Nelligan.'

At the name Jurnet looked up.

'Nelligan?'

'Tell him,' ordered the Superintendent.

Jack Ellers, obediently: 'Mrs Doran. Her and that broth of a boy she had living with her.'

'He was painting the window frames,' Jurnet said, he couldn't think why.

'She'll have to get somebody else to finish the job. Seems she got it out of him, pillow talk, that he was along of his brothers when they had no end of fun knee-capping her Terry, so she returned the compliment with interest. Had a great old gun she'd got from God knows where — damn near took his legs off. Being a nurse though, the caring profession, she had him bandaged up beautifully by the time the ambulance she'd rung for arrived. Saved his life, they said at the hospital.'

Jurnet got reluctantly to his feet. He sneezed, glad of the weakness he felt overwhelming him, dulling thought. Unconvincingly, he managed: 'I ought to talk to her.'

'No need. Everything under control.' The Sergeant smiled at his brother-in-arms, less concerned than his elders and betters to hide his affection. 'Matter of fact, Ben, she sent you a message.'

'Oh ah?'

'Near as I can remember it, she said to tell you anyone crazy enough to fall in love deserves all he gets.'

The Superintendent touched his gold pen again. In a voice once again vibrant with that comforting derision which advertised that the ball was once more in play between them, a passage cleared through emotional minefields, he commanded: 'Go home, Ben. And for all our sakes take something for that cold.'

Mario, his face wide with smiles, came hurrying out from behind the delicatessen counter to greet him. Pnina Benvista sat at one of the little white tables, an empty coffee cup in front of her. She took one look at Jurnet and said severely: 'You ought not to be up. I told Mario to have some hot lemon ready and put a hot water bottle in your bed.'

'I'm perfectly OK,' Jurnet asserted. He sat down at the table and sneezed. The Israeli girl looked annoyed, for a moment astonishingly like the Superintendent. The two had a lot in common, Jurnet thought with a sudden childish fit of the sulks. 'What about you?' he demanded accusingly. 'You got at least as wet as I did.'

'I? I am as tough as old boots.' Pnina Benvista hesitated, uncertain of the idiom. 'Why old? I am as tough as new boots. I never catch colds, wet or dry. All the Israeli sunshine I carry inside my body, it protects me.' She watched in silence whilst Mario placed in front of the detective a mug filled with a mixture from which steam, lemon and the scents of rum and cloves rose in equal proportion.

'Drink!' the delicatessen owner commanded.

Jurnet sipped obediently, angry though, with infantile weakness. *Who gave everyone the right to boss him about?* He longed for the oblivion of his bed at the same time as he hated it for its nothingness, his mind dwelling on the hot water bottle with enough malevolence to make the bloody thing spring a leak. Turning the knife in his own wound, he spoke to the Israeli girl in a voice strident with bitterness.

'I suppose you'll be off back to Israel.'

'Certainly not.' The suggestion was dismissed as beneath consideration. 'Already today I have been to the workroom, explaining to everybody what is the position, what we still owe to Miriam and to the people at Tel Tzevaim. They are good people, they understood. If we all work together the business, I think, can be saved. We have good products and as to the cause, there is no better.'

'You haven't wasted any time.'

'There was no time to waste.' The girl leaned forward across the table, her eyes bright and questioning behind the steam still rising from the hot lemon. 'And what about you, Mr Jurnet? Now that you know the truth, has time begun to run again for you too — ordinary, everyday time, one day following the other, the good and the bad equally? Is it enough to have found out at last how Miriam came to die?'

Low, Jurnet answered: 'It is not enough.'

'I am sure.' The girl sat back, nodded as if he had returned the right answer to a

411

tricky examination question. In some subtle way, the austere contours of her face had softened, the modelling of her lips grown fuller. 'But still it is something, is it not, to know that she was the one chosen by Uncle Rafi to die — that she did not die in mistake for you?'

'It's something. Not much.'

'Later,' she said encouragingly, 'it will come to mean more. You will see that I am right.' She called across to Mario. 'Is the bottle in the bed?'

'Two of them.'

Pnina Benvista stood up, shrugged on her white anorak. She stood looking down at Jurnet with love but without sentimentality. 'You will understand why I do not make the suggestion that I go upstairs with you,' she declared flatly. 'It is not the time.'

Jurnet said nothing. The drink had left him in a warm alcoholic haze which blissfully inhibited thought. The girl continued in the same matter-of-fact way that went with the sculptured starkness of her high cheekbones, the deep eye sockets, the wide mouth. 'Perhaps it will never be time. It is for you to say. Only for you to know that I am here if you want me.'

Jurnet went upstairs, feeling muzzy. The

bedside lamp was on, striking green sparks out of the eye of the Bingo bear. The central heating had been turned up, comforting.

Jurnet went to draw the curtains. He glanced down to the street, to where Pnina Benvista, her white anorak orange under the street light, was clip-clopping doggedly along.

As if she felt his gaze on her back, she turned, looked up and waved to him; then resumed her way, an indomitable figure melting into the darkness.

Jurnet watched until she was out of sight before joining the hot water bottles.